NEMESIS

A REALM OF FLAME AND SHADOW NOVEL

CHRISTINA PHILLIPS

PHOENIX 18 PUBLISHING

Nemesis
A *Realm of Flame and Shadow* novel
Book Two

ISBN: 978-0-6487568-5-9

Edited by Amanda Ashby
Cover Design by Covers by Christian

PROLOGUE

AZRAEL

 *omania: Nine hundred years ago*

THE STENCH of rotting flesh and corrupted humanity turned Azrael's stomach as he slashed through the vacant-eyed half-bloods guarding the castle's foul master. Hidden deep in the tangled forest, with only pale slivers of the crescent moon as illumination, the castle loomed black and foreboding. Exuding an evil that caused his skin to crawl with revulsion.

The vision of death that had haunted him for more than one hundred years was finally unfolding.

The vampires had fled beneath Azrael's blade, leaving behind their ill-equipped offspring to defend what remained of their domain.

Dhampirs.

Cursed creatures created from the union between vampire and human. Hair matted, skin filthy, they didn't stand a chance as he decapitated them with sickening efficiency. They didn't deserve this death, but they should never have existed in the first place.

Their destruction was a mercy, a release from their pitiful existence.

He strode through the dark, echoing halls. Torches flickered in wall sconces, enhancing the shadows that clung like monstrous spiders from the soaring vault, but he didn't hesitate.

The same unnatural vibration that he'd detected in the astral planes during the last few decades grew stronger with every second. Whatever it was, the source was here. And whatever it was, he had vowed to destroy it.

If he didn't, devastation would fall across the Earth as vampires and their spawn spread their evil. His vision had foretold it.

He'd been plagued only once before, millennia ago, by recurring visions of Earth-wide devastation. He hadn't understood the magnitude of what he was being shown, because he'd been blind to the truth. That the great Alpha goddess herself, who had created all the archangels, was the one his visions warned him of. The results had been catastrophic.

That would never happen again.

He followed the corrupt energy and surveyed the massive double doors ahead. The unidentified vibration soaked through the timber, permeated the ancient stone walls, and sank into his blood like an ethereal heartbeat. Whatever existed behind those doors had existed for countless centuries.

He tightened his grip on his katana and kicked open the doors. For a second the heavy fog of incense blurred his vision.

But only for a second.

What the hell?

His gut knotted as he stared at the creature imprisoned in the center of the chamber.

Bedraggled, dull, and clearly sick, the great bird huddled within its iron cage. Rage boiled through Azrael's veins.

It was a phoenix.

A magnificent, rare bird that flourished in myths and legends, yet it had existed in elusive enclaves for countless millennia. He had encountered two of the mystical creatures in the past and both times their majesty had filled him with awe. What the fuck was a pack of vampires doing with a phoenix?

"You dare penetrate my inner sanctum?" The voice was cold and dripped with aristocratic arrogance. Azrael tore his infuriated gaze from the phoenix and faced the vampire lord. The discordance in the astral planes might have originated from the phoenix, but the creatures weren't inherently good or evil. Something—or someone—had distorted its essence almost beyond recognition. The phoenix was no longer his prey. "Human scum."

He bared his teeth and slashed the powerful katana through the bars that held the majestic bird captive. The creature shuddered and sunk further into itself, as if the promise of freedom was nothing but an illusion.

The vampire reared in fury. Black shadows lengthened, claws extended, and sharp teeth glowed in predatory single-mindedness. He advanced, his intent clear, his ignorance of who—*or what*—he truly faced contemptuously evident.

Azrael dropped his glamour and extended his wings to their full, glorious extent. Not only to stop the vampire in his tracks but also to protect the cowering phoenix.

"Demon." The vampire spat the word at him, no longer speaking Romanian but ancient Phoenician. The patronizing air vanished as finally he realized his error in misjudging Azrael's heritage.

He still misjudged. But *demon* was a lot closer than *human*.

"Your filthy reign is over," he growled.

The phoenix emerged from its prison and lurched inelegantly in the air above him. He raised his katana, a sign of protection, and the vampire hissed in outrage as he retreated from the gleaming, blood-soaked blade.

"We'll meet again, *uniilă.*" The vampire reverted to Romanian. "This is not over between us."

With that he spun on his heel and dispersed into venomous black smoke.

Azrael swore furiously in the language of the ancients then swung around as the phoenix flew towards the narrow window. It shattered through the glass and as it soared into the black velvet night, free at last, it burst into flame.

CHAPTER 1

ROWAN

*L*ondon. Eight months ago

ROWAN MORETON SLAMMED on the brakes, mounted the curb and leaped from the sleek black Mercedes McLaren. She was parked illegally but it was three in the morning and the dark side alley was deserted. She drew her beloved katana and silently ran towards ominous shadows that pooled at the end of the alley.

Don't let me be too late.

But in her heart, she knew her quarry had gone. All she could detect in the air was the sharp tang of recently spilled blood and the acrid reek of terror.

But still she gripped her katana, ready for ambush, as she kept her back against the crumbling stone walls. Her eyesight adjusted to the gloom—one of the advantages of her tainted dhampir blood—and her preternatural hearing caught a faint, gurgling breath.

No rogue vampire remained in the area. Heart thudding, hoping she was wrong about the victim who huddled on the worn cobblestones, she advanced. With every step her rage magnified as impotent injustice seethed through her veins.

Of course she hadn't been wrong.

She crouched over the torn and bloodied young woman. Claws had slashed her face and ripped through her throat. Rowan's stomach knotted in futile distress at the unmistakable evidence that the creature hadn't stopped there.

With her free hand she gently brushed back the woman's blood matted hair. Without treatment she would die. But no human hospital could help her. Not now.

"It's all right. You're safe now." Four times over the last six years Rowan had whispered those words to victims, and she hated herself more each time. But what else could she say? What else could she *do*? "Can you hear me? What's your name?"

The woman opened one swollen eye. Terror oozed from every pore, every tortured breath. But her gazed fixed on Rowan, as if she was her lifeline.

"Lily." The word was guttural, barely coherent. "I can't—can't remember..."

"Try not to worry." Stupid words, but she kept her tone soothing, a form of mild hypnosis. Although her talent was nothing compared to the power wielded by full-blood vampires, the amethyst jewelry she wore helped enhance her ability. "I'm going to take you home with me, Lily. Look after you until you're better."

"Yes." Lily's whisper drifted on the fetid air as she slipped into induced unconsciousness. Gritting her teeth Rowan lifted the slender woman, hoping to hell that this time the vampire had failed to impregnate another innocent victim.

She wasn't going to hold her breath. All she could hope was that this time the woman would survive the birth itself, unlike the last victim Rowan had saved.

But first Lily had to survive this night. There was only one place Rowan could take her. The house she had called home since the day her own mother had died. *In order to give me this cursed life.* She shook off the memory and resolutely stalked into the night.

Back to the headquarters of the society that she'd pledged her loyalty to at the age of fifteen.

The Enclave of the Phoenix.

∽

LONDON. *Present Day*

"ROWAN, cheri, it won't kill you to smile a little." Marguerite, whose French accent was as pronounced now as it had, probably, been nearly two hundred and fifty years ago when she'd escaped from Madame Guillotine, prodded Rowan in the ribs. "You want to celebrate your birthday, non? Trust me, you won't get laid with that unbecoming scowl on your face."

Rowan slung the petite blonde vampire an irritated glare as the bouncers cleared a path for them to enter the hideously selective nightclub in Chelsea.

It was all very well for Meg. She only had to look at a male—mortal or otherwise—and he fell at her feet. Rowan had never quite got the hang of small talk. Being a half-human freak wasn't something she could ever share with anyone, and for some reason that was all she could obsess about on the rare occasion a guy attempted to flirt with her.

"I'm worried about Lily." Over the last couple of days Lily—who, at twenty-two, was only two years younger than her and the closest thing to a real human girl friend she'd ever had—had become lethargic and scarily forgetful. "I should be there with her, not out clubbing."

Meg shrugged, supremely unaffected by Lily's obvious decline.

"You're a hunter, Rowan, not a babysitter. The human has plenty of nursemaids. Now, tell me. Anything here you find tasty? It's been an age since you've had any fun."

As Meg dragged her towards the bar Rowan glanced around, unimpressed by the minor celebrities and desperate wannabes who littered the plush interior. It was true. Lily was safe at the Enclave, surrounded by those who knew how to care for her and the unborn child she carried. It was also true that it had been ages since Rowan had indulged in what Meg termed fun.

As in, sex.

In fact, her sex life was so pathetic she could remember the exact time and place of her last encounter. A year ago, tonight. On her twenty-third birthday.

On the back seat of a Bentley.

It had been rushed, frenzied, and sordid. Not something she liked to remember. Then again, she didn't much like recalling any of her infrequent couplings. None of them meant anything. None of them had ever meant anything after Steven, her first and only love, had been murdered in front of her eyes on her seventeenth birthday.

One day she'd get over that.

Maybe.

Given her lifestyle she should have got over it years ago but the hard knot of guilt in the center of her chest never eased. Because his brutal death, at the age of nineteen, had been all her fault.

As Meg flirted outrageously with a couple of guys at the bar, who appeared to be vying for the privilege of buying the drinks, she realized her hand was curling over her hip. She froze, then forcibly splayed her fingers and concentrated on trying to look normal.

But it was hard, when she knew that everyone in the club, except Meg, would run screaming into the night if they knew what she really was.

And besides, she missed her katana. She felt naked and vulnerable without it. The stiletto hidden inside her purple suede ankle boot really wasn't that much of a comfort.

Meg nudged her and handed her a lethal looking drink. "Lambs to the slaughter," she said with satisfaction. "Want to share?"

Rowan glanced back at the bar where the two guys remained riveted on Meg. They looked like a couple of American football players and their biceps bulged beneath their designer shirts. They'd shit themselves if they knew what Meg really was. And what she intended for them.

"I don't have the teeth for it. Remember?" She offered the vampire an insincere grin to hammer home her point. Meg tossed her hair in an impatient gesture.

"Always the same excuse." She sounded offended. "You know I'd get things started for you, cheri. You deserve a treat on your special day."

Before she could stop herself, she licked her lips. The lure of fresh blood was a temptation. A gut-burning, forbidden, temptation, she constantly fought to resist.

But it wasn't just the fact she didn't possess fangs. Her immune system was tarnished by her human heritage. No matter how her vampire half hungered to satisfy its primal bloodlust, she had to make do with a sanitized, medicated version.

Unless she wanted to die.

Of course, it depended on who she believed. The Elector High Council proclaimed it as a fact, while Meg, who'd cared for her since she was a baby and trained her in weaponry from the age of six, appeared keen for her to attempt something that could kill her. But the vampire was adamant Rowan would be perfectly all right. Then again Meg didn't care much for the Elector High Council. She didn't care much for authority, period. And while Rowan agreed that the Council, isolated in Eastern Europe, was an antiquated and possibly irrelevant blot of bureaucracy, she couldn't shift the fear that had been ingrained in her from her earliest memories.

Untreated blood would destroy her.

"I'll pass." She sniffed the drink. Was it worth downing the lot in one gulp? Alcohol affected her corrupted biology in unexpected ways. She never knew whether she'd be perfectly fine or plunge into a hallucinogenic nightmare. "Go play with your toys, Meg."

Meg narrowed her eyes, clearly intent on arguing the point, but then her burly lambs appeared as if they found it impossible to stay away. With one final condemning glance the vampire swirled on her six-inch stilettos and led them to their slaughter.

Slaughter by orgasm. She watched them disappear into the crowd. Maybe she should have taken up Meg's offer.

She craved that elusive, intimate connection with a man willing to hold her close, without any preconceived expectations. Someone she could share her fears and dreams with.

Someone to share her life with.

Despair trickled through her as she gave the clubbers another surreptitious glance. Anonymous sex wasn't what she wanted. But it was all she was ever likely to get.

The Elector High Council discouraged its dhampirs from embarking in long-term relationships. After what had happened to Steven, she understood why.

In her peripheral vision a tall, leather-clad figure strode into the club and her preternatural senses went on full alert. But even as she swung around, she knew he was no vampire. Irritation spiked through her. Couldn't she relax for even one night of the year?

She spared him a fleeting glance and then couldn't drag her gaze away. He was in profile, built like a warrior and was frowning across the sea of posturing humans as though he searched for something just beyond his reach.

Fascination washed through her. She'd never seen a human as

insanely arresting before. His dark hair looked deliciously windswept and just touched the collar of his black shirt. How would it feel to spear her fingers through that luxuriant hair as he wrapped those powerful arms around her?

Heat seared through her and her grip tightened around the glass. It was the kind of thing she fantasized about when she was safe, and alone, in her bed. But it was too intimate for an anonymous hookup.

Yet the captivating image wouldn't fade.

If she was going to have her annual one-night stand, he was the only one she wanted it with. Even if he was way out of her league.

And if she left it to chance, he'd barely give her a second glance.

She wanted more than that. She wanted to touch him, to inhale his scent and imprint him on her mind. To taste his flesh and feel his hard body possess her. But most of all she wanted, for a few magical moments, to pretend she was a normal human woman. A woman he found irresistible.

Her last wish would never happen, but neither would *anything* unless she gave Lady Luck a nudge. Her powers of psychic persuasion were limited. But when magnified by the power of her amethysts it should be just enough to snare his attention for a sex drenched hour or so.

It was the closest she'd ever get to the heart-deep connection she dreamed of.

He turned and walked towards the bar and the crowd parted before him like a subservient wave. She took a deep breath and followed him.

Happy birthday to me.

CHAPTER 2

AZRAEL

*A*zrael scanned the nightclub, but his mind was far from the surging horde of mortals surrounding him.

Nine hundred years ago, after freeing the captive phoenix, his visions of the vampire Sakarbaal and his dhampirs had abruptly stopped. Even though the vampire hadn't been destroyed, every shred of evidence of his existence vanished overnight. The discordance that had tainted the phoenix essence in the astral planes faded and eventually disappeared but Sakarbaal's escape ate into him like acid. It had taken centuries of fruitless searching before he allowed himself to consider the possibility the evil that had permeated his visions had finally ended.

Fifty years ago, they came back.

With a vengeance.

This time there was no filthy dhampir army. He never saw any faces. Only the aftermath of a blood-drenched apocalypse that ravaged the face of the Earth. But the same evil he recalled from before pervaded every scorched breath.

He'd spent the last half century in the Andromeda Galaxy, where countless mortal civilizations had flourished for millennia before any of those on Earth had arisen. But it didn't matter how deep into the past he searched for answers or how many vampiric creatures he hunted or unholy relics he destroyed.

The visions only became more frequent. More graphic. Showing him a future where humanity became nothing more than a feeding ground for a false, self-professed god.

And then a few months ago a chillingly familiar, elusive vibration began to haunt the lower levels of the astral planes.

It could only mean one thing. Sakarbaal had, once again, captured a phoenix.

As he had always known deep in his heart, nine hundred years ago he hadn't altered the future, merely delayed it.

He'd collated masses of intel on the vampire race, a scourge that polluted almost every mortal inhabited planet. But he uncovered no definitive link between vampires and phoenixes and there were no ancient sources of wisdom scattered across the universe that could help in his quest.

It was time to resume the hunt on Earth.

Before he did that, there was something else he needed to do. For six months, since one of his oldest friends, the Archangel Gabriel, had lost his immortality in a sadistic twist of fate, he'd avoided Gabe and his human-born bride, Aurora.

But it didn't matter how deeply he wished he could change things. Gabe was mortal, and although in the past they had gone decades without seeing each other, that was no longer an option.

Gabe didn't have endless centuries, anymore.

And he needed to meet Aurora. The woman who hadn't simply captured Gabe's heart, but had managed to shatter one of the fundamental tenets that archangels had lived with for millennia.

Yeah, he had to meet her. But he wasn't looking forward to it. And that was why he'd ended up in this club tonight, as a distraction from both his mission and tomorrow's meeting.

So far, it wasn't working.

A spiky-haired brunette, diamonds sparkling in her ears and

around her throat, offered him a sultry smile as she gyrated in time to the music. Desire and hunger radiated from her, and every sexy move of her body brought her closer to him, her invitation blatant. She was beautiful, but not appealing.

Not that he did humans as a rule. They were too fragile and brought back too many bad memories. Of a time, long ago, when archangels had lived openly on Earth, and he'd witnessed the devastating heartache of his immortal friends when their beloved soulmate had died.

Sex without any emotional ties was the mantra he lived by. Though now he thought about it, he couldn't even remember the last time he'd had sex.

He focused on the woman as she gave him another seductive glance from beneath her lashes. The flirtatious gesture did nothing for his libido. But since he was here, what the hell.

He might even enjoy the novelty.

As she twined around his body, his glance snagged on a woman who was glaring at the brunette as she gyrated against his back. Fascinated by her antagonism, he trailed his gaze over her midnight hair, piled on top of her head in a messy chignon. Long tendrils escaped their confines and framed her face, giving her a cute, vulnerable air.

Gods, had he just seriously thought a human was *cute*?

But there was something intriguing about the way she stood, like a warrior sizing up her prey. The short black dress gave a tantalizing glimpse of cleavage, clung possessively to her breasts and showed off her shapely thighs and calves. Purple lace—*stockings?* —matched her purple ankle boots and the jewelry in her ears and around her throat and wrists.

Anticipation thrummed through his blood. She might be merely a human, but there was something irresistible about her, and he took a couple of steps towards her.

She visibly started and shot him an uncertain glance, as her left hand curled around an amethyst that hung from a silver chain around her throat. It was a defensive gesture and before he could say anything she glanced furtively over her shoulder. Did she seriously think his focus was centered on something behind her?

Or was she playing games? He didn't care. She'd managed to take his mind off Gabe and Aurora and that was all he wanted.

"Hey." He accompanied his greeting with a smile guaranteed to melt the defenses of an ice goddess. Instead of dissolving into his arms with a seductive sigh, she stared at him, and confusion glowed in her captivating green eyes.

Why hadn't she expected him to speak to her? She was fucking gorgeous, and she had to know it.

"Hi." She sounded guarded and he had the strangest conviction she wasn't playing him. What *was* she doing?

He offered her another archangelic infused smile. She still didn't metaphorically fall at his feet.

Interesting.

"Do you two know each other?"

"What?" She blinked, severing their connection, before glancing at the other woman who was now stalking to the bar. There was no lingering hint of the animosity he'd seen just moments ago. "Oh. No."

She released her death grip on her necklace and flattened her palm against her thigh. He waited, but it appeared that was all she had to say on the matter.

Countless times in the past mortals had been rendered speechless in his presence. But this was different. She had no idea who he was, and the brief glimpse of celestial radiance he'd aimed at her hadn't appeared to affect her at all.

Which was intriguing enough. But combined with the heat in her eyes when she'd looked at him, her genuine shock when he'd spoken to her, and obvious disdain for small talk, she was one of the most fascinating mortals he'd ever met.

"Would you like to dance?" The incongruity of an archangel

asking a human to dance amused him, but he kept his grin to himself. Because right now, all he wanted was to hold her in his arms and feel her body meld against his. For the first time in forever his blood stirred and cock thickened.

Hello, libido.

"Dance?" She sounded amazed that he'd asked her such a thing.

"Sure. We're in a club. We could dance."

"Oh." Her fingers tightened around her drink. "I'm not sure."

She gave the impression she wasn't interested, but he knew that wasn't true. Desire spiked from her in a heady, intoxicating scent that sank into his skin and caused his pulse to quicken. He couldn't even recall the last time a woman had elicited such a reaction without them even touching.

"You're not sure if you want to dance with me?" This was a crazy conversation. He'd never had to work so hard to get a favorable response from a mortal.

He couldn't remember the last time he'd had as much fun.

She blinked at him, her long dark lashes a lethal distraction. "No, I mean I can't dance."

Neither could most of the humans in the club, but it didn't stop them trying to prove otherwise.

"That makes two of us."

"I'm sure you're great." She sounded serious. "And I'd love to dance, but I thought I should warn you that I'm crap at it."

"Are you trying to tell me to get lost? Because you don't have to sugar coat it to protect my feelings."

"No." Alarm flashed across her face. Shit, she thought he meant it. His flirting technique clearly sucked. "I don't want you to go. I'm still just… processing things."

He grinned, plucked her drink from her hand and placed it on a nearby ledge. "How about we process things together?"

"Okay."

He took her hand. It was small, fine boned, an unwelcome

reminder of her inherent fragility. But that didn't stop her touch from sending lightning sparks racing through his blood. It was insane how badly he wanted to pull her into his arms.

Once they were on the dance floor, she turned to face him. He slid his fingers along her bare arm, and she quivered, a breathy sigh escaping her crimson lips.

It was all the encouragement he needed, and he cradled her waist. After a moment's hesitation she flattened her palms against his chest. Even through his shirt, her touch scorched his flesh and he tugged her closer. But she didn't wrap her arms around him, and her resistance to his unspoken invitation was surprisingly strong.

"I told you I couldn't dance," she said, and he had the strongest sense that she assumed he'd agree with her. "Then again, it's not like I give it much practice."

She hadn't raised her voice to be heard over the pounding music and although he could hear her perfectly, it occurred to him he hadn't made any effort to speak over the volume, either. Yet she'd not missed a word. Odd when everyone around them accompanied their raised voices with exaggerated gesticulation.

"You know what they say." Deliberately he lowered his voice, but she didn't frown or lean in closer. "Practice makes perfect."

"I don't get out much." She offered him a glimmer of a smile. It damn well stopped the breath in his chest. "At least I haven't stamped on your foot yet."

She wasn't close enough to stamp on his foot. He slid one hand to the small of her back and slowly drew her unresisting body towards him. She gave a delectable sigh as her hands curled over his shoulders and at long last she melted against him.

Her face nestled against his shoulder, and her hair brushed against his jaw. He inhaled a ragged breath and caught an elusive hint of jasmine, and the scent mingled irresistibly with the faint undertone of aroused femininity.

His arms tightened around her, one hand gliding up the

length of her spine, the soft silk of her dress a sensual caress against his skin. She shifted against him and he was so damn hard it hurt. Then she linked her hands around his neck and gave a soundless sigh.

It was the most erotic sensation he'd experienced in centuries.

What had they been talking about? It didn't matter. He lowered his head and nibbled kisses along her neck, the taste of her skin a heady combination of temptation and desire. Tremors licked through her, heightening his own lust and she sank completely against him, a torturous delight.

"What's your name?" His question rasped against the delectable curve where neck met shoulder. It would take no effort to rip her flimsy dress from her. *Soon*. But he could hardly contain the primitive urge to possess.

"Rowan." Her voice promised everything. He waited for her to ask his name, but she didn't. Instead her fingers speared through his hair and gently tugged. Sparks of flame ignited across his skull, and as she twisted his hair around her fingers a certainty throbbed through his lust drugged mind. He didn't merely want a quick fuck with this bewitching human.

He wanted Rowan for the whole night.

CHAPTER 3

ROWAN

*R*owan dragged her fingers from his silky hair and trailed her fingertips across his nape. His hands, possessively splayed across her back, held her in a firm grip. Clearly, he had no intention of letting her go anytime soon.

His muscled chest pressed against her sensitized breasts and his rigid length branded her. A tremor raced through her, raising goose bumps on her arms and causing her breath to stumble in her throat. She shifted against him and his hot breath caressed her neck.

He wanted her. And she hadn't even had time to use the psychic powers of her amethysts to snare him. Not only was the hottest guy she'd seen in years in her arms, but he was there without any subtle manipulation on her part.

"Are you here alone?" The raw need in his voice was electrifying.

I wish I was. Then, maybe, she and this warrior like god could have more than a hasty coupling in a dark corner. Except it didn't matter if she was here with anyone else or not. A small pain speared through her heart at the reminder that no matter what, she could never expect anything more.

"No. I'm with a friend."

"Rowan." He made her name sound sinfully seductive and she was so entranced she lifted her head from his shoulder to look at him. And almost stopped breathing. She'd forgotten, in just those few short moments, how utterly compelling he was. Truly a god in the flesh.

She would savor these moments forever.

"Rowan." His voice dropped a couple of octaves and while it should have been impossible, he sounded sexier than ever. "I want to spend the night with you."

Illicit thrills spiraled through her. A whole night. Wrapped in his arms. She hadn't spent the whole night with a guy since Steven.

If she was a pureblood human, she'd never take such a risk. But even if this glorious stranger turned out to be a murderous psychopath it didn't matter. She could break his neck in a heartbeat.

But she, who trusted no one outside her small circle within the Enclave, inexplicably trusted this warrior-god. He wasn't dangerous. He was a hot, lust-fueled male and he wanted *her*.

She rose onto her toes and he met her halfway, his lips brushing hers in a caress so fleeting their flesh barely connected. Yet she felt the heat of his touch arrow through her breast and shatter with exquisite shards of lightning between her trembling thighs.

His arms wrapped around her pinning her against his hard body. It had been so long since she'd been held like this. So long since primal desire had thundered through her blood and clouded her survival instincts.

She trailed her fingers from his temple to his jaw. Faint stubble grazed her fingertips and his wickedly seductive smile tied pleasurable knots of desire in her chest. Cradling his strong jaw in her palm she leaned into him and savored the evocative hint of cinnamon on his uneven breath, before claiming his lips.

The cacophony of sound faded. All that existed was this man in her arms. Tingles cascaded over her flesh as if this was her first kiss. It almost was. She hadn't kissed anyone this way in seven years.

His tongue met hers. But he didn't invade her willing mouth. Didn't plunder the way she'd got used to. Instead he teased her with fleeting strokes between her hungry lips. Flicked the tip of her tongue. Seductively nipped her lower lip.

Wet heat blossomed between her thighs and she moaned, a low, sultry sound. She couldn't help it. Didn't care. She'd never imagined a kiss could be so amazingly erotic.

Her nipples chafed against the lace of her bra. She longed to feel his naked chest pressed against her, skin to skin. Her fingers clawed and from a great distance she heard an appreciative growl rumble through his body.

"Is this a yes?" His question scorched her lips. For a passion-hazed moment she had no idea what he was asking. His beautiful lips curved into a smile as though he guessed. "You'll stay with me tonight?"

Of course it was a yes. How could he imagine otherwise? But a tug of delight tightened low in her belly that he had taken the time to ask. To make *sure*.

Slowly she raised her head, his jaw scraping along the soft skin of her cheek. She wanted to look into his eyes. See his desire. She didn't want to spoil the moment. Didn't want to shatter these fragile tendrils of sensation. But she had to find the words to answer him.

"Rowan." Meg's imperious tone invaded her sensual cocoon and she stiffened. *No.* She would *not* have this precious moment interrupted. "Rowan, cheri, I need to speak to you."

She watched her warrior-god frown as his focus shifted to Meg. Impotent rage, disappointment, *futility,* swept through her. Why right now? There was nothing so important that Meg needed to interrupt her for. And surely she hadn't already finished with her two conquests?

His hold on her relaxed. More irritated with the vampire than she'd ever been, she twisted around. But he didn't release her. Instead he wrapped his arms around her waist and held her securely against his chest.

His cock scorched through the silk of her dress, an immovable reminder of exactly why she had no intention of letting Meg spoil this elusive encounter. With only the greatest difficulty she prevented herself from squirming in his possessive embrace.

Meg looked completely pissed off. As if the last thing she wanted was to spoil Rowan's fun. *Why the hell are you, then?*

"Is this your friend?" His breath tickled her ear. She tried and failed not to shiver with reaction. God, she'd been more aroused by a simple kiss than any of her infrequent encounters during the last few years. Then again, there'd been nothing simple about that kiss. Even the memory of it was enough to send renewed darts of dark pleasure arrowing through her.

"Yes." Her voice croaked, not sounding nearly as sexy as the guy's raw whisper. She cleared her throat, but it didn't help clear her brain. "What's the matter, Meg?"

Meg shot the guy an assessing glance and clearly approved, if her then lingering look was anything to go by. Rowan gritted her teeth and glared at the vampire, as an unfamiliar pain burned through her chest. If Meg thought for one second that she—

"We have to go." Meg, finally dragging her attention back to Rowan, sounded infuriated. "We have no choice."

She wrapped her hands around her almost-lover's wrists and tugged herself free. She wasn't sure whether to be grateful or insulted when he didn't try to detain her. He had a quizzical smile on his face as if this interruption didn't unduly disturb him. He was obviously confident that, no matter what the crisis, she would choose to go with him.

Somewhat mollified she stroked her hand over his chest. "I won't be a second," she said. "I'll be right back."

"Sure." He tucked his thumbs into the pockets of his pants. It was hard to drag her fascinated gaze from him and focus on Meg.

The vampire took her hand and pulled her closer. "*He* has returned," she hissed into Rowan's ear. "The London Enclave has been summoned."

Meg was trembling with outrage. She hated being dictated to, and over the last couple of years her dissatisfaction had become more vocal. But when the ancient lord of the Enclave turned up, vampires in his employ had no choice but to dance to his tune.

"Fine. But you don't need me." She glanced over her shoulder and relief washed through her. He hadn't turned his attention elsewhere. She turned back to Meg. "*He* won't know I'm not there. It's not as if he ever acknowledges any of *us* is it?"

Sakarbaal, head of the Elector High Council, despised dhampirs. She'd been in his presence on only a couple of occasions and she had no desire to repeat the experience.

"That isn't the point." Meg, who for all her faults at least didn't harbor any prejudice against Rowan for her half-blood status, scowled. "You know that isn't the point."

Of course she did. The Ancients who comprised the High Council, despite their mandate to shelter unwanted dhampirs, had decreed half-bloods were not allowed to mingle socially with humans. Dhampirs, unlike vampires, couldn't be trusted to keep the secret of their heritage.

As far as the upper echelons of the Enclave were concerned, highly trained dhampirs were nothing more than hunting dogs that needed to be kept on a tight leash when they weren't on duty. Thankfully that attitude didn't permeate throughout the entire organization, and they were—at least, those outside Eastern Europe—well paid for their services.

But if Sakarbaal discovered his wishes were being flouted

there was no telling what he might do. She had a terrifying image of being shipped off to the heart of the Enclave's administration in Romania and ice trickled through her veins.

She'd rather die than endure the kind of existence half-bloods suffered at the hands of the true ancients.

Sakarbaal would never call her into his presence. He wouldn't have the first idea whether she was in the London branch of the Enclave's Grosvenor Square mansions or not. But no matter how much she wanted to scorn the vampire lord the risk was too great.

The bitter truth was that when Sakarbaal was in town, all dhampirs who weren't on a mission had to go into lockdown.

Meg was right. Neither of them had a choice. She was going to have to bail on the hottest guy she'd ever met. One who'd managed to turn her on with nothing more than a kiss and seductive whisper.

And she would never see him again.

It was more than disappointment that ate through her breast. More than frustrated lust and impotent fury at how little control she really had over her life. It was crazy to feel this sense of loss, as though a fundamental piece of her was somehow disintegrating. She didn't even know his name. Knew nothing about him at all. And yet she couldn't shift the feeling that, if only she'd been given this one night with him, her future would have changed direction irrevocably.

Slowly she turned. Who was she trying to fool? Tonight would have been nothing more than mindless sex. Why did she still secretly crave a normal future? Normal was something she'd never be. *She* was something a normal man would never want. Her dreams were just that.

Dreams.

She tried to ignore the way her heart tugged as she walked back to him. He hadn't moved and appeared oblivious to the countless glances he was receiving from both sexes. She could almost believe he hadn't taken his gaze from her since the moment she'd left his side.

"I'm sorry." More than he'd ever know. "Family emergency. I have to go." And as soon she turned her back, he'd be hitting on another willing conquest. He wouldn't even remember her name by the end of the night. She didn't even try to pretend that didn't hurt.

His sinfully illegal smile faded into a frown, but instead of turning from her his focus sharpened, as if he saw something more in her words, a deeper meaning. What was the *matter* with her? Having a vivid imagination wasn't always such a great thing. It was far more likely he was just suffering from a headache.

"Are you free tomorrow night?"

"What?" The word blurted before she could stop herself. Had he just asked her out?

"Tomorrow." His lips quirked at her gauche response. "We could do dinner."

He *was* asking her out. On a *date*. She was so staggered her vocal cords seized up. Only when Meg gave her a savage prod on her shoulder did she realize she was in imminent danger of gaping.

"Sure." Her voice sounded unnaturally high to her ears but hopefully he wouldn't notice with the volume of noise in the club. "Do you know *Estella's* on the King's Road?" It was one of the few restaurants she knew personally. She and a couple of her fellow dhampirs hung out there on occasion.

"I'm sure I'll find it." He looked as if he was about to say something else, before changing his mind. "Eight o'clock?"

"OK." Was she supposed to say anything else? What was standard protocol in this situation? The last time anyone had asked her out on a proper date she'd been sixteen and madly in love.

Meg didn't give her the chance to agonize. She grabbed her

arm and pulled her away and Rowan didn't bother trying to hide the grin of triumph. What did it matter that Sakarbaal's unexpected arrival had ruined her plans tonight?

Because tomorrow she was *going on a date.*

CHAPTER 4

ROWAN

*T*he London HQ of the Enclave was two adjacent Georgian residences in Grosvenor Square. From the outside they looked perfectly normal, except maybe for the imposing stone phoenixes that flanked the doors. As far as the outside world was aware, both mansions were divided into luxury apartments.

It just went to show how very little the outside world knew of its internal affairs.

She checked on Lily in the medical wing, which comprised the entire floor of one of the mansions and would cause the top biochemists on the planet to salivate with envy if they ever caught a glimpse of it.

When Lily had regained consciousness after the attack, Rowan had often visited her, and as the weeks went by an unexpected friendship formed between them. Despite the horrible circumstances, Lily's wit was razor sharp and medically her pregnancy seemed to have progressed well.

But something wasn't right now. She sat on the edge of the bed and took Lily's hand. "Hey, it's me." She leaned closer and whispered in her ear. "Guess what? I'm going on a hot date tomorrow."

She hoped the secret might bring Lily out of the strange, lethargic state she'd fallen into a couple of days ago. But there was no reaction.

Rowan bit her lip and gazed into Lily's eerily lifeless eyes. Yesterday, when she'd asked one of the doctors what the problem was, he'd just sighed and said it was to be expected.

Whatever *that* meant. Although she hadn't asked, he must have seen the question on her face since he'd elaborated.

"They all go through this at the end. You remember the other human women you brought in? They were just the same."

She'd mumbled in response, but the awful truth was, she hadn't become friendly with any of the other three women she'd saved during the last six years. She'd taken them to the Enclave, and that had been the last she'd seen of them. They had given birth and, after their memories were modified, been allowed to return to their lives. Except for the last victim, Zoë. Rowan had discovered by accident that she hadn't survived the birth.

It had shaken her. Badly. To have gone through everything she did—only to die when freedom was so close.

She pulled her mind back to Lily. There was only one thing she could do to help her friend, and although in her heart she knew it couldn't work, she had to try. With a deep breath she closed her eyes and concentrated on allowing the healing properties of her amethysts to flow through her and into Lily. But the other woman remained as lifeless as a rag doll.

Feeling helpless, she plumped up the pillows. And saw the corner of a book poking out from beneath the bottom pillow.

Her heart slammed against her chest and she stealthily pulled it free from its vulnerable hiding place. It was her mother's precious journal that she'd lent to Lily just a couple of days before her health had deteriorated.

The journal was the only thing she had of her mother's. Lily had been visibly touched and promised to keep it safe.

It wasn't safe anymore. Heart heavy, Rowan slid it beneath her coat, and retreated to her attic bedroom.

Far from the drafty, depressing hovel she was certain the Electors envisaged for their dhampirs when they'd passed down that edict, the attic bedrooms *here* were the last word in luxury.

She retrieved her stiletto, pulled off her boots and curled up on the queen size bed before pulling out her phone. She was in dire need of some advice. And since her fellow dhampirs didn't date, and she didn't have the natural advantages Meg possessed, that left hunting down the answers herself.

"They hauled you back too, then."

She looked up from an article promising her *the best sex ever* and saw Brad, a dhampir two years her senior, glaring at her from the doorway. He had an irresistibly Byronic look about him and when he radiated leashed fury the effect was breathtaking.

Unfortunately, her admiration was purely academic. His dark beauty and undercurrent of restlessness only roused her affection, not her libido.

"Just as I was about to have my birthday shag." She dropped her phone next to her so he wouldn't see what she'd been reading. He could charm a human girl at twenty paces. He'd never need a step-by-step guide on how to flirt, but for some reason he was entirely oblivious to his lethal attraction.

Instead of making a sardonic response he kicked the door shut and prowled into her room, like a caged panther seeking escape. Coiled tension thrummed in the air and formless unease shivered through her, raising goosebumps along her arms.

Before she could ask him what the problem was, he abruptly sat on the edge of her bed, forearms resting on his thighs, hunched over as he rolled something between his hands.

"We're nothing to them but fucking puppets." Bitterness twisted each word. She shifted across the bed to sit next to him, and gave his shoulder a comforting pat. He wouldn't be this pissed off if he'd been summoned back from a mission. Maybe he'd been on an illicit night out tonight, like her.

"Were you about to get lucky too?"

He looked at her then, and the despair in his dark eyes stabbed through her heart.

"I've been seeing a girl for the last two months."

"What?" She gripped his arm, trying to ignore the hurt that twisted through her. She'd told him everything about Steven at the time. "Why didn't you tell me? You know you can trust me." She wouldn't even have told Meg without Brad's consent.

"It had nothing to do with trusting you." His voice was raw, and a shudder of presentiment inched along her spine. What wasn't he telling her? "I didn't want to put you in any danger."

"Danger?" She frowned, not sure what he meant. "Why would knowing that put *me* in danger?"

"I didn't want to risk it, all right?" He sounded savage. "But it's over. The fucking bastards got to her. Ripped out her *throat*. There was nothing I could do by the time I got there. She'd already gone."

Nausea churned as grief for Brad and the unknown girl crushed her chest, and she pressed her forehead against his shoulder. Crimson drenched memories clawed through her mind. Steven, holding her hands, telling her he didn't want to live without her. And then the blood, so much blood, spraying from his torn throat. The attack had been so swift, so unexpected, that she'd frozen for vital seconds and lost her chance for vengeance. But the stark truth was she should've been able to sense the danger before the killing strike. She should have been able to save him.

All her training, useless in the one moment when she'd needed it most.

"I'm so sorry." She threaded her fingers through his, trying to ease his pain. His guilt. They both knew this girl would still be alive if she hadn't become involved with Brad.

"But guess what?" He tightened his fingers around hers. "Before I even had time to process it, Alex appeared outside her window. I was so fucking messed up I let him in without thinking. Didn't take him a second to knock me out and bring me back here. But here's the thing, Rowan. How the hell did he know where I was?"

Alex, a four-hundred-year-old vampire who'd been turned at the age of twenty-five, was as close to Brad as Meg was to her. Surely he wasn't suggesting Alex had something to do with this murder?

"Maybe he followed you? God, Brad." She cupped his face and forced him to look at her. "You can't think Alex killed her. It's just not possible. He's your *friend.*"

His expression was bleak. "Who found you after Steven was murdered in the street?"

She reared back, denial pounding through her brain.

Meg had appeared that night, seemingly from nowhere, and dragged her from the murder scene before she'd had time to fully register what had happened. Before the police had arrived. Before she'd been pulled into the murder inquiry.

But how did she know where I was that night?

"No." She shook her head as if that might lend power to the word. "I don't believe it. You don't believe it either. We both know who's responsible."

Not all vampires pledged allegiance to the Enclave of the Phoenix. There were countless alliances across the world. Most of them posed no threat. A handful was a force to be respected but only one wielded power as great as the Enclave presided over by Sakarbaal.

The Strigoi Echelon, as ancient as the Enclave, was their one true enemy. They, like the ancients in the Enclave, despised half-bloods.

Unlike the Enclave, they didn't make any attempt to nurture the offspring of vampiric rapes. It was common knowledge they considered hunting down the loved ones of filthy dhampirs a fine sport.

Brad didn't answer. He uncurled his fingers and she saw a small phial of dark amber liquid in his palm. Uncomprehending, she looked at his grim face. Why had he brought his medication with him?

"Ever wondered what shit they put in this stuff?" He held the top of the phial between finger and thumb. "Ever wondered what would really happen if we stopped taking it?"

"You know what'll happen." She understood what he was saying. She'd gone through the same doubts seven years ago. And look where it had got her. "Don't you remember what happened to me when I stopped taking it after Steven died?"

Even now the memory was enough to give her nightmares. Without the synthetic blood substitute to curb her primal impulses she'd slid into a vortex of mindless self-destruction. And the pain, like acid eating her from the inside out, had been unimaginable.

"Withdrawal." His entire focus was on the glowing phial. Amber acid, they called it between themselves. "But if you could get past that, you'd be free." His eyes were glazed, lost in his own fantasy world. "Dhampirs don't need to be medicated in order to survive. You know that."

"Yes, but they live like savages, scavenging in the gutters." Free? What exactly did he mean by that? They would still be half vampire, half human. They would still neither fit nor be accepted in either world. What kind of freedom was that? Despite the restrictions imposed on dhampirs by the High Council, at least here in the HQ's mansion they were surrounded by every luxury. "That's no life. And they rarely live to see twenty."

He gave a bitter laugh and pity glowed in his eyes, as though she was an incredibly naïve human. "And our projected lifespan is so bloody great, isn't it? Can you name one of us who's lived to see their twenty-seventh birthday?"

I don't want to have this conversation.

She didn't want to think about all the dhampirs she'd known who had died horrible deaths while serving the wishes of the High Council. She especially didn't want to think about her dhampir friend Belinda who'd been slain less than six months ago, while servicing a high-ranking member of the Strigoi. Belinda's specialty had been going undercover as a brainless sex nymph and extracting vital Intel from her victims. She'd despised that part of her job, but it wasn't as though they were given any choice in their assignments, and Belinda had excelled at her duties. Right up until that last suicidal mission.

Rowan dragged herself back from the painful memories. It was her *birthday*. Tomorrow night she was going on a *date*. She snatched her hand from Brad's and speared her fingers through her hair, pressing her forehead against her palms.

She knew she was destined to die young. But had he really needed to thrust that down her throat today of all days?

"Rowan." His voice dropped to a whisper. "I've less than nine months left until I turn twenty-seven. I don't know what's going on, but I do know one thing. I won't find the answer here."

Dread seeped into her heart. There was only one place that might hold the answers he was searching for.

"You can't seriously be thinking of going to Romania? They might not torture our kind like the Strigoi do but—"

"This half-life isn't enough anymore." Savagery underpinned every word. "The only chance of finding out the truth is going to Romania. That's where our history is, Rowan. Christ, I need to get away from here. I'm sick of the lies."

Although it was the end of February and there was a hint of snow in the air, her room was warm. But shivers chased over her arms and chilled her blood. She got through each day by not thinking about her mortality, by not dwelling on the knowledge that she was now the second oldest dhampir in residence.

Ten years ago, she had been the eighth.

But now Brad was stirring up all the confused feelings and unasked questions that had seethed beneath the surface of her existence ever since Steven's death. She didn't want to face them. Didn't want to dig deeper. All she wanted was a *normal life*.

"You can't trust any of them." His whisper was so low she had to strain to hear his words. "Bottom line, Rowan. Vampires won't turn against their own for us. You have to remember that."

She couldn't bear seeing him so broken. "Brad." She took his hand and focused on his knuckles. It hurt too much to look at his grief ravaged face. "Don't make any decisions about your future yet. I know how much you're hurting, but things will get better. It took me a while, but I recovered after what happened to Steven."

Lies. She'd only pushed that night into the deepest recesses of her mind, but she hadn't recovered from it. How could anyone get over something like that? But pretense was all she had to offer Brad.

His lips twisted into a travesty of a smile, but his grip on her hand tightened. He knew what she was doing. And the hollowness of her words reverberated around her brain like a malignant echo.

Brad didn't have an unknowable future stretching out before him. He didn't have the advantage of time on his side for things to *get better*.

None of them did.

She leaned her head against his shoulder, the way she had so many times in the past, and the silence enveloped her and sank into her bones.

There was nothing left to say.

Azrael

THE FOLLOWING afternoon Azrael teleported to a narrow country lane on the outskirts of a village in Cornwall, where Gabe had made his home with Aurora. He eyed the large stone house, with its rambling, snow dusted gardens, that looked as if it had been standing for more than three hundred years.

He rapped his knuckles on the door. Contacting Gabe wasn't as simple as it used to be. Now he was mortal, he'd lost the archangelic ability of telepathic communication.

He didn't want to think about everything else Gabe had lost. The price of saving Aurora's life had been Gabe's immortality. How could he bear to survive as a *human*?

Gabe pulled open the front door. "Hey, stranger." Gabe thumped his back and grinned, as if he wasn't living in purgatory. "Come in, it's freezing out there. You're letting the heat out."

He wasn't sure what he'd been expecting. For Gabe to appear haggard? But he looked great. Better than great. And something else that he couldn't place but gnawed at the edges of his mind.

"Nice place," he said, as he stepped over the threshold and glanced around the flagstone hallway. A magnificent central staircase led upstairs, and although it was completely different to the villa Gabe used to live in, there was a surreal sense of similarity.

"No one's lived here for as long as Aurora could remember. It was falling apart and when we managed to hunt down the owner, he didn't want to sell. Something about it holding nostalgic memories from his childhood." Gabe grinned. "That's when I discovered I haven't lost all of my powers of persuasion."

"Is that the only power you've retained?"

"Az. It's okay. I haven't changed my mind. I don't care that I'm no longer immortal. Not when I have Aurora."

It was unnerving, the way he spoke about Aurora. It was blindingly obvious how much he adored her. For sure, she was unique, a remarkable human whose heritage straddled two different dimensions. But that extraordinary union of DNA wasn't the reason he was reluctant to meet her. It was because she was also the reincarnation of Gabe's first love, Eleni.

And Eleni had been part Nephilim.

Nephilim, the beloved children of archangels, weren't supposed to be able to be reborn and the revelation had seared the embers of his heart.

Long before any archangels had fallen, their great goddess had proclaimed any offspring conceived between her personal creations and mortals, and all their descendants, were soulless. Unable to ever reincarnate.

He'd believed her without reservation for their goddess would never lie to them.

How wrong I was.

Were the souls of countless Nephilim eternally trapped in an obscure fracture on the astral planes? Was that why it was so difficult for them to return to the corporal plane?

"Hi, Azrael." A woman walked across the hall towards him. There was a guarded note in her voice, as if she wasn't sure of her reception.

The blood pounded in his temples. She looked nothing like Eleni. Not that he had expected she would. *What are you?*

"Az, this is Aurora." Subtle warning threaded through each word, and the implication that he might snub the beloved of a fellow archangel grazed his soul.

Whether she was Eleni or not, she was still the one Gabe had chosen. He respected that, even if he couldn't agree with it.

"It's an honor." He took her hand, and her touch ignited a blast of psychic power, as images streaked through his mind. Of another time. Another life. Of an ancient civilization that had nurtured the archangels in their youth.

The same civilization that had, millennia ago, been mercilessly destroyed.

Renewed guilt scorched through him. As raw and devastating

as the moment he'd realized his fatal error so many thousands of years ago.

And the blistering betrayal of his goddess, that had shattered the fundamental core of his being.

He'd fooled himself into believing he'd overcome the guilt, buried the betrayal. But the two were inextricably entwined. He didn't deserve to forget any of it, even superficially.

"Aurora." His voice was hoarse as the last sliver of doubt vanished. Gods, it was true. Now he'd met her he knew she really was Eleni, the last surviving descendant of the Archangel Zadkiel.

And she had no idea that her untimely death had been *all my fault.*

The tension in her face faded. "Yes." Her smile was understanding. "I know this is strange and awkward. But's it's really me."

He released her hand, and Gabe threaded his fingers through hers. And then it hit him. The eerie sense of something being just out of reach.

Gabe looked happy. Really happy. Shock clawed through him at the realization of how long it had been since the other archangel had looked so contented.

He's no longer an archangel. But did the fact he'd lost his immortality really change his heritage?

They went into the kitchen, which resembled a demolition site.

"Renovations." Aurora plugged in a kettle. "Did Gabe tell you we're funding new science research facilities at several universities?"

He hadn't. Then again, since the immortality draining incident, he and Gabe had only spoken once, when Azrael had arranged to come and visit them today.

"Aurora's idea," Gabe said. "I planned on building a private research lab, but this way we get countless perspectives."

Their ideas were fascinating. To investigate the fringes of science without preconceived notions. But throughout the entire conversation his blood thundered in his temples and heart thudded against his ribs.

They wanted to achieve so much. Explore psychic develop-ment—or the lack of it—in humans and undertake archaeological digs to discover the ancient histories that had been hidden for millennia.

But it was futile. They'd never manage to accomplish even a fraction of their dreams. Within a few score years at most both Gabe and Aurora would be *dead*.

"Anyway." Aurora glanced at Gabe before turning back to him. "You're going to stay for something to eat, aren't you? We thought we'd go to the local pub."

His gaze dropped to their entwined fingers, and inexplicably it reminded him of the woman he'd met last night. Not for a second had he imagined she'd leave, when the desire between them was so potent. It must have been one hell of a family emer-gency. But he'd not detected any panic or shock radiating from her. Just frustration.

No woman had ever turned him down. But it added to her air of mystery. Anticipation sizzled through his blood. In a few short hours he'd see her again. And then he realized Aurora was still waiting for his reply.

"Sorry. Can't make it tonight."

Her look was calculating, as if she could see straight through him. "You have a date, don't you?"

Gabe gave a derisive snort of laughter. "Archangels don't *date*."

Gabe had got that right. He never dated. Except asking Rowan to join him for dinner tonight suddenly sounded very much like a date.

He hadn't meant to ask her out. But she'd looked so appealing with her hair tumbling around her face and her lovely green eyes filled with disappointment. The words were out before he'd realized.

And he didn't regret them.

"Don't judge everyone by yourself," Aurora said. "Azrael, your date is more than welcome to join us tonight if you'd like."

"Yeah, because an immortal would really want to hang out on planet Earth with a couple of humans." Gabe appeared to find the scenario amusing.

"You don't know that he's seeing an immortal."

"That's more likely than him hanging out with a human."

They continued to discuss his dating status, and it was fucking surreal. It was like he'd tumbled back in time, to when Gabe and Eleni used to be just like this.

They'd gently mocked his aversion to becoming even superficially involved with any of his lovers, and he'd let them—let everyone—think it was because he didn't want commitment.

He didn't, but not for the reasons they imagined. Unlike many of the archangels, he'd believed in their goddess' edict that they were forbidden to fall in love with humans.

She had created her archangels to worship and adore *her*, and only her.

He'd loved her unconditionally. Trusted her implicitly.

Had never, not even for a fleeting moment, imagined she was part of the cursed, recurring visions that had plagued him for decades and driven him on endless quests to uncover lost civilizations in the hope of unlocking ancient secrets. Knowledge that would give him the power to prevent the destruction of the Nephilim in the coming apocalypse.

The answer had never been hidden in the past. It had been staring him in the face all along. In the corrupted guise of his loving goddess.

I need to get out of here.

"Gabe's right." He shot them a sardonic grin. "I don't do dating. Sounds way too complicated."

"You should try it sometime." Aurora shot a pointed glance in Gabe's direction. "You might be surprised."

"That's the kind of surprise I can live without."

But as he left, with half-meant promises to keep in touch, an uneasy certainty weaved through his mind. It was more than simply sex he wanted with Rowan.

He wanted to unravel her mysteries and discover her secrets.

Did that sound like a date?

No. He didn't get involved. Ever. Rowan could keep her secrets.

He took a deep breath, and the chilled air filled his lungs. One mystery at least had been solved. Eleni truly had been reborn. But that reality only threw up a thousand more questions. Because her existence forced them all to face something they never had before.

Had any other Nephilim returned during the centuries?

CHAPTER 5

ROWAN

*R*owan parked the Mercedes McLaren in a private car park behind a small apartment block, using one of the many resident permits and gate keys she possessed. Not only was this space gated and secure, it was only a five-minute walk from the King's Road.

It was only seven-forty-five, so she had plenty of time. And although all the articles she'd ever read urged her to be at least five minutes late, she had no intention of playing that kind of ridiculous mind game.

She didn't want to risk him thinking she wasn't going to turn up.

Heart thudding against her ribs she slid out of the car. A frigid wind blasted her and in the same instant she tensed against the chill, the unmistakable odor of rogue vampire hit her senses.

No. The denial shrieked through her mind as she froze against the open door of the car. She'd ignore it. Holding her breath, she shut the door, but still the foul stink of decay sank into her flesh like a putrid blanket of fog.

She gritted her teeth and folded her arms as she strode

purposefully in the opposite direction to the scent. But it permeated her mind, like skeletal fingers scraping across a chalkboard. A primal imperative to hunt that was as much a part of her biology as her need to consume blood.

"Shit." The word hissed into the night, a puff of infuriated white mist. Clenching her fists, she marched back to the car and wrenched open the door. She retrieved her katana, concealed beneath the plush carpet, and grabbed a couple of hawthorn stakes. Of all the bloody times, she had to run across a rogue right now.

Sure, she was *supposed* to be out working. That was the only way she'd managed to escape tonight. Sakarbaal and his entourage were, it seemed, staying in London for a while.

Luckily her long leather coat hid her dress. Because who went hunting wearing a dress? Generally, she never bothered leaving her hair down either, but no one had remarked on it.

Not even Meg.

Swiftly she followed the reek of decaying blood. She left the dimly lit car park and strode down the narrow, gloom filled alley, towards a hunched shadow. There was no need for stealth. This vampire, lost in the bloodlust of attack, radiated only primitive cunning and need.

Rogues, whether they had once been civilized or had always groveled in the gutter, couldn't be allowed free rein. They drew too much attention with their undisciplined attacks and unregulated killings. Other vampires might want them destroyed but they rarely wanted to destroy them themselves.

They left that to the dhampirs.

The creature whirled, blood dripping from its fangs. Rowan bared her teeth. She was wearing her brand new high-heeled silver boots, completely inappropriate for fighting in. And they'd be ruined if they got splattered with blood.

The rogue dropped its victim, who began to crawl sluggishly

into the gutter, and advanced towards her. There was no spark of intelligence behind those blank, bloodshot eyes, only primal instinct. He was likely newly made and had been left to fend for himself by a vampire too ignorant or arrogant to give a shit.

Which just made her job a whole lot easier. If he had never used his inherent vampiric powers, the chances were he had no idea he even possessed any. She leaped out of the way as he jumped at her, and his shock at her speed radiated from him.

He hadn't a clue what she was.

Undeterred, he turned to leap at her again. God, what was the time? She didn't want to be late for her first date in more than seven years. She gripped her katana with both hands and severed the creature's head from its neck in mid-air, then hastily jumped out of the way. Had she managed to avoid the blood? How mortifying if she turned up with blood in her hair.

She stepped over the head and slammed her foot on the creature's abdomen. His hands blindly reached for her as she whipped out a stake and thrust it into his chest. Then, using the sole of her boot, *which was going to completely ruin it,* she hammered the stake all the way through the rogue's heart.

Its body crumbled, vanished and she glared around, looking for the victim. Although she didn't possess the power to completely wipe the memory of an attack, she did have the means to close any puncture wounds. And if there was no evidence, who would believe the rantings of a traumatized human?

She just hoped the victim wasn't so badly injured that she'd have to take further action. Why had this happened tonight? She could go weeks without finding a random rogue. Usually dhampirs hunted specific targets.

A faint scuffling caught her attention. The victim, a teenage boy, peered up at her through glazed eyes. Trying to curb her impatience, she gently eased his head back so she could get a look at the damage. Didn't look too bad. Lucky she'd caught the rogue when she had.

"Was that... a vampire?" His voice sounded strangled as he gripped her wrist.

"No." She unhooked his fingers so she could get the phial secreted in an inside pocket of her coat. Unlike full blood vampires her saliva didn't contain the healing properties required to close puncture wounds, but their pharmaceutical geniuses had come up with an impressive substitute.

"Are you... an angel?"

Despite the fact she was running late, his unexpected question made her laugh. She'd been called many things in her life. But no one had ever asked if she was an angel. She bent over him, phial in hand.

"Yes," she whispered. How nice to be thought an angel when most humans, if they knew what she truly was, would call her a monster or worse. She dripped a couple of drops onto the boy's neck and his skin sizzled as it healed.

With one hand she pulled him upright. He didn't fall over.

That was good enough for her.

She picked up the stake. She needed that as proof to claim her bounty. Then she turned on her heel and ran back to the car.

Azrael

AZRAEL FOUND *Estella's* without any problem. It looked casual and laid back, with a bar taking up the length of one wall and the restaurant occupying the remaining space. He'd even arrived a few minutes early so Rowan wouldn't have to wait for him. Except, as it turned out, *he* was the one waiting for *her*.

He'd never had to wait for a woman before. He wasn't entirely sure he liked the experience. It felt too—mortal.

His vague irritation vanished when he caught sight of her

hurrying along the road towards him. Her long hair was loose, and the bitter wind tossed her black curls around her face in glorious abandonment.

And he remembered why he'd wanted to see her again. Why he was waiting here, ten minutes after the appointed time, when under any other circumstances he would've walked when the clock struck eight.

It was because, quite simply and possibly bizarrely, he enjoyed looking at her.

"Hi." She sounded out of breath. "Sorry I'm late. I had to sort out a last-minute work thing."

She was wearing a long black leather coat with silvery boots. How high did the boots go? To her thighs?

He couldn't wait to find out.

"I hope they paid you overtime." He draped his arm across her shoulders in a blatant gesture of possession. For some reason he wanted every male in the vicinity to know that this woman belonged to him tonight.

And he had no intention analyzing why.

She gave a breathless laugh as they entered the warmth of the restaurant.

"I'm paid on commission. But even so, it was really bad timing." She raked her fingers through her hair, attempting to tame the windswept tangles.

He led her to the bar and as she sat on one of the high stools her coat flapped open revealing her black lace covered thigh. The boots only reached to just below her knee. He'd not seen anything so seductive in years.

"Sounds intriguing. What do you do?"

"If I told you, I'd have to kill you." She sounded perfectly serious.

He laughed. His question had been automatic as he had only a fleeting interest in what she did for a living. But her refusal to tell him made him genuinely curious. Especially since she *still* wasn't flirting.

She absolutely meant that she had no intention of telling him what her job was.

He leaned closer so he could breathe in her evocative scent of jasmine. "That's usually my line."

He waited for the inevitable questions. What woman could possibly resist such a provocation? But she merely nodded, and apparently had no intention of trying to coax the information out of him.

"Can you tell me your name?" She sounded as though she would completely understand if he said no. What's more, he got the impression she wouldn't especially care if he said no.

In the past he'd often not known the name of females he'd had. It had certainly never bothered him at the time. But now, with Rowan, he discovered he wasn't at all impressed by the notion that *she* might not care as to whether she knew his name or not.

"Azrael."

She repeated his name as if it was an exotic treat she was savoring on her tongue. "Like the angel of death?"

Right. He hadn't expected that. She hadn't struck him as an authority on archangels, even if the information in general circulation about them was complete crap.

He was saved from answering by the bartender taking their orders. Rowan requested an unopened bottle of water. And then they were ushered to their table in a secluded corner.

She took off her coat. She was wearing a long sleeved black and silver dress that clung to her curves and hugged her mid-thigh. Long silver earrings, a riot of tiny stars and half-moons, glinted against her midnight hair and she wore half a dozen or so silver bangles.

One bangle was encrusted with amethysts.

They sat down and she rested her wrists on the edge of the

table. A faint hum of electricity emanated from the semiprecious stones, a sure sign the quartz's inherent power wasn't dormant. She didn't wear amethysts merely for decoration. These unpolished stones had been cleansed and were well used. Rowan knew of their healing power. *Interesting.*

He trailed a path over the back of her hand. Her skin was smooth and cool to his touch, and he slid his finger into the tempting hollow between her thumb and palm. Her thumb closed over him, so slightly it might have been unintentional, but the sensation of entrapment was exquisite.

His gaze caught hers. Slowly he pushed his finger a little deeper. Without breaking eye contact she curled her fingers into a fist, creating a tight passage that cocooned him in seductive promise.

Long black lashes framed her entrancing eyes, and her delicate bone structure was enhanced by an ethereal translucent quality. He'd thought her beautiful in the nightclub. He'd been wrong.

She was stunning.

She didn't release his hand when a waiter came to take their order, and when they were once again alone, he leaned over the table until their breath mingled. "I've been looking forward to tonight, Rowan."

"So have I." Her whisper was husky, provocative, and like a smoky aphrodisiac weaved into his veins and smoldered his blood. "I'm glad last night fell through now."

So was he. An undercurrent of sexual awareness had sizzled through his blood since the moment he'd met her, and the postponement of consummation was deliciously erotic.

He curved his fingers around her fist and brushed his lips across her knuckles. "Tonight, I'll make all your fantasies come true."

She smiled, as if she thought he didn't mean a word.

"That'll be nice." Her polite response confirmed his suspicion.

His lips curved into a wicked grin against her knuckles. Tonight might be many things. But he had no intention of any of it being merely *nice*.

He was going to rock her world. But he had the strongest suspicion she was going to rock his, too.

CHAPTER 6

ROWAN

*R*owan gazed into Azrael's dark eyes. Fascinating golden flecks gave him an intriguing untamed appearance and she knew she was enjoying this encounter far too much for her future peace of mind.

She pushed the thought aside. It was just a one-night stand. The only difference was, for the first time, she was experiencing the novelty of seduction beforehand.

"Tell me, Rowan." His voice was sinfully sexy, and a wicked smile curved his delectable lips. It was obvious he knew his lethal charm could get him anything he wanted. "What's your most outrageous fantasy?"

He'd disappear faster than a staked vampire if she told him what she really wanted was to be a *full blood human.* He'd either think she was insane or into role acting so completely that reality was a distant memory.

No way was she going to spoil this moment with the truth. Well, not the whole truth anyway.

"My most outrageous fantasy?" Her voice sounded surprisingly husky. And although she'd spent an hour practicing to get her tone just right before leaving her bedroom earlier tonight, it had nothing to do with artifice.

It was hard to breathe properly when he held her hand as though it was something infinitely precious and when he looked at her with eyes that smoldered with blatant desire. It was a miracle she could speak at all when she could scarcely drag oxygen into her lungs.

"Yes?" He breathed the word across her knuckles, a sensuous whisper of possible promise.

She knew he expected her to say *bondage* or *ménage* or maybe even having sex in a public place. But she was sick of having once-a-year sex in cars and back alleys. She wanted so much more than that.

"My most outrageous fantasy would be offering absolute trust to my partner."

Shock flared in his gorgeous eyes. *Shit*. Should she have said something more predictable? Desperately she tried to recall the sex advice and dating articles she'd dissected since last night. And realized she'd just dropped a major gaffe.

He probably thought she was hinting at something long term. And no matter how much she did wish for that, it was something she'd never seek. Not after Steven.

Not after Brad's tortured confidences last night.

"That's what I call a challenge." Azrael didn't sound on the verge of beating a hasty retreat. He sounded intrigued.

Enchanted by his response she smiled back at him. It was an impossible challenge, but the thought of him even attempting such a feat caused warmth to drift through her scarred heart.

She concentrated on memorizing every tiny detail of Azrael's face. She'd never seen such a fierce combination of strength and beauty before—and she'd seen more than her fair share of astounding vampiric beauty in her life.

The door to the restaurant smashed open and voices rose up.

"Calm down, son." The waiter's voice was firm, and with a

faint frown she glanced over to the door. And froze. God, *no*. It was the boy who'd been attacked. Why hadn't he just gone home? Why had he come in here of all places?

Azrael followed her glance. She took a deep breath and deliberately looked away from the boy. It wasn't as if he'd recognize her. It wasn't as though she had anything to worry about. But even *so*. Talk about shitty luck.

"...think it was a vampire..." The boy's voice was edged with panic and it seemed everyone in the restaurant was watching him. She picked up her water and took a long swallow. Why didn't they take the kid into a back room?

Azrael looked back at her. "So," he said, "about this challenge of yours—"

"But an angel saved me," the boy said and from the corner of her eye she saw how the manager and another guy were attempting to usher the boy somewhere less conspicuous. Even Azrael appeared distracted as he threw the boy another glance.

They'd almost got him through the door that led into the staff area when he swung around. Even though she was focusing on her water with fierce concentration, she knew the boy was looking directly at her. Against her will, her gaze caught his.

He was riveted. Why didn't the management just shove him through the door? But instead he raised his arm and pointed at her, a look of reverential awe scrawled across his features.

"There." His whisper thundered through her head as if he'd yelled from the highest church steeple. She could feel the ripple in the atmosphere as the other diners turned to see who the boy was pointing at. Heat seared her cheeks and she forcibly resisted the urge to slide under the table and hide.

What a bloody idiot she was. She should have taken the time to use her limited powers of persuasion, combined with her amethysts, to cloud the boy's memory so he wouldn't remember the attack, or his subsequent rescue. But she'd been so eager not to be late for her date that she'd been derelict in her duty.

And this was what happened when she tried to cut corners. It came back and tore great chunks out of her arse.

"Hey." Azrael's low voice pierced her self-condemnation. "Are you okay?"

She risked shooting the boy another glance, but finally he'd been persuaded to leave the restaurant. She refocused on her water, not sure she wanted to see the expression on Azrael's face just yet.

"I'm fine." She'd just managed to make herself the center of attention, and not through something meaningless or innocent which could be easily overlooked. She'd made a basic error of judgment and errors that threatened the security of the Enclave weren't tolerated.

Dhampirs were supposed to flit like ghosts through the human population. Clearing up the messes left by rogues and carrying out assassinations ordered by high-ranking vampires. They weren't supposed to draw attention to themselves. Especially when that attention was connected to their line of work.

Especially when they happened to be *on an illicit date.*

"Are you going to kill me now?" Azrael's voice was gently mocking, but he still didn't relinquish her hand. "I know what you do for a living. You're an angel."

She didn't need to have a vampire's enhanced hearing to know she was the focus of every conversation in the restaurant. The sideways glances burned like lasers. All she could hope was the story went no farther than these restaurant walls. Because if it ended up online there was no hope of hiding her mistake from the Enclave.

Azrael was still waiting for her reply. She risked looking into his gorgeous eyes and almost forgot the mess she'd got herself into.

"I'm supposed to be undercover."

It was true, in a way. She *was* undercover. As a human. The last thing she wanted—especially right now—was for her cover to be blown.

The amusement dancing in his eyes died. "I see."

She knew he didn't. He probably imagined she was an undercover cop. But that was okay. Better than the truth. With a sick feeling in the pit of her stomach she pulled her hand free.

"I just need to go to the bathroom." Then, if he wanted out, he could just leave without fabricating some excruciating excuse. She left her coat on the back of the chair and weaved among the tables, keeping her head down. Not that it made any difference. Curious stares followed her right to the ladies' room.

With a heavy sigh she planted her hands on the vanity bench and braced her weight. She was probably making too big a deal of it. People would more likely think the boy was high, than he'd really been attacked by a vampire. No one was going to guess what she was, based on the rantings of a spaced-out kid. As far as she knew no-one had sneaked a photo of her, which meant the chances of the Enclave finding out about tonight was close to zero.

She straightened her shoulders. There had been plenty of time for Azrael to make his getaway. Steeling her nerves, she re-entered the restaurant and despite her best intentions her focus zeroed onto their table.

Her heart lurched. It was empty. He *had* left her. And although she'd expected him to, deep down she'd harbored the hope that he wouldn't.

Stop. It was a good thing he'd left. Now she could get out of here without drawing any more attention to herself.

She made her way back to the table, avoiding all the pointed looks. Except there weren't any. She risked glancing at the nearest group of diners, and they were completely ignoring her.

Not one person in the restaurant was looking her way. Considering how nobody had been able to tear their attention from her less than five minutes ago it was a bit weird to feel so invisible.

She pulled her coat off the back of her chair and tried not to remember the way Azrael had looked at her just before she'd gone to the bathroom. She could have sworn she'd seen sympathy in his eyes. But, as always when it came to deciphering human emotions, she'd been wrong.

It hadn't been sympathy. He'd been calculating how soon he could escape.

"Let me help." Azrael's dark, seductive voice drifted against her ear as his hands grasped her coat. Her heart jerked against her ribs and tremors raced along her arms at the contact. Yet a discordant thought vibrated through her jangling nerves. *How didn't I know he was behind me?*

But that puzzle faded into insignificance beside the over-whelming knowledge that he hadn't left. "Thanks."

He wound his arm around her waist and held her securely against his side, as if he was publicly declaring territorial rights. She shot him an uncertain glance as they made their way to the door before she pulled to a halt.

"I'll just go and settle the bill," she said. Azrael might never set foot in *Estella's* again and not give a damn about wasted food, time, or paying his way, but it was one of her favorite places. Even if she never came here again after tonight's spectacle.

"It's done, Rowan. I always pay my debts."

He pushed open the door and the February wind whirled with icy intent. His arm tightened around her, drawing her into the seductive heat that emanated from his body. He might no longer want to share dinner with her, but he still wanted her. She shoved her foolish daydreams aside and focused on her reality.

"Is your car nearby?" At least in a car she'd be out of the cold. She could close her eyes and pretend they were somewhere less sordid.

She felt his big body shake with silent laughter.

"No. It's not far. I'll soon warm you up." He tugged her closer and she sank into the fantasy that this was more than an anonymous hookup. Well, it wasn't anonymous for a start. She knew his name.

What am I thinking? She'd broken the golden rule of the Enclave. Dhampirs were supposed to be all but invisible in public. They should never be the focus of questioning glances. She needed to get back to the mansion and lay low. Not follow through with this illicit birthday present to herself anymore.

Without warning, an eerie shiver skated along the back of her neck and she stiffened, instantly alert. *Something's watching me.* She looked across the road and in her peripheral vision saw— could have sworn she saw—a shadow lurking in a dark doorway.

But there was nothing there. And nothing, not even a vampire, could move so fast that she wouldn't have seen it, even if it had vaporized. Once a vampire was in their sight, tracking its movement was one of the dhampirs' strengths.

She was seeing shadows when there were none.

But this is still too dangerous.

He suddenly pulled to a halt and looked down at her with a quizzical frown. Then, before she realized what he was doing, he shrugged off his long winter coat and flung it around her shoulders.

She stared at him, staggered by his gesture. Sure, she was a bit chilly, but her reaction just then had been more psychic than physical. But he hadn't just noticed her shiver. He'd given her his *coat*.

"Don't want you catching a cold."

She'd never had a cold in her life, thanks to the immortal side of her heritage. And the frigid weather didn't affect her much, although he must be freezing after his act of chivalry. His coat was heavy, encompassing her in a mantle of heated masculinity. But instead of handing it back to him she drew in a deep breath, luxuriating in the heady male scent of autumn forests that permeated the expensive wool with tantalizing promise.

"What about you?" Her voice was husky as she reached out and flattened her palm against his chest. Despite the fact he wore only a shirt, heat warmed her hand as though she touched a living furnace. "You're hot." The words slipped out without her meaning to, but instead of biting her tongue at her stupidity she smiled up at him. Because he *was* hot. He was the hottest damn thing she'd ever met in her life.

"So are you." His teeth flashed in an appreciative grin. "You even look great in my coat."

She could feel the thud of his heart beneath her fingers, an erotic tattoo that increased in tempo as she leaned towards him. *Don't do this.* But she couldn't leave him. Not yet. *Let me have tonight.* "You look great *out* of your coat."

His hands slipped beneath his coat, pulled open her leather one and cradled her waist. "You haven't seen anything yet."

CHAPTER 7

ROWAN

*R*owan dragged her fingers over his rock-hard chest and deliciously defined abs. She didn't doubt his word. Couldn't wait to see in the flesh what she could feel in the dark. Recklessly she pushed against him, desperate to discover if he was as ready for her as she was for him.

His erection jammed against her, promising her everything and more. A soft sigh escaped, and her fingernails dug into his ribs as his grip on her tightened.

"Is that a promise?" His coat slipped from her shoulders, but she didn't care. It wasn't his coat that heated her blood or caused her pulse to race.

"You bet." His voice was little more than a growl as he grabbed his coat before it fell onto the ground. He wrapped his powerful arms around her shoulders and pulled her sideways into a deeply recessed shop doorway. "I always keep my promises."

Once again, his teeth flashed in the dark as he offered her a smile of pure sin.

Before she could stop herself, she gripped fistfuls of his shirt and feverishly pulled the designer cotton from his pants. She wanted—*needed*—to feel naked skin. God, how much she wanted to press her naked body against his. To wrap her legs around his back. To experience the sheer luxury of sharing not only a bed but a whole night with him in her arms.

Through the pounding in her mind she realized her back was against a wall. No security lights glowed. No streetlamp threw incriminating illumination. An unobservant human would never know she and Azrael were buried in the shadows of the shop's portico.

Just a foretaste of what was to come. That's all she wanted right now. Her hands slid beneath his shirt and his firm abs sent tremors of need spiraling through her.

"I'll hold you to that." Her voice was uneven. She wasn't sure why she even answered him. She needed no promise from him and would never hold him to one even if, in a crazy moment of passion, he promised her the world.

"I'm counting on it." His hard thighs jammed her securely against the wall, his coat a welcome cushion against the damp stone. "Gods, I can't even remember the last time I wanted a woman as much as I want you." He cupped her face, his thumbs stroking her cheeks. As if she was something precious. "Are you an enchantress?"

"Yes." It was a sultry whisper, and yet laughter bubbled beneath the surface of her lust. In the space of one night she had been likened to both an angel and an enchantress. "But don't worry. It's not your soul I'm after."

His fingers speared into her hair, undeniably possessive. Her fingernails dug into his back, needing him closer.

"What is it you're after, Rowan?" One hand fisted in her hair, as if he was a conquering barbarian and she his helpless captive. It was a tantalizing fantasy. Especially when it was an impossible scenario. She could never be the helpless captive of a human.

But she could pretend.

"Your body, Azrael." She wanted to explore and tease and taste every inch of him. Wanted to memorize every second of their time together. Store it up, so she could relive every moment in glorious detail later.

That's what she wanted. But she had no intention of letting him know just how desperately she craved his touch.

Still gripping her hair, he curved his other hand around her throat. Her pulse hammered against his fingers, so deceptively fragile she could almost imagine he held her life in his hands.

"I have no problem with that." His raw whisper branded her lips. She had no idea what he meant. "Tonight, my body is yours."

His mouth was so close to hers. She wanted to lose herself and find mindless oblivion. How far away was his car?

She pushed one hand between their bodies. His erection filled her palm and it was all she could do not to rip open his pants and take him where they stood.

He gave a hoarse growl and rammed her back against the wall. His free hand roamed over her shoulder, briefly cupped her aching breast, and then he tugged her dress up to her waist.

Disappointment burned through her before she crushed it to dust. A quickie in a doorway was all she could offer him, and all she could expect in return. It wasn't as though she could risk seeing him again. Not when it might put his life in danger.

But I want so much more.

It could never happen.

He palmed her naked thigh, clearly appreciating the fact she'd worn suspenders and tiny lacy knickers tonight. His mouth claimed hers, savage and demanding as his fingers ripped the lace from between her thighs and teased her swollen lips.

Lust thundered through her veins, clouded her mind. But she never risked unprotected sex. She tilted her head to the side and loss shot through her when he released her tender mouth.

It was hard to find the words, but she sucked in a ragged breath and pressed her hand against his chest, to give herself a breathing space. Before she did something stupid.

As if this isn't risky enough.

Azrael

AZRAEL FROZE as Rowan stiffened in his arms. What the hell? He'd been seconds from fucking her up against a rough stone wall. Disgust flooded through him, but still couldn't dampen the raw need that rampaged through his blood. The lust that had obliterated everything but the need to possess this woman—*this human*—in his arms.

"Rowan." He sounded rabid. No wonder she flinched. He sucked in air between his clenched teeth, tried to beat back the ravening imperative to cast a glamour and thrust inside her welcoming heat.

Except she was trying to stop him.

He'd lost control. *I never lose control.* And now she was looking at him with those great green eyes of hers as if she was having serious second thoughts.

It wouldn't take a second to enter the very edges of her mind and erase the last few moments, just as he had with the diners in *Estella's* so none of them recalled the incident between Rowan and the confused boy.

But he couldn't do it. Because that would be just as despicable as shoving her up against a wall in the first place.

"Sorry." He brushed silky soft strands of midnight hair from her cold cheek and again cursed himself. She was slowly freezing when, by now, they could be back in his hotel suite. "It's not the right weather for outdoor games."

Without waiting for her answer, he straightened his coat around her shoulders before tugging her against his side. It was odd, this compunction he had to protect her from the elements. Logically he knew she was warm enough in her long leather coat, but something compelled him to wrap her in his own coat.

If a human had done something similar it would smack of

primitive male wanting to publicly brand his mate. But since he wasn't human, it obviously wasn't that.

"I suppose not." Her voice was guarded as though she wasn't convinced he wouldn't sweep her into the next available shop doorway. "So how much farther is it?"

"Just around the next corner." Damn, it hurt having to walk when his cock was so hard. He'd never appreciated how much he relied on teleportation when the going got tough. He clenched his teeth and concentrated on putting one foot in front of the other.

Despite his discomfort, amusement flared. This was the first time in his long existence that he'd had to wait for gratification. Archangels never needed to. Then again, they didn't go around picking up oblivious humans either. At least, he never had.

"Okay," she said. "It's just I don't think you should be walking around without your coat on. It's making me feel guilty."

"Don't. I'm as tough as they come. The cold doesn't bother me." He couldn't recall anyone showing such simple concern for his welfare before. If she knew what he was, she wouldn't waste her time. He guessed there were some unexpected bonuses in hooking up with an unaware mortal. Who would have thought he'd find her solicitude so inexplicably charming?

"Hmm." She didn't sound convinced, but she did snuggle closer to share her body warmth. There was no need. He could feel the heat from her body radiating from her despite the two coats.

Not that he was complaining. She could crawl all over him if she felt the urge. Preferably when they were both naked.

"Here we are." He hoped she couldn't hear the relief in his voice. They crossed the road and approached the Victorian hotel, its gothic architecture quaintly imposing. Rowan paused and frowned as if the place didn't meet with her approval.

What would she prefer? A tropical island retreat? A secluded cabin with breathtaking mountainous views? If it wasn't for the fact that his method of transportation could tip her into hysterics, he could take her anywhere in the world she wanted to go.

Make that the universe.

"We're going in here?" She shot him an uncertain look. "Did you book a room?"

She sounded as though such a notion had never crossed her mind. Where had she imagined he was taking her?

"I did." He gestured for her to precede him into the brightly lit foyer. "It's the closest hotel I could find to *Estella's*."

"Impressive." She sounded impressed too, but when he looked at her, she wasn't admiring the ornate interior. She was staring at him and for a second the soft, unguarded look on her face caused an odd pain to stab through his chest.

Unguarded? The thought jangled in his mind. Did she usually guard her expression? It hadn't occurred to him she might do such a thing. But now she was simply smiling at him, with no hint of the vulnerability that had so fleetingly illuminated her delicate features.

He wound his arm around her waist and led her to the elevators. *Never* had it taken so long to get the female he desired where he wanted her. But, despite the inconvenience, he wouldn't have forsaken that walk with her. It had been... different.

Everything about her was unique. A crystalline certainty glittered in his mind, a warning he had no intention of heeding.

One night wouldn't be enough.

CHAPTER 8

ROWAN

*A*s Rowan entered the lift with Azrael, she tried to stop grinning. He'd think she was insane. But she couldn't help it.

Tonight, she was going to share a bed with a guy who surpassed every fantasy lover she'd ever conjured from her fertile imagination.

The door closed. She turned in the possessive circle of his arms and looked at him. His eyes were dark with passion, the golden flecks that highlighted his irises giving him a seductively wild air.

She shoved him back against a gilt-framed mirror. Shock flickered in his mesmeric eyes. Had nobody ever shoved him before? He looked as if he couldn't believe she had been capable of such a feat.

She wound her arms around his neck, pressing herself against him and this time when his coat slid from her shoulders, he didn't try to rescue it.

"You pack a powerful punch." He sounded impressed. "Got any more surprises up your sleeve?"

He probably wouldn't appreciate it if she demonstrated her

true strength by lifting him from the floor and tossing him across the lift. All he saw when he looked at her was a deceptive fragility. But that was only an outwardly human shell that contained the tainted DNA of a hybrid abomination.

She only wanted him to see the shell. Because if he saw any deeper this encounter would be over before it had even begun.

"If I told you what I had in mind, it wouldn't be a surprise." Her whisper was ragged as she forked her fingers through his hair.

The lift stopped and the door opened. Azrael didn't move. "It's been a while since anyone managed to surprise me." Amusement threaded through the heady lust in his voice. "Looking forward to it."

Not as much as she was. Flirting might be beyond her grasp, but she had no intention of missing this golden opportunity of indulging in a night of glorious sex. *That* didn't require small talk. Didn't require fielding awkward questions about her private life. And unlike the infrequent one-night stands she'd experienced over the last few years, there was no dull sense of despair knotting her gut.

For the first time since Steven's death, being with a guy didn't make her feel cheap.

"Unless you intend to take me where I stand, you're going to have to release me." There was no mistaking the hint of laughter in his voice. "I can see why you go undercover now. If anyone messes with you they're in for a shock."

"Oh." Hastily she peeled herself from him. She had to be careful. It was all very well for a guy to think she worked out or whatever but even that wouldn't account for him being unable to push her out of his way unless she let him.

He picked up his coat and swung it over his shoulder, his other arm wrapped around her waist. Within moments they found their room and he opened the door for her.

As the door swung shut the wall lights winked on, bathing the room in a low golden glow. He tossed his coat across a chair, wound his arms around her and pulled her back against him, his lips nuzzling her throat.

She leaned back, her hands cradling his, thrilled by the latent strength in his rock-hard muscles that embraced her. It hadn't even occurred to her that he'd hired a room for the night. Because hiring a room for an anonymous hookup made it... *personal.*

Her eyes drifted shut as his lips teased the sensitive skin behind her ear. It didn't matter what distinctions she made. This encounter with Azrael had become personal the second she'd agreed to meet him again. But this was as far as it would go. She couldn't do *personal.* It was too dangerous for the human involved. But god, she would do it tonight. And in the deepest recesses of her heart she would make-believe it was as personal as anything could be.

"I've never met an enchantress as seductive as you." His whispered words were an evocative caress against her ear. "Or an angel." There was a hint of laughter in those last words and although she wasn't sure why he found that amusing, his humor warmed her deep inside, in a hidden place she had thought forever frozen.

"How many have you met?" A tiny warning in the back of her mind urged her to skip this verbal foreplay. She didn't need it. It didn't stop her craving it.

And that was the danger. But she couldn't bring herself to shatter this illusory façade of intimacy.

She felt him smile against her sensitive skin as he began to leisurely unbutton her coat.

"You'd be surprised." Again, there was that hint of amusement in his voice, as if there was more to his words than simple flirting. "I've never had an angel like you in my arms before."

"Well don't worry." She looked at him over her shoulder as he slid her coat down her arms. His languid seduction was unbelievably alluring. "You haven't got an angel in your arms tonight, either." Not that she minded if he thought of her as an angel. At least that was a beautiful fantasy, unlike the ugly truth.

Her coat pooled on the floor and he turned her to face him. His hot gaze raked over her as though branding her features into his mind. "If I didn't know better, I'd swear you possessed the blood of immortals."

What a strange thing for him to say. Not that she was complaining about his odd word choice when he was clearly thinking of pure and angelic rather than dark and vampiric. She knew he was only flirting, that it was all a part of his inherent charm. But it didn't stop her hugging his words in her heart, to cherish and replay them in the future, during the dark times when she struggled to accept the reality of her existence.

"And if I didn't know better, I'd say you were descended from archangels." Was she flirting? Could it really be this easy?

His teeth flashed in a smile, but it seemed oddly false, as though he didn't find her comment amusing. Then it fled her mind as he began to tug her dress up her thighs.

"Rowan." His fingers skated over her naked thighs and she quivered in anticipation. "Means ancient protection against enchantment." He found her barely-there lacy thong and teased her wet cleft with one finger. She fisted his shirt and tried to focus. *Buttons.* She had to undo his buttons... "Were you named well? Will you resist my enchantments, Rowan?"

Hardly. How would he react if she told him the truth of her name? That her mother, with her last coherent thoughts, had called her unborn daughter Rowan. Not to protect against witch-craft or enchantments. But to keep the dead from rising.

It was all detailed in her mother's journal.

"Never," she said.

"Take this damn dress off." His voice was raw with need. "Before I rip it off you with my teeth."

She flashed him a grin as she took a step back and gripped the hem of her dress. "I'd like to see you try."

Before he could respond she pulled the dress over her head and flung it across the floor. His eyes smoldered and there was no need for words when his look said it all.

Thrilled by his reaction she planted her hands on her waist and very slightly tilted her hips. The black and silver corset she'd bought earlier that day—along with the rest of her outfit—was simple, elegant and utterly decadent.

She'd never worn anything like it before. But the thought of wearing it for Azrael had hooked into her mind and not let go. And now, seeing the way he couldn't tear his gaze from her, she preened with delight.

"Do you want to rip this off with your teeth?" She tugged provocatively at a silver ribbon as she backed up another couple of steps. "Or do you want to watch me strip for your pleasure?"

He moved so fast she was stunned into silence. They were so close her breasts grazed his chest with every ragged breath she took.

"You can strip for me later." It was a hoarse command. "Enchantress."

She wasn't sure whether it was an endearment or curse. Did it even matter? Before she could think of a suitable response, he swept her into his arms and strode towards the bed.

She clung onto his neck, heart ricocheting against her ribs. It had been years since anyone had picked her up like this. Not since she was a small child.

It was intoxicating. He made her feel fragile and vulnerable. As if she was truly a human woman without a secret life.

He lowered her onto the bed then tossed his shirt across the floor. As he kicked off his pants her gaze drifted from his face to drink in the magnificent sight of his broad shoulders, naked chest and taut stomach. He was built like a powerful god from antiquity. Bronzed, perfectly sculpted and completely irresistible.

"Enjoying the view?" His voice was raw with need but shot through with amusement as though her avid scrutiny pleased his ego.

"Yes." The word was little more than a croak as her heated gaze fastened on his glorious cock. Never had she seen such an enticing sight. The room blurred, and all that existed was Azrael standing before her like a proud unabashed god of pure desire.

"So am I." His intense gaze raked along the length of her body, and flames smoldered beneath her skin as though he branded her on a cellular level. Her heart hammered erratically as he focused on her wet sex, barely concealed by the whisper of black lace that passed for modesty. He knelt at her feet, tugged the flimsy material along her legs and eased her thighs apart.

"Beautiful." His voice was husky and soaked into her like potent whiskey. "Your scent is driving me out of my mind."

"Azrael." His name was a seductive aphrodisiac on her tongue. She speared her fingers through his dark hair, urging him closer, silently begging for something she hadn't craved in seven years.

The tip of his tongue teased her swollen lips. She gasped, gripped him harder and tried desperately not to buck beneath him. She felt him smile, his teeth grazing her sensitized flesh. Then his tongue licked over her clit, a caress of sheer hedonistic delight and her last shreds of self-control incinerated.

"I want you." It was a hoarse command and she wound his hair around her fingers and pulled him up. He swallowed, savoring her taste. It was so damned arousing she'd come if he so much as licked his lips. "God, Azrael, I need you inside me right *now*."

He kneed her thighs farther apart and planted his hands on the bed either side of her shoulders. His dark hair tumbled in wonderful disarray and she hooked her booted ankles around his waist.

Something nudged her lust-fogged brain. With a frustrated

groan she dragged one hand from his head and fumbled down the side of her boot. Where the hell was it?

"Are you all right?" His raw whisper flayed her senses. "Do you want to take your boots off? What's—"

She gave a grunt and yanked the packet from her boot. He eyed the pack of condoms as if she'd just whipped a cobra from her corset.

"Here," she panted. "Do you want to do the honors or shall I?"

For a second she had the oddest feeling he'd never been in such a position before. But that was mad. No one with a sliver of sense would have a one-night stand without using protection. Before that worrying thought could take hold, he shot her a manic grin.

"Be my guest." He rolled off her and sprawled on his back, and she ripped open the packet without taking her gaze from his massive cock. Her mouth watered. God, he was big.

With shaking fingers, she eased the sheath over the slick head of his cock. It was so tempting to wrap her hand around him, to explore his heavy balls, to taste and lick but if she did that he'd come. And then she'd have to wait ages before he was ready for her again and all she wanted right now was to fuck him so hard the world exploded.

His hand tangled in her hair as she labored over her task. "Is this some form of torture you've devised?" His voice rasped in the heated air. "Is it supposed to be this tight?"

She rolled back onto her knees and admired her handiwork. The condom reached nowhere near his root but hopefully it wouldn't pop off at an awkward moment.

"So long as it's not interfering with your blood flow." She couldn't tear her fascinated gaze away from him. Even encased in the luminous orange latex he was beyond outstanding.

He muttered something in a language she didn't recognize and then, so swiftly it took her breath away, he reversed their positions.

"Got anything else hidden down those boots?" He loomed over her, biceps straining as he braced his weight on his hands. She scrawled her fingernails over them, thrilling at the way his flesh tensed at her touch.

"I might have." No way was she telling him about the strategically concealed stiletto. She wrapped her legs around his hips, but he refused to obey her unspoken demand. "Azrael. What are you *waiting* for?" She was begging and she didn't care. Because they only had one night together, and she didn't want to waste a single moment of it in needless suspense.

His cock nudged her wet entrance and she sucked in a sharp breath. It had been so long since she'd had sex. Why was he taking so long about it? If he didn't hurry up, then to hell with his masculine pride. She'd pin him to the bed and ride him until she fried his brains.

His smile all but fried *her* brains. "Are you sure you're ready for me?"

Despite her frustration, laughter bubbled. "Don't worry. Your *ego* isn't that big. I'm sure I can manage anything you throw my way."

"Ouch." With infuriating self-restraint, he refused to succumb to her desperate wriggles. "Remember you said that."

She hooked her ankles around his waist and gripped his tight butt. His killer smile vanished, and he gritted his teeth, still fighting to maintain control.

But she wanted him out of control. She slid her finger over his butt and his pupils dilated, obliterating the last sliver of iris. He growled something unintelligible and then thrust inside her, so suddenly that for a second reality ceased to exist.

"F-fuck," she gasped, her nails tearing into his taut butt. He filled her so completely, she wasn't sure if she could even breathe anymore.

"Yes." The word was feral. But he didn't move, just remained locked inside her, giving her time to adjust to his absolute penetration. "You still with me?"

She hitched in a ragged breath, her mind reeling, as she attempted to unlock her rigid muscles. "Your ego is bigger than I first thought."

He laughed out loud. Entranced, she gazed at his perfect face that could surely make angels weep.

She would remember this moment for the rest of her life.

"You're exquisite." Slowly he raised his hips, and the sensual friction against her clit sent spears of lightning through her tender flesh. "You feel like hot liquid silk around me."

No one had said anything like that to her before. It was only sex talk, but thrills of pleasure sparked through her heart, regardless. Experimentally she tightened her internal muscles and he let out a groan of ecstasy.

"Rowan." He sounded tortured. "Gods, you're pushing me to the edge."

"I want you at the edge." She had no idea how she managed to gasp the words aloud. "I want to push you *over* the edge."

His thrusts became frenzied. He hammered her into the bed, and she lost all sense of time or place. There was only Azrael. Only this moment. Only this mind-blowing, incredible connection.

The thunder of her blood pounded in her head, a frantic counterpoint to the erratic staccato of her heart. She met each demanding slide of his cock. Savored each rasping gasp. Reveled in every tiny ripple that licked through her senses.

Her climax shattered through her, fierce and primal, like nothing she'd experienced before. And as sanity receded, Azrael's hoarse roar of release echoed through her mind and catapulted her from the precipice.

CHAPTER 9

AZRAEL

*A*zrael collapsed on top of Rowan. His lungs seared with the effort of dragging in air and he was still deeply embedded inside her glorious body. He couldn't recall the last time he'd had sex but gods. He couldn't recall it ever feeling this damn great.

It was an effort to raise his head. The curve where her neck met her shoulder was so deliciously enticing. But he was no lightweight and she was only a human. He didn't want to crush her.

Although she'd surprised him with the iron-like grip around his back. If he'd been human, he would've been in danger of a couple of cracked ribs. Last night in the club he'd never guessed she possessed such hidden strength, and it was a gratifying revelation.

He braced his weight on his forearms and looked down at her. Her long, dark lashes fluttered over her eyes, hiding their expression. Her cheeks were flushed, and her midnight hair spread over the ivory pillows in enticing disarray. Her corset concealed and revealed in equal delectable measure, and he was torn between leaving it on her and ripping it off. But there was no denying how it accentuated the curves of her body. The swell of her breasts rose and fell with every erratic breath, the valley of her cleavage an irresistible challenge yet to be conquered.

He eased out of her and lay on his side, head propped on his hand. A flicker of guilt burned through him. He'd used her more roughly than he'd intended. It didn't matter that she'd urged him on or matched him thrust for thrust. The last thing he'd wanted to do was hurt her, but he'd lost control. There was no excuse. She was strong, but she was still mortal.

She opened her eyes and looked at him. Never had a woman's gaze so entranced him.

"You're still awake." He couldn't tell whether that was censure or surprise in her voice. "I thought you would've passed out after that."

"I never pass out after sex." He shifted his hand to her thigh. "Are you okay?"

"I'm perfectly okay." Her voice was a seductive purr as her fingers traced over his chest and circled his nipple. Distracted, he followed her gaze along the length of his body and caught sight of a lurid orange *thing* hanging off his cock.

Before tonight, he'd never used a condom. Archangels neither caught nor transmitted infections. And as a form of contraception it was redundant. Archangels had been genetically designed to be incapable of procreation. Just because some, in the distant past, had managed to conceive the beloved Nephilim was irrelevant.

Conception required an archangel to fall. He never had. And he didn't intend to.

Not because of his cursed goddess' edict. It was because to *fall* required trust. And there was no way in hell he'd trust anyone but a handful of archangels again.

Since he couldn't share any of that with Rowan, he'd gone along with the whole condom fiasco.

"Why don't you get rid of that?" She glanced at the offending item. And then flicked the tip of her tongue across his nipple.

His cock jerked with anticipation and he grabbed a wad of tissues from the bedside table. Seriously, *this* side of things had never occurred to him when he'd picked up Rowan.

But it was a small price to pay if it eased her mind. They had all night and this time he'd take it slow. He'd worship her body the way he'd wanted to earlier. Hear her scream his name as she—

She gripped his shoulders and shoved him onto his back. *How did she do that?* Before he even managed to catch his breath, she straddled him, knees pressed against his hips, hands still clamped on his shoulders. Her smile was wickedly decadent, and her hair tumbled over her shoulders like a midnight waterfall.

He speared his fingers through her hair and luxuriated in the sensation of her teeth and tongue and lips on his flesh. If she wanted to be in charge that was fine by him.

As she worked her way down his body the ribbons and lace of her corset teased with tantalizing promise of what he had yet to discover. *Next time* he'd strip her first. There was still plenty of time for him to do everything to her that he intended.

She sat on his thighs, a delightful distraction in black and silver, her stockings an erotic whisper against his flesh. He could do without those damn boots though.

Carefully, as though she imagined he might break, she cupped his heavy balls. He choked back another groan and dug his fingers into her lace-covered flesh. The heat from the palm of her hand sank into him, tensing muscles and tightening the need. Yet for all her confidence when it came to sex, she handled him with a strange air of innocence.

She rose onto her knees and leaned over him. Her cleavage mocked him, laced into that devastating corset, and he palmed her delectable ass as she fiddled with something beyond his shoulder.

He should have guessed. She held a violently purple condom between her finger and thumb, and he was torn between biting out a curse or a laugh.

Luckily, she didn't appear to notice.

"Won't be a sec." She snaked down his body and her hot breath panted across his groin as she began her task.

He clenched his fists as she eased the condom over his swollen head. Damn, it was torture feeling her hands on him and seeing the look of awestruck concentration on her lovely face. Her lips were parted and all he had to do was buck his hips and his cock would slide inside her wet mouth.

"Rowan, you're killing me." He collapsed onto the pillow as she nibbled kisses around the base of his cock, one hand gripping his erection in a satisfyingly tight embrace.

Her teeth grazed his sensitized flesh as she smiled, and then a chill whispered over his damp skin as she rose onto her knees. She flattened her hands onto his chest, and her eyes were more black than green.

"Wouldn't want that." Her voice was uneven, and a growl rumbled in his throat as she hovered over his throbbing shaft. "Are you sure you're ready for me?"

Despite his discomfort he managed a feral grin at how she so artlessly tossed his own words back at him. "You're the expert on my *ego*. What do you think?"

Her smile was a captivating enigma of sultry seductress and disarming innocence, and fascination beat a heady tattoo through the lust that consumed him.

"I think you're more than ready for me," she gasped as she sank down the length of his shaft, and the sensation damn near turned him blind.

He cradled her breasts, her corset a feast for his senses and when she tensed her internal muscles, starlight exploded in the back of his mind.

"Ride me, Rowan." It was a hoarse command, and she sank

onto him, all the way, taking him up to the hilt. Such exquisite pleasure he all but came right then.

"Like this?" She sat back, black hair tumbling over her shoulders, eyes dark with passion and her lips provocatively parted. She looked like a goddess about to devour her prey. The image scalded his senses.

"Harder." It was a raw demand. "*Faster.*"

Her thighs tensed as she braced her weight but as she slid back down his cock, he bucked into her with such force she fell forward. She gave a breathless laugh, hands flattened against his chest, and matched him. The world became an unfocused blur and all he could see, all he could feel, was Rowan as she rode him as though her life depended on it.

Her bewitching gasps filled his mind and as her tight sheath convulsed around him, the little control he'd managed to cling onto shattered.

With a primal growl he came violently, blood pounding in his temples, lifting them both off the bed in a ferocious thrust. She sprawled in delicious abandon across his heaving chest.

He couldn't speak. Could scarcely think. So he just held her close, as their hearts thundered and breath shuddered in lingering ecstatic bliss.

Idly he played with her hair, twisting her curls around his finger and admiring the rich midnight hue. She raised her head and smiled down at him. She looked delightfully disheveled, and his suddenly insatiable *ego* swelled with pleasure. Gods, he was certainly making up for lost time tonight.

She lowered her head. He caressed her naked thighs and sexy stockings and waited for her kiss.

A knock on the door echoed through the room and before he could move a muscle Rowan catapulted off him like a streak of lightning.

He discarded the human protection, swung off the bed and wrapped his arms around her. She was practically vibrating with tension and he pulled her back against his chest. Who did she think was at the door?

Arms still around her, he walked her to the bathroom and grabbed a towel and bathrobe before draping the robe over her shoulders.

"It's room service," he breathed into her ear. "Aren't you hungry?"

She blinked at him. "*Room* service?"

He knotted the bath towel around his hips, shot her a salacious grin and opened the door. The waiter wheeled in the trolley, laid the table and left, all without so much as giving Rowan a sideways glance.

"I arranged it back in *Estella's*." While she'd been in the bathroom, he'd not only paid off their bill. He'd persuaded the manager to contact the hotel and relay their exact order. He pulled out a chair. "I invited you to dinner, Rowan. I'd hate to see you go without."

"Don't worry." She sat down and smoothed her napkin across her lap. "I definitely haven't gone without tonight."

He laughed and pulled the bottle of wine from the basket. "Glad to hear it. Wine?"

She put her hand across the top of her glass to prevent him from pouring. "No, thanks. Not when I'm—I'll stick with water."

"Not when you're what? On duty?" He had no idea why the possibility she was still actively on an investigation and had used him as part of her undercover operation pissed him off, but it did.

Her eyes widened in obvious surprise. "Of course not. I was going to say not when I'm having so much fun—but then I thought you'd think I was being an idiot."

One of them was being an idiot. And it wasn't her. It was a novel experience, and not one he wanted to repeat.

"I'm flattered you prefer me to a drop of good red." He swirled the deep rich liquid in his glass. She glanced up from her plate and then appeared riveted on the lead crystal. "How's your meal?"

She tore her gaze away from his wine. Maybe there was more to her avoiding alcohol than she'd told him. It would account for the fleeting look of desperate need that had flashed across her face.

He placed his glass on the table and reached for a bottle of water. Human alcohol did nothing for him in any case. He'd only ordered it because he thought she might enjoy it.

She licked her lips before turning back to her plate. "Just right," she said as she speared her fork into a bite-sized piece of steak.

It was an effort to tear his gaze from her, but he couldn't stare at her all night like a besotted mortal. And there was something he wanted to know. "Who did you think it was at the door just now?"

She shrugged one shoulder and avoided eye contact. "No idea."

"So you usually leap up like that? All you needed was a sword in your hand and you'd have looked like a warrior princess."

She didn't smile at his attempt at humor.

"You can never be too careful." She focused on her meal as though it was the most intriguing sight she'd ever encountered.

"Because of your job?" What the hell was she, a spy?

She made a non-committal *hmm* that stoked his curiosity higher.

She was the woman he was spending the night with. That was all. Why the obsession with wanting to find out more about her? Her job wasn't of any importance to him, and it didn't matter whether she was single. But the irrational need to know burned through him.

"Are you in a relationship with anyone? Someone who would consider you their personal property?"

"No." Her voice was guarded. "Are you?"

"That would be a no." He shot her a dazzling archangelic smile. She was beautiful, surprising and a revelation in bed. But none of that meant this was more than a one-night stand. He didn't want to give her the wrong idea. "I don't do relationships."

She visibly relaxed and instead of experiencing relief that she hadn't misunderstood him, macabre fascination flared. She was, after all, a *mortal*. Mortals were irresistibly drawn to archangels and invariably wanted a lot more than a single encounter. Why then did she appear perfectly fine when he'd basically told her tonight was all they would ever have?

Not that he wanted a messy emotional scene. *What the fuck do you want?*

"Neither do I." She smiled at him but for a fleeting second, he saw desolation in her eyes. "Too complicated."

Damn right it was. For a brief encounter, this was already more complicated than anything he could remember.

AZRAEL STIRRED, as Rowan stealthily untangled her limbs from his. After using the third and final condom—a lurid pea-green monstrosity—they'd fallen asleep on the bed, her head on his chest and his arm wrapped around her shoulders.

Another novelty, but this one he liked.

The side lamps glowed, and he watched her bend over to pick up her corset from the floor. Her tangled black hair cascaded over her shoulders, and his cock stirred as she struggled to lace up the corset, hiding her luscious curves from view.

Damn, she was seductive. Even when she didn't mean to be. They'd had sex three times tonight after which he'd discovered she didn't have a second packet of those hideous condoms tucked down her boots.

But now they were awake, he'd teleport to the nearest all-night pharmacy to restock. A minor inconvenience. He had no intention of prematurely cutting short this night. Not when it was the only one they would have together.

"Hey." He didn't know why she felt the need to pull her clothes on when she was only visiting the bathroom. "You okay?"

She swung round and guilt wreathed her features, as though he'd caught her trying to steal one of his wing feathers. The seductive image flooded his mind of wrapping his wings around her and seeing awestruck wonder fill her eyes.

It would never happen. He ignored the bizarre, hollow ache that flared deep in his chest. It meant nothing.

"I didn't mean to wake you."

He had no idea why she whispered but for some reason found it enchanting.

"You didn't. Hurry up and come back to bed. It's cold without you." Gods alive, had he really said that?

She clutched her dress to her breasts in a bewitching gesture of modesty. "I have to leave. It's late."

She had to *what*? He'd thought she was going to the *bathroom*. It was almost three in the morning and Rowan had intended to slip into the night *without a word.*

He was all but fucking speechless.

Except she didn't look like she was used to creeping out of hotel bedrooms in the middle of the night. Damn it, he couldn't work her out at all. She was a mass of contradictions. Not least when it came to sex. She was a sizzling siren who'd scorched his reason, but conversely appeared oddly inexperienced when it came to foreplay. And it seemed she didn't have a clue how to confront a male pissed off by her early morning flit.

He threw back the sheet and left the bed. Her swift glance to his groin only stoked his need further. There was no fucking way she was walking out until they were both thoroughly satisfied.

"Stay." His voice was low, persuasive. He didn't turn on the archangelic charm, but he wasn't far off. "For breakfast." He trailed his finger along the silken curve of her cheek. Another few hours, another few fucks, and then he'd be willing to say goodbye.

"I'm sorry." She sounded breathless and for a second he thought he'd misheard. "I can't, Azrael. I need to get back."

He'd never invited a woman to stay for breakfast before, and the first one he had—*refused*.

"Thank you for tonight." Her voice was soft. Seductive. Except she wasn't seducing him, she was leaving him. "I'll remember it forever."

She stepped back and smiled, but her eyes glittered with what looked suspiciously like tears. It was those tears and that wobbly smile that tipped him over the edge.

Fuck it. So what if he saw her again? He needed some down time from his current mission.

"How about we repeat the experience tonight?"

She didn't answer right away but her fingers clenched around her dress. Was that a good sign? Damn, now he was looking for *signs*?

"I'd like that." And yet worry filled her eyes, as if she'd just agreed to something incalculably dangerous.

She was hiding something. He was certain it was to do with her job. Was she in the middle of a mission and concerned about jeopardizing it?

"Same time same place?" He grinned. It was crazy how much fun this was.

"No." Suddenly she sounded decisive. "I'll meet you at ten inside the *Slug and Cabbage*—it's a pub about fifteen minutes from here. Does that sound okay?"

Her suggestion was fine. It was just intriguing that she hadn't automatically agreed with his. Then again, she was tantalizingly immune to his archangelic charms.

"Sure." He watched her sigh with apparent relief and then she pulled her dress over her head. Clearly, she was still intent on leaving. "Give me a minute and I'll escort you to your car." He assumed she had a car. When she opened her mouth, he waved away her inevitable objections as he sauntered into the bathroom. "You're not walking the streets of London alone at this time of the night."

Didn't matter if she was used to doing such a thing. He wasn't having it when she'd just spent the last seven hours in his company.

He came back into the bedroom. The only sign of Rowan was her stockings, discarded on the floor.

What the fuck? He pulled on his pants and grabbed his crumpled shirt. Would it have killed her to hang on for half a minute? He glanced down the corridor, but she was nowhere in sight, so he teleported to the ground floor to wait for her. Except within thirty seconds he had to accept that she had damn well eluded him.

A *human* had out maneuvered him. Admiration flowed through him at her rare skill. She'd better turn up tonight. Otherwise he'd rip London apart until he'd hunted her down.

He'd never hunted for pleasure before. The prospect fired his blood.

CHAPTER 10

ROWAN

"*A*re you seeing sexy-arse again tonight?" Over the last week Lily's condition had dramatically improved. From the lethargic, forgetful girl of less than two weeks ago she was now more like the woman who had emerged from the induced coma six months ago. She clearly remembered Rowan's attempt at healing with her amethysts last week and was convinced that was the catalyst that had *woken her up.* Rowan was more inclined to think it was down to whatever the medics were giving her.

Curled up on Lily's bed in the luxurious room adjacent to the medical wing, Rowan flapped her hand at the younger woman.

"Not so loud. Do you want the whole house to hear?" But despite her words she couldn't stop her inane grin. It happened every time she thought of Azrael, and he was on her mind a *lot.* She'd even stopped stressing that she would be summoned into Sakarbaal's presence for her negligence regarding the *Estella's* debacle. It seemed Lady Luck had been on her side that night.

"The door's shut and it's made of solid oak."

True, but Lily still couldn't grasp the scope of preternatural abilities vampires possessed. She didn't want any of them suspecting she had seen the same guy seven times over the last ten days. She hadn't even confided in Meg. Not after the suspicions Brad had sowed in her mind the other night.

"I'm seeing him tomorrow." She wrapped her arms around her knees. "I know I need to break it off, but I just can't."

"Screw that." Lily pushed herself from her chair and rubbed the small of her back. There was a frown on her pretty face, the face that had been brutally scarred on one side by her attacker more than eight months ago. "It's about time you got a life of your own. I'm telling you, as soon as this baby's born you and me —we're out of here."

A dull ache gripped her heart. What Lily suggested was impossible.

"You know I can't leave. Where could I go?" She only just stopped herself from reminding Lily that in the eyes of pure-bred humans she was a monster. Because Lily was pregnant with another such hybrid and no matter how much the other woman professed indifference for the creature she carried, it still possessed half her DNA.

"If you really wanted to escape, you could." There was a hard note in Lily's voice. "They don't *own* you."

She knew that and was a little irritated Lily seemed to think otherwise. But it wasn't that simple. Not just because Rowan owed the Enclave for her existence. She was a dhampir. There was nowhere else she *could* go.

But Lily was another matter. If she survived the birth—*please let her survive the birth*—Rowan would do anything to help her friend reunite with her family.

Even if it meant she'd never see her again.

The Elders would never allow Lily to retain her memories of these last few months. It was standard practice to scrub the minds of the human mothers before they were allowed to return to their own lives. She wouldn't even remember that Rowan had once been her friend.

Pain squeezed her heart. She'd miss her human friend.

There was a knock on the door and Lily sank back onto her chair and stared vacantly into space as one of the doctors entered the room with her medication. Rowan blinked, and her face heated as understanding blasted through her.

She's faking it.

Rowan grabbed her phone and stared blindly at the screen so her eyes wouldn't betray her friend.

"Hello, Lily." The doctor's words were perfunctory. Lily continued to stare into space. The doctor shot Rowan a glance. "No change?"

She shrugged and concentrated on pretending to read something on her phone. *Don't ask me anything else.* She was a terrible liar but luckily the vampire didn't appear to expect her to have any great insights about the situation. She spoke to Lily as if she was a small child who didn't understand what was going on. After checking her blood pressure and various other procedures the doctor pressed a variety of pills between Lily's lips and waited until she obediently swallowed.

As soon as the door shut behind the vampire, Lily turned to her and spat out her pills, one by one, into the palm of her hand.

"Well?" There was an accusing note in the other woman's voice.

Chills skated over her arms, and Brad's voice echoed in her head.

Ever wondered what shit they put in this stuff?

"They were medicating you *into* that zombie state?" Why would they do that? After she'd brought Lily here, on the brink of death, their medical expertise had saved her. They'd kept her in a coma so her body could recover and then they'd woken her and looked after her.

By that time Lily Cartwright, university undergraduate and only daughter of a prominent High Court judge had been declared missing, presumed dead. It was another two months before Lily had regained enough strength to demand to go home and by then it was too late.

As a result of the attack, and the growing baby, her blood was poisoned. Termination was too dangerous and only the continued medical intervention of the Enclave's doctors was keeping her alive. Once the baby was born her blood would return to normal and then the Enclave would be able to repair her damaged face.

That's what the doctors had told Rowan when she'd asked. They'd seemed surprised by her questions, as though they didn't understand her concern for a human. Then again, she'd never asked after the other women she had saved.

Had *their* blood also been poisoned? Was it an inevitable side effect of incubating a dhampir?

Why didn't I ever question that before?

Lily's lip curled in contempt. "A mindless dhampir-maker is easier to control than a human with a fully functioning brain."

"But why would anyone want to control you?" She was, after all, within two weeks of her delivery date. What did the Electors —all orders came from the Electors—think she was going to get up to in her current condition?

Lily heaved a sigh. "You never cease to amaze me." It wasn't a compliment. "Seriously. A year ago, I would've laughed myself sick if anyone had told me vampires existed. As for the offspring between a vamp and human, well come on. That's just something out of a horror movie, right?"

Since that was exactly what Rowan thought, she folded her arms and tried to ignore the pain that pierced through her heart. Lily was human. She regarded her as a friend. And yet even Lily thought she was nothing more than a monster.

She would die, literally *die*, if Azrael ever discovered her secret and she witnessed the admiration in his eyes turn to disgust.

"Yet here I am." She heard the defensive note in her voice and made up for it with a scowl.

Lily shook her head. "You're an assassin. A hunter." She sounded as though she was ticking off a shopping list. "By rights you should be one hell of a hard-arsed bitch. But you know what? You're one of the most trusting people I've ever met. You believe *anything* you're told."

The accusation stung. "The hell I do."

"I'm not going to argue with you. I'm not even saying that, in different circumstances, that's such a terrible thing. But living here the way you do? I'm telling you, Rowan. You need to start asking some hard questions."

"For your information, I don't trust *any*one." Apart from Brad. After their conversation the other night, where he'd all but accused his friend Alex of being an accessory to the murder of his lover, she was no longer sure about Meg, which hurt more than she'd ever let on.

"I know." Lily didn't appear to realize she had just contradicted herself. "That's not what I mean. You're half vampire, sure. But I think you're a lot more like your mother than you give yourself credit for."

"What?" This conversation was spinning into the surreal. "How can you even say that?"

"Her journal." Lily sounded surprised by the question. "Sometimes it was just like I was reading something you might have written. Don't tell me you hadn't noticed?"

She wasn't like her mother at all. Her mother had been *human*. And she was only a hybrid.

"My mother was a medical student at Great Ormond Street." How different could they get? Her mother's ambition had been to save sick children. Rowan killed enemies of the Enclave.

Lily heaved an exaggerated sigh. "I *mean* she believed everything this lot told her. Why do you think they let her keep her journal? Why do you think you were allowed to inherit it? Because she never said a word against them." Lily gripped the arms of her chair and leaned forward. "Until her final entry. The one where she listed all the reasons why she wanted her daughter to be called *Rowan.*"

To keep the dead from rising.

Unease trickled over her arms. That sentence had always haunted her, but she'd never raised it with anyone. Certainly not Meg, who'd looked after her since birth and presented her with the journal on her seventh birthday with the strict instruction to *keep it safe.*

In other words, to keep its continued existence a secret. She'd been so thrilled at the prospect of owning something that had once belonged to her own mother it had never crossed her mind to wonder at the vampire's command. None of her dhampir friends had been allowed to keep anything from their human parent.

"They didn't let me inherit it." Her voice was hoarse as she finally faced how strange that really was. Why would the Electors care if she had her mother's journal, unless there was something in it that they wanted to keep from her? But the only possibly controversial entry was the one about her name. Surely that couldn't be the reason? "Meg gave it to me. She made me promise I'd never let anyone know about it."

"And you never wondered why, right?"

No, but only because until now she'd never analyzed it. She'd just accepted everything Meg had said.

Keep it safe. So, she had.

Tell no one you have it.

Well, maybe she'd bent that rule. Before Lily, she had shared the journal with both Belinda and Brad.

But never with another vampire.

"Well I'll tell you this," Lily said. "Your mother's journal saved my sanity. If you hadn't let me read it, I would've had no idea what was happening to me."

What the *hell* was she talking about? She'd lost count how many times she had read her mother's journal. And there was nothing in there about being medicated into a zombie state.

Something snagged at the edge her mind. Something her mother had written a month before Rowan's birth about there being a problem with the baby. How she needed more rest…

"It struck me at the time." Lily's voice had dropped to a low whisper. "Her style changed, about three weeks before that last entry. She became more disoriented. Vague. But it was only after you did your amethyst healing sorcery on me that it hit me."

"They changed her medication." Rowan glared futilely at the ceiling. *Is this what the Electors wanted to hide from me?* Or was she being paranoid? "Because there was a problem with *me*."

"*That*," Lily jerked her thumb at her swollen belly, "is the excuse they gave me. God, Rowan. Without her journal I might never have made that connection. Don't you see? They do it towards the end of pregnancy, so the mother becomes completely malleable."

She wanted to tell Lily she was talking rubbish. But she couldn't. Because the doctor's offhand comment regarding the three other women she had saved in similar circumstances echoed through her brain.

"They all go through this at the end. You remember the other human women you brought in? They were just the same."

"That can't be the reason. Not the only reason." She stared into Lily's angry face and the hollowness of her words echoed in her ears. "Maybe it's just an inevitable side effect?"

"Maybe it is." Lily didn't sound in the least convinced. "But I'm not prepared to suffer it. I don't want this *thing* growing inside me and I'm not taking anything that makes me feel that way again, no matter how much good it might be doing for their precious dhampir."

"God, Lily." She pushed herself off the bed and gripped the arms of Lily's chair. "You make it sound as if they think we're something special to be nurtured. You know that's not true. Most vampires hate us because of our tainted blood."

"Of course you're special. You do all the vampires dirty work for them."

She was in danger of splintering the timber. But she couldn't move. Could hardly breathe. Because Lily's words pounded through her head and squeezed the air from her lungs.

Sure, she'd known for years she and her fellow dhampirs at the Enclave hunted rogues and assassinated the unsavory because the vampires preferred not to get personally involved in that side of things. It was the flip side to being accepted. Having a place to call home.

A form of repayment to the Electors for having taken in her pregnant mother and saving the tainted offspring.

But now, for the first time, doubt dug in poisoned claws. Was it possible that instead of the Enclave merely taking advantage of a situation, they might actively be *encouraging* it?

What am I accusing them of? How could she suspect them of something so abhorrent?

"They all go through this at the end." She'd assumed the doctor had been referring to the women she'd brought in. But what about all the other victims? Had they suffered from the strange lethargy towards the end of their pregnancies?

Chills raced over her arms. Zoë had died. She'd always thought the others had survived. But now the doctor's words took on a sinister implication. Had he been referring to the end of their pregnancies—or the end of their *lives*?

Had they *all* died?

Why hadn't she asked any of the *hard questions* before? Was it because, deep in her heart, she feared what she might discover?

CHAPTER 11

AZRAEL

*A*zrael teleported to a remote forest in the heart of Romania. It was midday, bitterly cold, and the stark outline of Sakarbaal's ruined castle was barely visible through an eerie fog that clung to the ancient stones like a belligerent curse.

It had been too much to hope that he'd find any answers here, where it had all begun. The castle had been abandoned since the night he'd freed the phoenix and was already falling into disrepair the last time he'd checked the place out, more than five hundred years ago.

But he'd needed to see it again. Just to be certain the vampire hadn't arisen from the ashes in a depraved inversion of the phoenix's rebirth almost a millennium ago.

A shudder inched over his skin. A ghostly remnant of the evil that had once haunted this land.

Wherever Sakarbaal had made his new lair, it wasn't here.

He got out of there and returned to the place he called home. Brooding, he flung himself onto a chair on his veranda but for once the view of blue tipped mountains surrounding a lush valley didn't help his mood. He'd discovered this planet four thousand years ago, hidden in a backwater of Andromeda III. The world was a paradise, inhabited by millions of exotic birds and wildlife. The indigenous humanoids were too primitive to interest any other immortal and so he had a perfectly secluded bolt hole.

But he couldn't get the image of the phoenix from nine hundred years ago out of his mind. How it had huddled in its cage, all but broken by whatever endless torture the vampire had inflicted upon it.

That Sakarbaal was obsessed by possessing one was clear, if he'd now managed to imprison another of the creatures.

What was he doing with it?

In every ancient culture on Earth, and across the universe, the phoenix was a potent symbol of renewal. Rebirth. During his research over the centuries he'd uncovered long-buried archives that spoke of how the great bird escorted the souls of the dead to the afterlife.

And he'd also discovered something else.

Long ago, he and fellow archangels Mephisto and Zadkiel had taken a desperately wounded Gabe into the highest, healing, realms of the astral planes. It was a tranquil realm, where immortals through the ages had basked in its calming presence. A level where the souls of mortals could rarely ascend, even after death.

But the phoenix had unfettered access. Not only could the magnificent creature's consciousness enter the highest levels at will, but when it died, its soul instantly ascended.

He'd witnessed the rare phenomenon only once, a dozen years ago. The phoenix's soul blazed, a starburst of power that for a heart stopping instant had illuminated unparalleled energy pulsing in shrouded fissures of the astral planes. But within a moment its soul vanished, as it once again resurrected in the mortal world, and the glimpse of unimaginable forces vanished with it.

It was obscene that a foul creature such as Sakarbaal had found a way to not only capture the elusive bird but corrupt its pure essence for his own ends. Was he attempting to use the phoenix's ability of resurrection to transcend his own undead status?

Hey, Az. Where are you?

The telepathic demand buzzed through his mind and he stifled a groan. The last time he'd spoken with Mephisto—the oldest and most powerful of archangels—was six months ago, just before Gabe's loss of immortality.

Home.

He'd barely sent the communication when Mephisto teleported onto the shady veranda, pulled out a chair and flung himself onto it.

"Have you set yourself up as a god here yet?"

"No. And don't think of starting one of your cults here. The mortals are surprisingly peaceful and that's how I'd like it to stay."

"Your pets haven't evolved enough to interest me."

"You didn't come here to tell me the indigenous mortals don't do anything for your libido."

Mephisto's feathers rippled in the late afternoon breeze as he hooked out a second chair with his foot. Frowning, he gazed across the valley before slamming his booted foot on the chair. "I've just come from an insignificant little planet that possibly harbors the last two Nephilim in the universe."

His vague irritation at the interruption vanished. Six months ago, Zad had told him Gabe and Aurora had discovered living descendants of an archangel.

For millennia he'd believed all Nephilim had been killed —*murdered*—because of his goddess' betrayal and his own refusal to see the truth in his vision. But he'd been committed to his hunt in Andromeda, and Zad's revelation had been pushed to the back of his mind.

"Is it true? They are of archangelic blood?" He'd never fallen. Had never had a child of his own. But before the great devastation had ravaged Earth he'd loved and protected the offspring of his fellow archangels for they were precious and rare.

Except I failed to protect them when it mattered the most.

Because he'd trusted his goddess.

"After so many millennia, can they truly be Nephilim?"

"If there's no doubt as to their ancestry then yes. They're Nephilim." He considered Mephisto's brooding profile. "Any idea who the archangel is?"

Mephisto didn't answer right away, and that was answer enough. He never liked to admit that he didn't know something.

"Even now," Mephisto said at last, "there are archangels who refuse to answer my call."

Azrael transferred his gaze to the valley. He knew that only too well. One of his closest friends shielded his existence from at least half of all archangels, including Mephisto. And had done so ever since the great civilization of their youth had been annihilated, eleven thousand years ago.

"Zad's convinced Aurora reincarnated because of her unique heritage," Mephisto said. "We don't know for sure if, after this life, she'll come back again. Fuck, we don't even know if Gabe will be reborn, seeing as his soul is inextricably entwined with hers." He exhaled a frustrated breath. "Was she reborn because of her heritage, or not? I need to know the truth, Az."

He wasn't the only one. After the great devastation, Azrael had sworn a pledge to protect the astral planes from hostile forces. While the higher levels were accessible only to those mortals who had passed on, the lower levels could be invaded not only by spiritually attuned mortals but by entities hell bent on countless forms of destruction.

It had served as a small salve to his conscience. He hadn't been able to save the lives of the innocent humans he'd lived among but at least he could protect the wellbeing of their souls.

Had he also been protecting the fragile essence of the slain Nephilim?

"After all this time we might never know the truth." He shot Mephisto a glance. "If Nephilim *do* possess souls, does that mean the offspring of demons do, too?"

"Wouldn't that be fucking brilliant?" Mephisto's wings fluttered in outrage at the notion. "I need distraction. Let's hit a nightclub on a civilized world and wallow in some mindless adoration from nubile mortals."

Nubile mortal conjured up an alluring image of Rowan, black hair spread over his thighs, wet mouth worshipping his cock. Far from tiring of her after their second night together he'd suggested a third. And then a fourth.

Each time she'd dictated the hour and location. It was obvious she was cautious about being followed. But who did she think was following her?

"I'll pass." Why did he need to hit a nightclub to pick up a mortal, when he had his very own human he was seeing the following day?

"That's the smug grin of an archangel who's being well and truly laid. I thought you were in the middle of a celibacy rut."

Smug grin? He hadn't realized the memory of Rowan's foreplay had reflected on his expression. He'd thought it was all centered between his thighs.

Her beautiful face and enchanting green eyes invaded his mind. "Celibacy is overrated."

"Preaching to the proverbial." Mephisto flashed him a lascivious grin. "Catch you later."

Rowan

ROWAN WAS on her way to the suite of offices, located on the second floor of the mansions, when she heard Meg's voice floating down the stairs. *Shit.* She hadn't spoken to her in days and after her conversation with Lily she wasn't sure she'd be able to even look the vampire in the eyes without Meg guessing her traitorous thoughts.

She wasn't up for a confrontation with Meg. Not yet.

Ask the hard questions.

First, she needed more evidence than merely her own suspicions. Which was why she was here tonight, and why she couldn't let Meg see her. She darted through the nearest door into a lavishly decorated eighteenth century bedroom and held her breath until she heard Meg and whoever she was talking to descend the stairs.

She waited a few more minutes just to be on the safe side, before she left the room and went to the offices.

She'd never realized what an advantage it gave her, being considered the dhampir version of a Goody-Two-Shoes. The couple of vampires working this evening barely glanced at her when she strolled in and said she needed to check something in Lily Cartwright's files.

But why would they suspect her of doing anything underhand? She'd toed the line since Steven's death. She'd never put the Enclave's existence in danger—luckily there had been no repercussions over the incident in *Estella's*—and she'd never needed an intervention due to drug or alcohol abuse.

She just did her job. And didn't ask questions. Well, this evening she wasn't asking questions either, but she was damn well going to find some answers.

Lily's medical history scrolled over the screen. As far as she could tell everything appeared to be progressing normally, apart from the note, sent by one of the Electors from Romania, recommending a change in medication. There was nothing to indicate it was due to a problem with the baby.

She took a deep breath. It wasn't too late to walk away. What did she think she could do, if she *did* discover some terrible conspiracy involving the human women? Confront the mighty Enclave?

They'd squash her like a gnat.

Her fingers hovered over the keyboard, as Azrael filled her mind. His irresistible smile, his wicked sense of fun, and his small acts of chivalry that were like second nature to him but meant so much to her.

The way he made her feel so… human.

Trepidation spiked through her chest.

For years she'd ignored the uneasy ripples in the back of her mind. The questions she refused to face, because it didn't matter what the answers were. Nothing could change her fate.

But I've never even tried to change things. The one time she had broken the rules and fallen in love, Steven, an innocent human, had died, and she hadn't dared step out of line since.

Until she met Azrael. And now she craved so much more than the Enclave allowed.

All she'd ever wanted was a normal life. But even if her life *wasn't* normal, that didn't mean she had to accept the status quo forever. She might not like the answers she found. But she couldn't hide in the shadows of ignorance any longer.

She opened Lily's personal file and the coiled tension in her chest tightened as she scanned the in-depth analysis of Lily's background.

Why did they need that level of detail? She could understand the medical history, but what did her parents' occupations or Lily's education have to do with anything? It was more like a dossier than a medical record.

Rowan glanced across the office, but the vampires appeared supremely uninterested in what she was doing. Dread slithered through her as she found the file on the previous woman she had rescued, Zoë Burton.

There was the same detail on her background, including her education and achievements. A full medical history, ending in the birth of her child and the death of Zoë.

She scanned the records of the first two women she had

saved, and the clinical reports on the progress of their pregnancies seared into her brain. Neither had survived the birth of their child.

She dug deeper. Sweat beaded on her upper lip and her hands were clammy. She'd always assumed that the many others in the past had had their memories wiped before being returned to their previous lives.

That, after all, was the Enclave's official line. They would keep the dhampir and return the mother home. Except she'd now gone back more than twenty years in the archives and the terrible suspicion that had surfaced when she'd been talking with Lily now confronted her, stark statistics on the screen.

Not one woman had survived the birth.

That wasn't all. There were other cases where the embryo had spontaneously aborted within the first few weeks—not that *that* was unusual. But without fail, the woman died at the same time. She didn't need a degree in medicine to know something wasn't right about *that*.

She checked her own mother's files, but there was nothing there that Meg hadn't shared with her. Nausea churned in her stomach, as she went back further in time to Brad's mother. And then she skimmed the records of her friends who had died over the last few years. Shivers prickled over her arms and inched along her spine and with chilled fingers she finally logged out.

Dhampirs weren't immortal. They died young. A steady stream of fresh blood was needed to continue the work the vampires preferred not to undertake. Whenever a half-blood was killed in action another was nearing the completion of their training. Why hadn't she found that suspicious before?

Because I never wanted to think about it before. The Enclave was her home, and although sometimes it was little more than a gilded cage, it was all she had.

Maybe the Enclave *was* simply taking advantage of the dhampirs that came their way. It was easier to accept what she'd been taught all her life, without questioning the facts.

But she'd opened the box. Looked inside. And there was no turning back now from the doubt gnawing through her heart. She'd avoided the *hard questions* because she'd always been grateful that the Enclave had saved her.

Did they really save me?

Every single victim of vampire rape they had taken in over the last fifty years had been between the ages of eighteen and twenty-three.

Each young woman had been highly educated and apparently poised on the brink of a demanding career.

Coincidence? Could be. She wanted to believe it. And if that was all she'd discovered, maybe she would.

But it wasn't. There was one last piece of damning evidence she couldn't make excuses for.

Because what were the chances that every victim *also* possessed the rarest blood group on Earth— AB Negative?

The same blood type as me?

CHAPTER 12

ROWAN

*A*s Rowan left the tube at Waterloo the following morning, a shudder inched along the back of her neck and she glanced sharply over her shoulder. No one suspicious lurked on the platform. She'd taken an insane amount of precautions with her journey today, hopping on trains, buses and the Underground after leaving her car in Kensington, in the hope of completely misleading anyone who might be following her.

She'd not experienced anything like that odd sensation the night she'd left *Estella's* with Azrael, but she had no intention of taking any chances. Not when it came to his safety. He might possess strength that most humans didn't, but that didn't mean a thing. Vampires were immortal, and he wasn't. He wouldn't stand a chance if a hunter from the Strigoi Echelon decided to eliminate him.

Or if one of the Enclave decides to assassinate him, either.

All because he'd been sleeping with her.

She tried to squash the thought, but it buried deeper in the back of her mind, a poisonous seed of doubt. With one last piercing glance she straightened her shoulders, ignored her bruised ribs she'd damaged during her assignment last night, and powered up the stairs. Only ancient vampires could venture out in full daylight without any adverse side effects and she wasn't so vain as to think any of that elevated rank would be tailing her.

She was just being paranoid. But she couldn't help it. Because the more she saw Azrael, the more she feared he might end up like Steven.

It was more than enough reason why she should have ended things already. But every time they parted, she couldn't bring herself to do it. Not when he gave her a lingering kiss goodbye or held her hand like he never wanted to let her go.

She couldn't stand him up, either. Because even when they weren't together, the memory of his smile warmed her heart.

Not good enough. She had to let him go. Disappear from his life, for his own safety. And she would.

Maybe tomorrow. But not today.

Because today was different. It wasn't dark. And most importantly, this date was all his doing.

He'd told her to meet him on the South Bank at nine forty-five. A small smile curved her lips.

It's not just about the sex anymore. The accusation pounded in the back of her mind no matter how she tried to ignore it. Well so what if it wasn't just about the sex anymore? Couldn't she simply enjoy spending time with him? Enjoy feeling like a normal human being? It wasn't going to last forever.

She focused on the iconic cantilevered observation wheel that towered ahead of her, silhouetted against the frosty blue March sky. It was insane to be so excited at the thought of going on it with Azrael.

"You look edible in daylight." The seductive whisper against her ear sent tremors of need through her blood and she turned to where he stood by her side, smiling at her. How did he manage to surprise her like that? It wasn't the first time he'd appeared by her side, seemingly from out of the blue. He had the stealth of a vampire. Except, by virtue of her mixed blood, no vampire could move so swiftly towards her without her knowing about it.

It was just one of the many things about him that fascinated her.

"You look pretty tasty yourself." She licked her lips and moved in closer, so she could breathe in deep his evocative, sexy scent. Probably not a good move, considering where they were and the unlikelihood of slaking her desire anytime soon. But he was just so completely irresistible. She wanted to wrap herself around him and never let him go.

He laughed and slung his arm around her shoulders. His long winter coat was unbuttoned, and as the wind whipped against them his silk shirt molded his sculpted pecs with tantalizing promise.

"Stop seducing me in public." Then he looked down at her, an evil gleam in his gorgeous gold-flecked eyes. "Screw that. I'd very much enjoy you seducing me in public."

"Tough luck. You said you were taking me on this date." She hoped he couldn't tell how much that thought thrilled her. It was great meeting him for food and sex, but this—this was something else. "I haven't forgotten you once told me you always keep your promises."

His big body shook with silent laughter as they bypassed the shivering queue. "I do keep my promises." He shot her a glance that was so full of sin the breath caught in her throat. "Never doubt that for a moment."

Azrael

Rowan's eyes widened when he led her into their own private capsule. Well, hell. She didn't think he was going to share their time together with anyone else, did she?

Apart from the requisite host, and he'd already subliminally manipulated her mind, so she'd recall nothing of what happened for the next half hour. He shot a telepathic probe at the security cameras and they died an ignoble death.

"Wow." Rowan sounded awed as the host poured non-alcoholic champagne into elegant flutes. "I didn't expect this."

"I know." He threaded his fingers through hers and led her to the other side of the capsule. Not once in all the times they'd been together had she suggested they do anything but meet late at night for sex. Not that he was complaining. It was an ideal arrangement. Except he'd wanted to do something different with her today.

She hadn't been easy to persuade. Perversely, that had made him more determined than ever to convince her. It was both bizarre and enchanting having to coax a woman to spend time with him.

"Lucky it's such a lovely clear day," she said as she gazed out of the capsule at the River Thames. "The view is amazing."

He stroked the back of her hand with his thumb and realized he was staring at her profile. But why wouldn't he? Her profile was a study in ethereal beauty and with that look of suppressed excitement on her face she radiated an irresistible allure. "You've never done this before?"

"Never got around to it." There was a wistful note in her voice. "We weren't much for family outings."

Her aura of anticipation faded, and he couldn't work out why her pensive expression tugged at something deep inside. *Or why he was digging into her private life.* What did it matter? It was her secret career that intrigued him.

"That makes two of us." He raised her hand and pressed their fists against his chest. "Family outings were never on our agenda."

"Do you have brothers and sisters?" She sounded genuinely interested, as though her previous reluctance to broach anything personal had been left behind, along with the ground.

That was a loaded question. Although all the archangels had

been created by the one Alpha Goddess, the only strands of genetic material they shared for certain were the manufactured ones she'd used for their incomparable wings.

He didn't want to think about her. Although he'd had nothing to do with her since the great devastation, the depth of her betrayal and how utterly he'd believed in her burned his soul, even after all this time.

"No. We're more a blended hot pot of numerous parental genetics."

It was as close to the truth as he could get. He could hardly tell her his goddess had stolen DNA from all the Alpha Immortals of antiquity to create her bastardized offspring.

She smiled, as if she found his confession charming. "Your family sounds a lot like mine. Kind of hard to pin down."

"My family is the definition of dysfunctional."

"I bet my family could put yours in the shade."

He laughed, then kissed her knuckles. "That's something I'd like to see."

"Trust me." She brushed her lips across his knuckles in a sensual reflection of his gesture. "You really don't."

"Do you see much of them?"

Why was he asking her about her family? He wasn't interested in her family. But conversely, he wanted her to talk about them. Because then she was sharing a part of herself with him that until now, she had kept under ironclad cover.

"Yes." She glanced down at her flute and swirled the pale gold liquid. "Well, it's like a family business. There's no getting away from them, really."

"Bit like the Mafia?"

She laughed. "Exactly like the Mafia. There's no escaping from the Godfather."

"Unless you really want to."

He'd meant his comment as a joke, but a shadow flickered over her face as if his words hit a raw nerve. His gaze sharpened.

He'd assumed she'd been exaggerating about her family but the look on her face suggested she hadn't. Who the hell were they?

"It's not always possible to have everything you want." Her gaze locked with his. "Sometimes you just have to make the best of what you have."

"That sounds ominous. You should introduce me to your family. I'll sort them out for you."

"Tempting." Her smile was beautiful and tugged at something deep in his chest. "But I'm quite capable of sorting them out myself."

"I'm sure you're more than capable of sorting anything out." He battened down the illogical urge to demand she tell him her full name, her place of residence and details of this mysterious family of hers. Why did her reluctance to confide in him rub his feathers the wrong way? "But remember, sometimes the bond of blood isn't everything."

"Oh." She rose onto her toes and her breath fluttered across his lips. "Azrael." The way she said his name, lingering over every syllable as if they were an indescribably exotic treat, stoked his smoldering lust. "Don't you know that blood is *everything*?"

CHAPTER 13

ROWAN

"Only if you want blood ties to be everything." Azrael inched her backwards, towards the center of the capsule. "Is that what you want?"

No. Denial vibrated through her, but she kept it locked inside. There was so much she could never tell him and trying to deflect his questions was getting harder.

Because in her heart she desperately wanted to confide.

What a disaster that would be. She couldn't stay with him. She didn't want to leave him. Never in a million years did she want him to discover the truth about her and yet, despite it all, she yearned to spill her fractured soul.

The back of her legs came up against the oval bench in the middle of the capsule. Instinctively she gripped his fingers tighter, before she lost her balance and fell onto the bench.

His arm was around her in an instant. In her peripheral vision she saw the host turn her back on them to look at the view. *If only we were alone.*

She leaned over and put her glass on the edge of the bench before winding her arm around his neck. Sharing her personal life was nothing but a dream, but it wasn't the only thing she craved.

"I want you." She breathed the words against his lips, her gaze locked with his. "I want you inside me, wrapped around me. Saying my name when you come."

His breath meshed with hers, and he dropped his glass onto the bench before he began to unbutton her coat.

"Your wish is my command." There was laughter in his voice as well as lust and she melted, as she always did when he spoke like that. It was as though he didn't have a care in the world, that life was one long amusing adventure. It was just another thing she loved about being with him—he could find humor in the most absurd things. And because he did, so could she.

"I didn't mean right *now*." But she made no move to stop him because of course she had. She didn't want to wait. But she didn't want to get arrested, either. "Anyone could see us." And yet despite her words she began to feverishly tug at his silk shirt.

He slid his arms around her waist beneath her coat, and the warmth and strength of his hands as he explored the small of her back and curve of her bottom was enough for her to discard any lingering protest.

"What if they do see us?" His whisper tickled her ear. "Let them watch." He pulled her around, so he was the one with his legs against the bench. "Before we steam up the glass."

She risked glancing through the glass at the neighboring capsule. None of the guests were looking their way. They all appeared intently preoccupied at the far end of their own pod.

"You have a wicked mind." She shot another glance at the host, but the woman still appeared completely oblivious to what her guests were about to get up to. A nervous giggle escaped, and she shoved him down onto the bench. "We'll have to be *very* quiet."

His smile was original sin and tremors of pleasure rippled through her. He pulled her onto his lap, her thighs spread wide.

Luckily, she'd worn stockings today instead of her usual leather pants.

But then she always wore stockings when she met with him. Stockings and suspenders, scandalously seductive corsets and deliciously decadent knickers. They made her feel feminine and desirable and she loved seeing the look in his eyes when she stood before him in her sexy lingerie.

"Keeping quiet is no problem for me." His husky whisper caressed her lips like an illicit kiss. "*You* are another matter entirely."

She tugged at his fly as he wrapped her thighs in the folds of his coat. "And still the size of your ego continues to astound me."

He laughed. Obviously, he didn't care whether the host heard him or not.

"I see no need for false modesty where my ego is concerned." At least he kept his voice down to an irresistible smoky growl. "Grotesque ribbed condom, inside pocket."

"Glad to see you came prepared." She smothered a giggle at the pained expression on his face.

She found the packet, ripped it open under cover of his coat, and gently released his glorious cock from his pants. She loved when he went commando. Not least because it made *things* so much more convenient.

"Rowan." He sounded as though he was being strangled. "Much as the look of adoration on your face stokes my insatiable ego, if you want to come as Big Ben chimes then you need to get a move on."

"Big Ben chimes?" She snorted and then slapped her free hand across her mouth to contain her mirth. "*Big Ben?*" she repeated and looked pointedly at his groin.

Still clutching the ends of his coat as a barrier against the outside world, his fists smashed into her ribs to keep her still. Usually it wouldn't have bothered her, but her ribs were still tender from the previous night's messy assignment. But that was her problem and luckily it wasn't as if Azrael could see the bruising to ask probing questions. She shifted into a more comfortable position and once again couldn't tear her fascinated gaze from his erection.

He swore under his breath, in that language he sometimes used in the throes of passion. "Do me a favor." He sounded aggrieved. "I'm talking about Big *Ben*." He jerked his head to the view behind her. "If you time it right you can scream my name in ecstasy just as it chimes the quarter hour. It'll drown you out."

"Oh, I see." She had the urge to giggle again. "Got it all planned down to the last detail, haven't you?"

"My plans tend to go awry when they concern you."

Just as her plans always tumbled into disarray whenever they concerned him. It was nice to know she had that effect on him, as well.

"Hold still." She rolled the condom over the head of his cock. Heat radiated from him, as though a furnace glowed beneath the rigid flesh. How would it feel to have sex with him without any barrier? She couldn't imagine it though. Not really. Because she'd never had unprotected sex before.

Never wanted to. But with Azrael... it had become a recurring dream.

An obsession.

It would never happen.

He let out an agonized groan. "I swear you do this as a form of medieval punishment."

"*Sssh.*" She darted a glance at the host. Who still appeared entirely preoccupied with the view that she must have seen a thousand times before. Talk about discreet. Was she used to couples misbehaving in midair?

"Fuck, Rowan," Azrael growled. "Forget about the host, will you? She can't hear a thing." He pulled her closer, and her lace-covered sex cradled his erection. "It's just you and me here, all right?"

She panted into his face and lost her senses in his gold-flecked eyes. Had he somehow drugged the woman? *Do I even care?*

She wrapped one hand around his neck and hooked her lacy knickers aside with one finger. She was wet and ready for him even though he had barely touched her. But his words, his smoky looks, the very scent of him were all potent aphrodisiacs that her body responded to instinctively.

"Prepare for docking procedure." She had no idea where the words came from but they made her laugh, especially when he shot her another of his pained looks.

He dropped one side of his coat, gripped his cock and nudged her deliciously swollen clit.

"Incoming," he growled, and shudders rippled through her as she sank onto him.

The breath hissed between her teeth as he stretched her tender flesh. He palmed her butt, forcing her down the length of his shaft.

"How does it feel?" The words were raw, savage with need, and his eyes were so dark they appeared black. "Different?"

She tried to speak but words hovered just beyond her reach. Instead she gripped his neck and biceps and gave a jerky nod.

"Better?" It was a rabid demand and he pushed upward, penetrating deep inside. She gasped and clung onto him, unable to move. Not wanting to move. Not sure she would ever be able to again. "You like it?"

She sucked in a strangled breath. "Yes." She attempted to make sense of her spiraling thoughts. "But it's not *better*, exactly."

The added friction from the ribbed condom sent her sensitized nerve endings trembling on a knife-edge. She liked it but she wasn't sure if she *loved* it. She had the vague, unsettling feeling that she might splinter apart if she wasn't careful.

Still holding one side of his coat around her, his other hand trailed from her butt over her hip, before cradling her face. It was a strangely tender gesture and caused a pleasurable pain to squeeze her heart.

"Are you okay?" The words were uneven, but concern threaded through his question. As if her comfort was more important to him than simply finishing what they had started. Warmth flooded her veins and the lingering tendrils of discomfort vanished beneath a rolling wave of need.

"Yes." Her gaze locked with his and she curled her hands around his shoulders to use as leverage. She was always okay when she was with Azrael. More than okay. *If only I could always be with him.* "What do you think? A couple of minutes?"

He grunted. Clearly, he couldn't give a damn how long they had before the quarter chimed. "Ride me, Rowan. Ride me hard."

Raw desire arrowed through her core, a pleasure so intense it hovered on the precipice of agony. She pumped her hips, grinding into him, welcoming his answering thrusts with ragged gasps of delight.

His fingers speared through her hair. He wound her curls around his fist and tugged her closer. Their hot breath mingled and then he leaned in and nipped her lower lip.

The world shattered. She forgot where they were. Forgot the need for quiet. Forgot everything except for the man she clung onto as volcanic pleasure erupted and consumed, scattering her senses and shattering her psyche.

Through the turmoil that raged, the haunting chimes from the clock tower echoed through her mind. But they faded into nothing as he ground one word against her mouth.

"Rowan."

CHAPTER 14

ROWAN

*A*fterwards, they strolled in the direction of Westminster Bridge. Rowan had no idea whether Azrael had anything else in mind for today and didn't want to shatter the moment by asking. In any case, she could hardly keep the inane grin off her face never mind construct a logical sentence.

"Thank you for a lovely morning. I'll have to think of something spectacular to surprise you with in return."

His laugh was deep and rich that warmed her from the top of her head to the end of her toes. He looked at her as if she was the center of his existence. *If only.*

And then his gaze turned speculative. "How badly injured are you?"

"I—what?" How did he know she was injured? Did she *want* him to know she was injured? "How do you mean? You didn't hurt me."

He ignored her pitiful attempt to deflect his meaning. "I saw you wincing a few times."

Wincing? No, she hadn't. Well, okay maybe she had shifted slightly on his lap into a more comfortable position but—god.

Was that why he'd asked her if she was all right? Because he had noticed she was in pain?

She had the ridiculous urge to melt into a puddle at his feet. "Oh, it's nothing." She could hardly believe he had noticed. Yet he *had*. It was slightly alarming to realize just how much that thrilled her. "I misjudged a couple of moves last night, that's all. Entirely my own fault. You should see the other guy, though."

Not that such a thing was possible. Because the other guy, a vampire who had crossed the Elders of the Enclave, was now nothing more than dust on the wind.

"If I did, I'd break his neck for daring to hurt you."

Enchanted, she smiled up at him. "That's a lovely thing to say."

The words were out before she could stop them. Except she *did* think it was a lovely thing for him to say. But was it normal to think like that? Would a regular human woman have responded that way?

He gave a huff of laughter, as though her response had taken him completely by surprise. Clearly, a regular human woman wouldn't have given the same answer. But her worry faded, because he hadn't judged her for it.

He never did.

Azrael

IT WAS late afternoon before Azrael teleported home. After the boat trip Rowan had taken him out to lunch at a riverside pub and then they'd spent a couple of hours in the Jubilee Gardens.

He couldn't remember the last time he'd spent such a day. In the past his sexual encounters had been exactly that. There had been no strolling hand in hand by a river. No sideways glances to admire the female's profile. No constant sensual sizzle in the air between them, or an undefined reluctance to end the day.

Truth was, he hadn't wanted to end the day at all. It had been Rowan who'd ended it, because she'd had to check into work. But not before she'd arranged their next meeting for the following night.

He still knew nothing about her elusive job, let alone her family. But it was all part of her allure. When he'd asked if she operated under the official radar, she'd told him the world would be a far more dangerous place if not for her family business.

He had the feeling she wasn't joking.

It wasn't that much of an inconvenience, being enthralled by a human. It wasn't like it would last. Once her secrets were out, there would be nothing left for him to discover and her irresistible aura of mystique would fade. He just wasn't ready to let her go yet. That was all.

He went into his bedroom that boasted magnificent mountainous views through the wall of glass that opened onto the veranda. He tossed his shirt onto the end of the bed, rolled his shoulders and unfurled his wings. It was a relief to drop the glamour.

Later tonight he was seeing one of his closest archangel friends, Nathanael, and the elusive contact he'd wanted to meet with for years. Why the contact had finally agreed to speak with him, he had no idea.

Guess he'd soon find out. In the meantime, there was something else he needed to do. After speaking with Mephisto yesterday, he'd vowed to spend a couple of hours each day on the astral planes specifically searching for a trace of Nephilim soul.

The astral planes were a haven of tranquility and beauty and he could never understand why the majority of his fellow archangels avoided the realms like humans avoided the proverbial plague.

They had always fascinated him. Even before the catastrophic devastation that had decimated humanity and obliterated Nephilim from the face of the Earth. He'd been drawn to the complexity of the many realms and the intricate passage each soul traversed after its physical body died.

He sank to the lower levels, the realms that brushed against the physical universe. These were the levels frequented by the living who entered the astral planes by way of dreams or meditation. Before this week he'd rarely entered these realms because the souls of the dead bypassed them.

Which made them the perfect place to start his search for an elusive Nephilim.

He filtered through the cacophony of countless energy signatures. His strategy was simple. He'd untangle every spiritual thread, identify their origin, and by a process of elimination discover the truth.

One way or another.

It could take centuries. But if there was one thing he had in abundance, it was time.

A distant echo of discordance reverberated along the outer reaches of the realm and his soul shuddered in response. Three times during the last few months he'd encountered this anomalous ripple and the elusive hint of the essence of the phoenix was unmistakable.

Nine hundred years ago he hadn't recognized the discordance for what it was. The pure phoenix essence had been corrupted by the evil of Sakarbaal.

This recent disturbance wasn't the same as before, but the subtle differences couldn't disguise how the purity of the phoenix had been contaminated by something unnatural.

If he could find the source, he'd be that much closer to discovering how Sakarbaal was infiltrating the astral planes with slivers of a phoenix's soul.

He followed the elusive signature, and unease stirred as he ascended through the myriad levels. He knew phoenixes could access the highest realms, and it appeared whatever had corrupted its essence hadn't hampered this ability.

As he entered the highest level, a rainbow starburst of energy shimmered before him, breathtaking in its beauty but at the same time a debilitating desolation slammed through him from the entity. Shreds of phoenix soul inextricably bound with humanity —yet it was something not human at all.

The answer was in front of him, but it was hard to face. The tarnished soul tainting the phoenix didn't emanate inherent evil. Even though it should.

Because it was a creature that should never have existed.

Dhampir.

Even the most spiritually advanced mortals in the universe could rarely ascend to the highest level. But by harnessing the essence of the phoenix, Sakarbaal's corrupted creatures had invaded the sacred realm.

Whatever the vampire was planning, it involved more than Azrael had suspected. And he had the ice-cold certainty that time was running out.

CHAPTER 15

ROWAN

"**A**re you avoiding me, Rowan?" Meg entered Rowan's bedroom without so much as knocking on the door first. She finished zipping up her boot, with its concealed dagger, and refused to glance at the vampire.

Except evading the issue wasn't going to make it go away. But it was more than that. She loved Meg. And deep in her heart she didn't want to discover Meg had been instrumental in Steven's death. Didn't want confirmation that she knew no dhampir's mother had ever survived the birth of their damned child.

The gnawing suspicion that far from helping the victims of vampire rapes the Enclave was, somehow, behind the attacks haunted her. But even worse was the fear that Meg knew about that, too.

How could she pretend everything was fine when in her gut she knew it wasn't?

Her days of believing everything she was told were over. They should have been over the night of Steven's murder, but she'd chosen the cocoon of safe familiarity over digging for the unpalatable truth.

Finally, she turned to face Meg, who looked highly irritated at having been ignored. "How did you know where to find me the night Steven was killed?"

Meg's eyes widened in obvious astonishment. She couldn't blame her. The question had come out of left field and she hadn't mentioned Steven's name to her in years.

"They called me. Told me where you were. What is this all about?"

"Who called you?"

Meg looked at her as if she had lost her mind. "HQ." The heart of the Enclave. Here, in Grosvenor Square. "Who else, Rowan? They contacted me as soon as they heard from you."

"I didn't call anyone. You arrived within seconds of Steven being attacked. I was still paralyzed with shock. It didn't even occur to me to call anyone, let alone actually do it."

Meg didn't answer but her lips flattened as though Rowan's words offended her deeply. Then she stepped farther into the room and kicked the door shut with her stiletto.

"What are you saying?" Her voice was low, deadly, her French accent more pronounced than Rowan could ever recall.

She stepped towards Meg until only a couple of inches separated them. "I'm saying you were called before Steven was murdered."

Silence screamed between them, filled with countless accusations she didn't want to voice, didn't want to examine, but she had to know the truth. Scarlet flickered in Meg's eyes and while she had witnessed that phenomenon countless times in the past, it had never been directed at her.

It wasn't directed at her now.

"How can you be certain?" Meg's words were a whisper in the charged air. "You were very young. It was so many mortal years ago for you. What's happened, Rowan?" And then she gripped her hand as comprehension flared in her eyes. "You're still seeing that one from the club, aren't you? You're afraid for his life?"

She ignored Meg's questions. "If it was the Strigoi behind

Steven's murder then the Elders knew about it in advance." She hesitated, unsure whether to voice her deepest suspicion. "That's if the Strigoi were behind it at all."

Meg's grip tightened around her hand. "Who have you spoken to about this?"

"Who do you think?"

"Keep it that way." It was an imperious command. "If Sakarbaal discovered you were even thinking such things he would have your head."

You can't trust any of them. Brad's bitter words echoed in her mind. *Vampires won't turn against their own for us. You have to remember that.*

Despite Lily's harsh accusations she didn't think she was completely gullible. Meg's shock just now had been genuine. But that didn't change the facts. Meg was a vampire and Rowan was only a dhampir. Unease slithered along her spine. Had she just made a terrible mistake by confiding in Meg?

As she made her way to the underground tunnel that led from the basement of the mansion to the mews in the back street that had been converted into garages, she met up with Brad. She hadn't seen much of him, either, during the last week, but he didn't look in bad physical shape. Maybe he'd changed his mind about ditching the medication.

She hoped to god he'd changed his mind about going to Romania.

"You're glowing, Rowan." He sounded accusing.

"I'm *what?*"

"You've never been any good at lying. But if you don't want anyone suspecting anything you've got to stop going around looking like"—his condemning glance flicked over her like a whip—"a Christmas tree fairy."

They marched through the tunnel for a few moments in silence. Finally, she couldn't help herself.

"Is it really that obvious?" She'd been so focused on ensuring she wasn't followed whenever she met with Azrael it hadn't occurred to her that her constant warm glow of excitement might be glaringly obvious to anyone who bothered to look at her.

"Yes." He slung her a sideways glance. "It is to me. It is to anyone who really knows you. Hasn't Meg said anything?"

"I haven't seen much of her this week." And when she had, how long had it taken her to guess she was seeing Azrael? A few seconds at most. Alarm streaked through her. She couldn't afford to take any chances. "I'll be more careful."

I have to finish this wonderful thing with Azrael. It would break her heart. But it might be the only way to save his life.

But why? If the Enclave were behind Steven's death, if they were behind the death of Brad's lover, what was their reasoning?

"What do you think he'd say, this guy of yours, if you told him the truth? Would he stick around?"

She tried to ignore the hard knot of dread in the pit of her stomach at the thought of Azrael ever discovering her true nature. Even if they never saw each other again, she didn't want his memories of their time together to be contaminated by that knowledge. "No guy in his right mind would stick around if I told him the truth. You know that."

They'd reached the garages. Brad turned and gave her a brooding look. "He must be something special if you've fallen for him. And if you have then he deserves to know the truth. Deserves to be given the chance to choose his future."

She gave what she hoped was a derisive snort. She couldn't figure out whether she was more shocked by Brad's casual assumption that she'd fallen for Azrael or his naïve conviction that a human might willingly choose to be with a dhampir. *No one* would willingly choose that.

"It's not like it's anything permanent." The words echoed in her mind, a hollow reminder of how desperately she wished it could be otherwise.

Fallen for him? Who was she trying to fool? Of course she'd fallen for him. Hard. But it didn't change anything.

"But do you want it to be permanent?" There was an odd tone in Brad's voice. "Sometimes you have to take a chance. I did. Told her what I was. And she was willing to do whatever it took for us to be together."

She stared at him, as his words spun around her mind in an endless refrain. He'd told his lover what he was, and she hadn't run screaming for the hills? Was that even *possible*?

"You—but—"

"I've spoken to Sakarbaal." His flat interruption strangled the words in her throat as another fear gripped her. The vampire lord had spent the last few days with the Enclave in Edinburgh. She hadn't even realized he'd returned to London. Dhampirs didn't speak to Sakarbaal to simply pass the time of day. There was only one reason why Brad was telling her this. *Please let me be wrong.* "When he leaves England, I'm returning with him to Romania."

CHAPTER 16

ROWAN

The penthouse was sleek, with enviable views across the City. It was the early hours of the morning and only a faint glow from the outside world pierced the velvet darkness as Rowan methodically wiped blood from her katana.

At her feet lay a pile of ashes.

Her mark hadn't been a rogue, but a vampire whose entrepreneurial activities had encroached too far into the Enclave's business portfolio. Her assassination was a warning to others not to cross the Enclave, but for the first time Rowan didn't dismiss the nagging thread of doubt that tightened her chest.

Had the vampire deserved to die?

Until now she'd always accepted her assignments at face value. Read the Intel and agreed that for the Enclave to survive they couldn't afford to let other clans forget the ancient hierarchy. Only the Strigoi Echelon matched them in power and prestige and that was a war that was only rarely fought on the street.

Yet she couldn't drag her gaze from the ashes, a physical condemnation of all the choices she'd made in her life.

Except she'd never been given an option. She'd only followed orders.

Isn't that a choice in itself?

When she finally returned to HQ she made her way to the back stairs, which had originally been constructed for the use of servants, and flexed her throbbing fingers. Either her feelings for Azrael were adversely affecting her reflexes or she was getting too old for the game. Twice the vampire had caught her unawares, fracturing a couple of ribs in the process. If she didn't want to die before her time—*three more years if I'm lucky*—then she either had to sharpen her concentration or get the hell out of the Enclave.

It was a terrifyingly seductive notion. Something she had never seriously considered before because where could she go that the Elector High Council would not be able to hunt her down?

Dhampirs didn't hand in their notice when the going got tough. There were no workplace negotiations or early retirement plans. They could put in for a transfer to another Enclave branch in the UK or abroad, but their basic job description remained the same.

To her knowledge no dhampir had ever left to follow their own destiny away from the Enclave. But then again, what did she really know? Only what she was told.

But she didn't have to be told one thing. Even if any dhampir had walked, they wouldn't have lasted long. If the lack of amber acid didn't kill them then she was damn sure the Electors would see to it that they didn't survive.

Because, at their core, the Electors didn't believe dhampirs should survive at all.

"Rowan Moreton." The voice purred through her mind, deep, sensual and saturated with latent power. She spun on her heel, adrenaline pumping through her body in futile preparation to fight or flee.

She could do neither. Because lounging against the wall was Sakarbaal.

The seductive compulsion to sink onto her knees and grovel before him whispered through her, paralyzing her instinctive, human, need to flee. She'd been in his presence only twice before, and the same conflicting urges had consumed her on both occasions.

But she'd never been alone with him. And he'd never focused his formidable attention her way or looked at her with his piercing emerald eyes.

Somehow through the pounding of her heart and rushing of her blood she realized he was waiting for her response. She swallowed, her mouth parched, and grasped at her fleeing courage.

"Yes, my lord."

He smiled, and raw terror scraped through her chest at the sight. *What does he want with me?*

His finger, long and elegant, beckoned her closer. Ice trickled along her spine, but she could no sooner disobey his unspoken command as she could dissipate into smoke.

"Rowan." There was a contemplative tone in his voice as he hooked his finger beneath her chin and forced her to meet his eyes. From a distance he was imposing. Up close, he was breathtaking. Even in a twenty-first century suit with his silk tie tugged loose and black hair curling over his collar he emanated a dark, otherworldly magnetism. And although he could easily pass as a human in his mid-thirties, the aura of the ancients clung to him like an ethereal breath.

And no wonder. He was the founder of the Enclave and almost three thousand years old.

Sakarbaal scrutinized her face as though he wanted to peel back the layers of her skin, prise open her skull and claw through the secret corners of her mind. She remained rigid, her heart thundering in her ears as she pushed all memory of Azrael into the deepest recesses of her brain.

"Beautiful, of course. Intelligent, naturally." He sounded like he was checking off a mental shopping list. His finger abandoned her chin and trailed along the line of her jaw and she shuddered with a combination of revulsion and fascination. "You've never fully utilized your abilities before. How disappointing."

Did he expect her to answer him? It wasn't as if she didn't know what he meant. Before she'd met Steven her friend, Belinda, had accompanied her to an initiation ceremony to gauge her potential as a spy. Meg had been livid at the possibility of Rowan prostituting herself but as it turned out she never even passed the basic induction.

When it came to lying, she sucked. And since her life would depend on lying, if she went undercover and climbed into bed with the enemy, her use to the Enclave in that respect was zero.

She kept silent. It was safer than inadvertently angering the most powerful vampire in existence.

"You're damaged." Sakarbaal withdrew his finger and ran an assessing glance over her. She had the sudden certainty he could penetrate her hunting gear and see the bruising beneath. "You completed your assignment?"

"Yes." Did he want the evidence? The stake she'd used to plunge through the vampire's heart was in her pocket. But she made no move to retrieve it as a horrifying conviction gripped her. Was he questioning her abilities? Reconsidering her usefulness to the Enclave? If he chose to kill her now, she wouldn't stand a chance against him.

"Naturally, you did." There was a thread of amusement in his voice, as though he had not doubted her success for a moment. A gleaming athame appeared in his hand. Ice speared her heart and instinctively she backed up against the timber banister.

Sakarbaal pointed the blade at her face. "For your next mission you must be fully functional."

She couldn't tear her mesmerized gaze from the tip of the

ceremonial athame. One thought pounded through her mind. He didn't want her dead. He had a mission for her.

And she had to be *fully functional*.

"My injuries are superficial, my lord. They'll soon heal."

"Not fast enough." The way he swept his glance over her, left her in no doubt of what he really thought. She was only a dhampir and while she healed a lot faster than a human, it was nothing compared to the regeneration rate of a vampire. "You must be in optimum condition by the end of this day."

It was four in the morning. She was meeting Azrael tonight. Somehow, she didn't think Sakarbaal's mission would be easily accomplished, certainly not something she could finish in time to see Azrael afterwards.

It was only one night. She could reschedule. But disappointment scorched through her, a burning reminder that she was far from a free agent when it came to forging her own destiny.

Without taking his gaze from her, Sakarbaal pushed his jacket and shirt sleeve up his forearm. Paralyzed, she watched him slice open his wrist.

Saw the crimson blood gush.

Terror raced along her spine and flooded her reason.

Her back was flat against the banisters. Sakarbaal stood directly in front of her. There was nowhere to run. And the scent of his rich, evocative blood invaded her mind, blurred her vision and distorted reality.

He couldn't mean what she thought he did. *Untreated blood will kill me.*

"Drink." His command whispered through her senses, and a part of her wanted to fall on him and wrap her lips around what he so freely offered. But another part of her, the human half that she so desperately wanted to embrace, recoiled with repugnance.

It wasn't because of the blood. Her vampiric instincts could override such queasy sensibilities. It was because of *whose* blood it was. And the knowledge that once she had the vampire lord's blood in her veins, she would be irrevocably his.

His fingers slid through her hair, his athame grazing her skull, and he forced her head to his wrist. Her temples pounded, her heart hammered, and her gums ached in response to a primitive imperative she was incapable of fulfilling.

But she had no need of fangs when fresh blood flowed inches from her parched lips. Need overrode caution. Desire vanquished fear. She sank onto his wrist and sucked with a desperation she couldn't control. Fire scorched her mouth, incinerated her throat, and blasted through her arteries. An agonizing burning that both fed her hunger and starved her fractured soul.

Shattered images flashed behind her closed eyes. Somewhere in a sane corner of her mind she understood them as memories from Sakarbaal. Memories he was sharing through his blood. Feverishly she gripped his arm, swallowing convulsively, trying in vain to block the terrifying visions. But instead they became stronger, more visceral, impossible to ignore.

A dark demon, hunting her kind through the ages. Slaying them without mercy as they fell to their knees beneath his bloodied katana.

"Yes." Sakarbaal's irresistibly seductive whisper encompassed her mind. "Witness the slayer of dhampirs. Your deadliest enemy." His fingers tightened on her hair and he pulled her sharply upwards. Like a salivating dog she whimpered and struggled uselessly in his merciless grasp. But even as she frantically licked the blood smeared on her lips, his wound healed as though it had never existed.

The fire burned through her blood, healing and corrupting in equal measure. A hoarse scream flayed her throat as fractured bones knitted, battered organs regenerated and damaged skin resealed.

Gasping, she fell onto her knees as he released her. His blood hadn't killed her. She was healed. But she could feel his blood pumping through her veins, an eternal part of her whether she wanted it or not.

I don't want it. But it was too late now. Yet even as she recoiled from what she had done, her body embraced it. Demanded *more.*

"I know of your lover with whom you've been meeting this week."

The frenzied craving to once again taste his blood, to lose herself in his dark, entrancing thrall receded as ice speared her heart. He knew of Azrael.

Meg betrayed me.

Sakarbaal eyed her as though she was a vaguely interesting bug he had just stepped on. She staggered to her feet and clung onto the banister as he idly licked the blood off the blade of his athame.

She couldn't let him know how much Azrael meant to her. If Sakarbaal imagined he was merely a passing body in the night, he might overlook her indiscretion.

"My lord—"

"A demon of extraordinary power."

"What?" The word slipped out involuntarily. "No." There were no such creatures as demons. And even if there were, why would he say such a thing about her lover?

Sakarbaal's lips thinned and leashed rage hummed in the air between them. She'd just disagreed with the High Lord of the Council. Inferred he was lying. Her knees turned to jelly, and she gripped the banister tighter to stop herself from sliding onto the floor. Frantically she tried to undo her potentially fatal mistake.

"My lord, he's nobody. Just a human I picked up one night. He's—"

"Using you to get to me."

Her heart thudded erratically, and it was becoming harder to breathe by the second. It wasn't true. Sakarbaal was lying.

Azrael had never pressed her for any personal details. But he'd made several references to her job and people she worked for. Yesterday she'd told him more than she'd ever told anyone before.

He'd likened her family to the Mafia. In fact, he'd seemed amused by the analogy.

But that didn't prove he had any idea who her family was.

And I don't have any idea who his family are.

"No." She unhooked her fingers from the comfort of the banister and pushed herself upright. "He knows nothing about you, my lord. He's—I don't know anything about him. He was just a one-night stand."

"Ah." A chilling smile curved Sakarbaal's lips. "Now I understand why you failed to achieve your potential. If you want to survive this night, Rowan Moreton, you'll have to mask your true feelings far better than this."

She had thought the most terrible thing that could happen was for her secret to be discovered. But this was worse. Unimaginably worse.

There could be only one reason why he was questioning her about her illicit lover.

Because Sakarbaal expected her to *kill* Azrael.

"I have no feelings for—him." He wasn't a demon. But if she wanted to survive long enough to warn Azrael then she needed to convince the vampire lord that she swallowed every word he uttered.

"Excellent." Sakarbaal's voice gave no indication as to whether he believed her or not. "Should you require more incentive, access the memories I've shared with you. This demon—angel, whatever you wish to call it, exists only in order to wipe dhampirs from the face of the Earth." Once again, he tilted her chin with his finger, so she had no choice but to meet his merciless gaze. "Make no mistake. Once you've served your purpose, he'll slaughter you with as little regard as he slaughtered the Ancient Ones' children nine hundred years ago."

Denial screamed through her brain, lodged in her throat.

She'd been taught of the Great Massacre but until now had believed it was more myth than true history. An allegory, on how the outside world viewed dhampirs. And a warning that they were only safe because of the protection of the Enclave.

The memories Sakarbaal had forcibly shared with her rampaged in gruesome, vivid detail through her mind. The black forest, the looming castle and the pitiful shrieks of untrained dhampirs as they fell before the hunter's blade.

And this time she saw his face.

Azrael.

Panic thudded through her and she struggled to think straight. Sakarbaal could easily have corrupted the memories for his own purpose. Azrael wasn't evil. He wasn't using her to get close to the vampire lord.

Why would an angel want to wipe dhampirs from the face of the Earth?

There are no such things as angels.

Most humans thought the same about vampires.

Grief splintered through her at the callous genocide of those long-ago dhampirs. She might not like her tainted blood, but she was inextricably linked to them because of it. There was nothing she could do about the past, but she wouldn't let Azrael become another victim.

She'd have to tell him his life was in danger. That he needed to disappear. *Tonight's the last night I'll ever see him.*

"Tonight, when the demon is sated and sleeping," Sakarbaal said, as if he channeled her thoughts, "this is what you will do."

CHAPTER 17

AZRAEL

The exclusive Soho club Nathanael had chosen for their meeting was called *Archangels' Paradise*, which Azrael presumed Nate found amusing. The interior was a lavish confection of gold and scarlet, with strategically placed angelic statues and half-naked beautiful girls who attended to the patrons every indulgence.

He found Nate in one of the private booths. "Don't tell me your contact's changed his mind."

"No." Nate tipped the contents of a shot glass down his throat. "After all this time *he* wants to meet *you*, Az. Got nothing to do with your repeated requests at all."

He sprawled on the semi-circular sofa and scrutinized the other patrons. Far as he could tell they were all fully human. It was a little intriguing why Nate's contact now wanted to meet him, but the important thing was they were finally going to speak. "Where is he then?"

"Behind you." Nate slung him a grin that bordered on a smirk. What the hell? Before he could stop himself, Azrael leaped to his feet and swung around. How had he missed a two-thousand-year-old vampire?

Except there he was, lounging against the end of the sofa. And he still couldn't sense a damn thing. Irritation sizzled through his veins. The bloodsucker not only had impressive powers, but he'd felt the need to display them.

"Hey, Nico." Nate sounded amused by the whole thing. "You've made your point. Park your ass and stop glowering."

The vampire circled the front of the booth before finally hooking a gilded chair with his boot and dragging it towards the table.

They eyed each other across the table. It was equally obvious the vamp had no intention of sitting first, either.

Azrael gritted his teeth and sat, as though the upholstery were made of jagged glass. He'd give the vampire this small concession, seeing as he wanted information, but he didn't have to like it.

"Just so you know," Nico said as he lowered his lean frame onto the chair, "you're not as aware as you like to think."

He stifled the urge to unfurl his wings. It was always a pain in the ass having to maintain a glamour concealing them when he was pissed off. And Nico's attitude was pissing him off big time.

"Is that so?" He'd waited nearly two hundred years for this meeting, ever since the night he'd discovered the seedy acquaintances Nate hung out with. Why Nate wanted to associate with filthy bloodsuckers Azrael couldn't fathom but Nico, at least, was no ordinary vampire. He could hold the key to finding Sakarbaal.

Nico flashed a mirthless smile, his fangs gleaming in the subdued light. "Yes, that is so, archangel. You couldn't sense me a moment ago and you had no idea that I've been tailing you for the last two weeks."

He almost laughed at the vampire's gall.

"Why would an Elder of the Strigoi Echelon want to stalk an archangel?" He injected a good measure of derision into his tone. "You know who I am. You know why I want to speak with you. Do you get off on subterfuge?"

"Azrael, archangel of tact," Nate said, as he caught the attention of one of the girls and ordered drinks while Azrael and Nico continued to glare at each other. "Though I've got to admit, Nic. I'm intrigued. Do you suspect Az is a double agent working for Sakarbaal?"

"No." Nico retracted his fangs and offered another insincere smile. "The archangel works only for himself."

"That's what we all do." Nate broke off and gave the girl who brought over their drinks a smile that caused her to wobble on her six-inch heels. He waited until she was out of earshot before he turned back to them. "We don't take orders from anyone. And when the shit hits, our priority is to look out for number one."

"Your philosophy amuses me, Nate." Nico didn't sound especially amused, and neither did he take his intense gaze from Azrael. "Your fellow archangel's, on the other hand, doesn't."

"You have a problem with me wanting to destroy Sakarbaal?" He grabbed the nearest glass and drained the contents. It was only human alcohol and did nothing for him, but it was either that or reach across the table and grip the arrogant bastard's throat.

He understood Nico's antipathy towards him. The feeling was mutual. But they shared a deadly enemy. That was no secret. And although it was less well known that once, in the distant past, Nico and Sakarbaal had been as close as father and son, that bond had shattered almost a thousand years ago.

Nico was the only vampire still in existence, outside of the top tiers of the Enclave, who might know what Sakarbaal had been doing with a phoenix in Romania.

"The way you tried to nine hundred years ago?"

The last thing he needed was to be reminded of how he'd failed in that mission.

"I crushed whatever he'd been planning." Although not, unfortunately, for good.

"Yes." For a second he caught a savage gleam in the vampire's eyes. "I witnessed the aftermath."

Was Nico referring to the pitiful horde of dhampirs he'd slain while searching for their master's lair? It didn't seem likely. Why would one of the ancients give a shit about any of those misbegotten creatures?

They certainly hadn't nine hundred years ago.

"I have no intention of allowing him to escape me for a second time."

Nico's gaze didn't waver. "And you won't hesitate to slaughter any dhampir that comes between you and your target?"

Did the vampire know Sakarbaal had managed to infiltrate the spiritual realms? "Dhampirs are polluting the astral planes. What the hell's going on there?"

Something flared in Nico's eyes. Hadn't he known of that development? "Dhampirs are merely following their master's orders. As they always have. Sakarbaal doesn't encourage free will in his slaves."

He recalled the filthy, vacant-eyed creatures that had shuffled, zombie-like, towards him on that bloodied night in Romania. Disgust churned his gut.

"He's raised another mindless army?"

Why surround himself with dhampirs? They might hold off inept humans, but they were no match for trained warriors, never mind anyone with even a trace of immortal blood in their veins.

"He's raised another dhampir army, yes."

Frustration tore through him and he leaned forward, forearms across his thighs. "But what the fuck is he doing with them? What's the phoenix connection, Nico?"

Nico didn't answer right away. But if he had no intention of sharing any information then why had he decided to meet with Azrael after two centuries of refusing?

"We suspected he'd captured a second phoenix about fifty years ago." Nico sounded reluctant to share that fact, but it answered the question why Azrael's visions had returned half a century ago. "It took us several decades before we were certain. Whatever it is he's planning, he's close to execution."

"And that's why you finally agreed to see me?" Azrael leaned back against the sofa. "Because I'm the only one who can finish this?"

Nico gave a derisive laugh that grated on his nerves. "The reason I agreed to see you is because *you* are the one in danger of being finished by Sakarbaal."

He'd waited two hundred years for Nico to tell him this? Was this all the information the vampire possessed? "No fucking vampire is going to be the end of me, no matter how powerful he thinks he is."

"Az is right," Nate said. "It'll take more than a pissed off vampire to kill an archangel."

Nico smiled. For the first time that night it looked genuine. Something in the conversation had clearly amused him although he couldn't think what the fuck had. "Sakarbaal engages others to do his dirty work. If I'm not mistaken—and I'm not—he won't strike the killing blow until you're utterly defenseless."

"Not going to happen. You got anything useful for me or has this been a complete waste of time?"

The amusement fled and Nico leaned forward, hostility radiating from him. "You wanted to know if Sakarbaal has raised another dhampir army. In your prejudiced view, what did you see when I told you he had? A repeat of Romania? Do you think he learned nothing from that massacre?"

"I don't give a shit about his fucking dhampir army. I want to know what he was doing with a phoenix nine hundred years ago and what the hell he's trying to achieve by shredding its soul."

Nico's lip curled in blatant derision. "I could tell you a great deal, archangel. Let me start with this. Your cover is compromised."

The only cover he maintained while on Earth associating with humans was the illusion of being a mortal himself. For a reason known only to the vampire, Nico had brought him here tonight with only one intention. Of wasting his time.

He stood and turned to Nate who looked supremely unconcerned by the non-events unfolding. "I'll catch you later. There's nothing here to interest me."

And then Nico spoke. "Tell Rowan, the Strigoi Echelon send her our regards."

CHAPTER 18

AZRAEL

*N*ico's mocking words slammed through Azrael's chest, stopping him dead. How the hell did he know about Rowan?

Because he really has been following me. And he'd led the vampire to Rowan.

He swung round, rage and something akin to fear blazing through him at the realization he'd put her in mortal danger.

"Stay away from her." It was an archangelic command and if Nico didn't acknowledge that then his damned nights were numbered.

"Why?" Nico reclined in his chair and had the nerve to sling him a smile that raked like barbed lightning through his chest. How dare a vampire question him? How dare the bloodsucker attempt to threaten Rowan? "Is she that good a fuck?"

Primal fury whiplashed through him at the insult. No one spoke of Rowan with such arrogant contempt. He grabbed the vampire's throat and slammed him up against a gilded Corinthian column. The column cracked, faces turned their way, and he was barely aware of the concealing glamour that Nate flung up around them all.

"Touch her and I promise I won't just come after you. I'll destroy every fucking Strigoi in existence."

The vampire's eyes glowed crimson but the mocking smile remained fixed on his lips. As though, far from the warning it was intended to be, Azrael's reaction revealed something far more intriguing.

"Hey, Az," Nate said. "You can't throttle Nic, no matter how hard you try. Who the hell is Rowan anyway? Another vampire?"

He snatched his hand from Nico's throat and slung a glare of such feral disgust Nate's way it would have pulverized a lesser being. "Rowan is not up for discussion."

"She's the reason we're having this discussion," Nico said. "Why I agreed to this meeting."

Whatever game Nico was playing, he'd had enough. The vampire couldn't harm Rowan. All he had to do was give her his official protection and no other immortal would dare touch her.

He'd never done such a thing before. But if she was in danger because of their association then he would do nothing less to ensure her safety.

"What the fuck's going on?" Nate stood up, his attention fixed on Nico. "What does Az's current lay have to do with anything?"

He gritted his teeth and took a step back. Just because she *was* his current lay didn't mean Nate should refer to her as such. It was... disrespectful.

Nico ignored Nate, his focus entirely on Azrael. "It was Sakarbaal I was tailing two weeks ago. I can get closer to him without detection than any other can, and we hoped to discover the reason for his unexpected return to London."

"Go on." The words scraped his throat raw, but if Nico was finally going to say something worthwhile then he had no option but to swallow the acidic rage poisoning his reason.

The pause lengthened, fraught with words unsaid, until the vampire deigned to respond.

"His dhampirs bear no resemblance to those you encountered

in Romania. For the last fifty years he's bred only the beautiful and intelligent." Anguish scorched the last few words, and Azrael's gaze sharpened. *What the hell's that about?* Nico's features turned granite as he met Azrael's eyes, and his voice turned cold. "Attributes that, combined with vampiric abilities, he can use to his utmost advantage."

"He's been genetically engineering dhampirs?" Nate sounded fascinated. But then, he hadn't been there that night. Hadn't witnessed that decrepit army or heard their haunting screams as they'd died at his feet.

"Yes." Nico spared a fleeting glance in Nate's direction. "But not in the way you might imagine."

"Fine." He all but spat the word at the vampire. "You're saying he has dhampirs in London? And he has them hunting me?"

"He has dhampirs in every major city in the world. And yes. He assigned one of his premier assassins to take you down."

The idea that he was the target of a dhampir didn't concern him. But there was a connection to Rowan, and he didn't like how Nico had failed to address that. "Are you suggesting this dhampir is attempting to get to me through Rowan?"

"How would that work?" Nate said. "You could just teleport her somewhere safe until you'd neutralized the threat."

"Sakarbaal's dhampirs aren't merely highly trained warriors. He uses them as spies. You can guess how the most beautiful serve his wishes." Nico paused to let that unpalatable bit of information sink in. Who in their right mind would want to fuck a dhampir? He didn't care how different they were from the ones he'd encountered before. Some things just didn't—couldn't —change.

"Whoa." Nate sounded impressed although he had no idea which part of the sick plan could have done that. "She must be spectacular to have blindsided you, Az."

"What?" He glowered at his fellow archangel. Was Nate daring to insinuate that *Rowan*—?

"Fourteen nights ago," Nico said, "I discovered that Sakarbaal was tailing one of his senior dhampirs. This didn't much interest me. Until I saw her pick up her mark."

That was the night he and Rowan had met outside *Estella's*. He shoved Nico back against the column, the tip of his dagger against the vampire's throat.

He didn't even recall pulling the dagger from its sheath. "Don't go there."

Nico didn't appear intimidated by either the words or weapon.

"I kept my distance. I might be able to conceal my presence from Sakarbaal but your pretty little dhampir is another matter. Nevertheless, I saw you leave the restaurant. Saw you pull her into the doorway. And watched you enter the hotel."

Raw fury blazed and he plunged the dagger through the vampire's throat. Except the vampire was no longer there, and only lingering tendrils of black vapor wrapped around the blade.

"I wasn't Made last millennium." Nico's whisper grazed his ear and he swung round to where the vampire stood, as solid as ever. "And I'm no feeble dhampir you can destroy with a thoughtless decapitation."

"Rowan's not a dhampir." The words corroded his throat and offended his soul that he even had the need to utter them. "You're mistaken."

"And yet I'm not." Nico's lip curled in disdain. "She's the second eldest dhampir in the London branch of the Enclave of the Phoenix. Dhampirs don't live to a great age under Sakarbaal's rule."

"I don't know what you think you can achieve by this." He reined in the savage desire to rip Nico's foul heart from his chest. He knew, in his current state, he'd fail. But gods, he'd find a way to slaughter the bastard when his guard was down. "If Sakarbaal had sent one of his agents then she would have come onto me. *I* was the one who picked up Rowan."

A memory seared through his brain. Of how Rowan had glared at the woman in that nightclub, the one who had attempted to seduce him on the dance floor.

It didn't mean she'd been planning to make her move. If she was a dhampir *I would know.*

"You forget she's been trained in the art of seduction. And by your reaction she is obviously exceptional in her field of expertise."

But she hadn't struck him as being experienced in the art of seduction. In the distant past he'd fucked countless females on myriad planets who specialized in pleasure. Rowan's sexual awakening this week had *not* been manufactured.

"She's mortal." The words sounded feral to his ears, but he couldn't help it. Nico's accusation was repellent on every level. "Do you think I can't tell the difference between a human and a fucking anomaly of nature?"

But he'd never scanned her aura. Why would he? They'd met in a human club. And she was too beautiful, too fragile, too enchanting to be something so fundamentally aberrant.

Except for her surprising strength. But there could be a dozen reasons for that and none of them involved vampire blood.

"Anomaly of nature?" Derision dripped from every word. "You should know all about that, *archangel.*"

Yes, he knew all about that. Archangels were anomalies of nature and he had been called worse during his long existence. But they weren't talking about him. They were talking about Rowan and there was no way she could have fooled him into believing—

Believing what? That she was just a regular human woman? A woman who fascinated him to such a degree that he'd met her more frequently over the last two weeks than any other female he could recall in millennia?

The woman who had allegedly, the night they'd met at *Estella's*, saved a boy from a *vampire attack?*

"You have no proof." He pulled back from Nate's restrictive grip. "*Your* word means nothing to me."

"Az, I've known Nico a long time." Nate sounded serious. "He's telling the truth. The female is working for Sakarbaal. You need to deal with the problem."

This was crazy. No one who had ever met Rowan could think for a second she was anything other than human. Once again, the nightmare from nine hundred years ago flooded his mind. The dhampirs were rank, filthy. Their eyes were blank and dried blood stained their gaping mouths. To accuse Rowan of sharing that tainted heritage was obscene.

"It's easy enough to prove." Nico lounged against another Corinthian column, giving the infuriating impression that they were speaking of something trivial. "Invade her mind. You'll discover all her secrets. You'll feel her blood connection to Sakarbaal. Then you can eliminate her. After all, she's just a disgusting dhampir coming between you and your target."

Azrael forcibly unclenched his fist. There was no need to probe Rowan's mind. Although he'd clouded the surface memories of the diners in *Estella's*, that wasn't the same as invading their brains in search of answers. That was a weapon he used for his enemies, and the results could be ugly. All he needed to do with Rowan was scan her aura. It would be enough to show she was fully human and innocent of Nico's accusations.

And when he did, Sakarbaal would no longer be the only Ancient One he planned on hunting down.

CHAPTER 19

ROWAN

The restaurant was a quaint Tudor inn nestling against the bank of the River Thames. As Rowan walked across the cobblestone path, her stomach heaved with nerves and she flexed her numb fingers. Grief shredded her heart and a futile, white hot rage burned her mind.

Her fleeting glimpse of how a normal life could be was over. The dreams she'd woven around Azrael were nothing more than ephemeral mists that had blinded her to reality.

She'd always known they could have no future. But it didn't make this any easier. Because she'd been foolish enough to fall for him.

Stop. She wasn't going to spoil their last night together with regrets. He was the best thing that had ever happened to her. *No one* was going to take that away from her.

Even before her encounter with Sakarbaal she'd known tonight was the last time she could meet Azrael. But now, after she said goodbye to him, she wouldn't be going home.

Not when she had disobeyed a direct assassination order from not merely a senior Elder of the Enclave, but the Master of the Elector High Council.

She'd spent the day pulling together a hasty escape plan. With the wealth of information the Enclave had amassed over the years, it wasn't hard to discover the best place to buy a fake birth certificate and other documents. She'd emptied her bank accounts—at least the Enclave paid their dhampirs well—and had managed to smuggle a stockpile of amber acid into her car.

It wasn't a great plan, but it was better than nothing. Better than continuing to live under Sakarbaal's rule.

Stealthily she eyed the dark night, trying to catch a shadow among shadows. She could sense no vampire nearby, but Sakarbaal had plenty of humans he could call on to tail a dhampir he didn't trust.

And she was under no illusion he trusted her. While he might not imagine she'd blatantly disobey his command to incapacitate Azrael, he'd known she was lying about their relationship. He must have guessed she wasn't as invested in this assignment as she'd tried to pretend.

Not that it mattered. After tonight she would either be dead or starting a new life as a fugitive. And while a hopeless part of her still dreamed of spending what remained of her life with Azrael, she knew better.

It could never happen. For so many reasons.

At the oak doors she hesitated, her hand pressed against the aged timber. Concealed in her car was six months' supply of amber acid. By reducing her daily dosage to half, that gave her a year's grace. And during that year she had to discover how to replicate the blood substitute, or she was as good as dead anyway.

She took a deep breath and pushed open the door. Warmth blasted her, from the open log fire in the hearth and from the human patrons who were blithely unaware of what creature had just entered their haven.

I'd do anything to join their oblivious ranks.

But that was never going to happen. Despite her best intentions, Sakarbaal's cold words invaded her mind.

This demon—angel, whatever you wish to call it, exists only in order to wipe dhampirs from the face of the Earth.

But that was only Sakarbaal's truth. She no longer believed everything she was told without cold, hard evidence. And warped memories from an ancient vampire *didn't count.*

And then, at the back of the inn at an intimate, candlelit table for two, she saw Azrael. Her breast compressed, as if a fist squeezed her heart, and her throat constricted in unbearable sorrow.

She'd give anything if only she could prolong their time together.

He looked up, and the rest of the world faded into insignificance. Even from this distance an aura of leashed power radiated from him. Despite being tucked into a cozy corner, and the black, casual shirt he wore, nothing could disguise the inherent magnetism his presence invoked.

As she made her way across the floor, she was aware of the glances he attracted. The crackle of raw sexuality in the air, like an approaching summer storm, and that he appeared entirely oblivious to. It was easy to believe immortal blood ran in his veins, and right now she didn't care whether that blood was from an angel or demon.

She would never be responsible for spilling it.

He stood up as she reached their table and his chivalrous gesture tugged at her heart.

"Hi." She smiled at him, their gazes meshed, and an unaccountable shiver prickled along her spine.

He smiled back, helped her with her coat and waited until she sat, but still the eerie chill flickered over her flesh like an arctic caress. Had she imagined that iced expression in his eyes? The odd sense of disconnectedness in the smile he'd offered her?

"You look edible by candlelight." His husky whisper sank into her senses but instead of delight at his compliment unease curled deep in her belly. He'd said something similar to her only yesterday. But yesterday his glance had been warm, his words a sensual promise.

Tonight, his words gave the impression of a threat.

Stop. She was imagining things. Letting Sakarbaal's accusations poison her mind. There was nothing odd or strange about Azrael's behavior. She was seeing shadows, but they were of Sakarbaal's creation and had nothing to do with the truth that was Azrael.

"I'll remind you of that later." They had one last night together and she was going to make a million memories, before it all crashed down. She planned on waiting until after they'd made love, when they were in each other's arms, before she told him of the danger. Before she warned him that his life had to irrevocably change if he wanted to survive.

"I'll look forward to it." Again, he smiled at her as he picked up the menu, and again ice invaded her veins, as though he sent a subliminal message that her subconscious couldn't decipher.

Despair stabbed through her. Sakarbaal had managed to tarnish her final hours with Azrael.

She picked up her own menu and pretended an interest in the dishes that she no longer felt.

"How has your day been?" She'd never asked him about his day before. It was too intimate. But she would never again have the chance to ask, so what did it matter?

If he was surprised by her question, he didn't show it. "Same as usual. Scraping the dredges from the gutters and sending them into their own personal version of hell."

Azrael

Rowan kept her gaze fixed on the menu, as if it was the most fascinating thing she'd ever seen. He fought the urge to reach across the table and snatch the damn thing from her hand.

She sat there in her soft forest green sweater, her gorgeous black hair curling over her shoulders. Her long lashes concealed her eyes and a pale rose blush highlighted her aristocratic cheekbones. If Nico had told him Rowan was descended from a demon, he could believe it. Her beauty was ethereal, her presence addictive, and to learn she had immortal blood in her veins wouldn't surprise him at all.

But a dhampir?

And still he hadn't scanned her aura. It was the first thing he'd intended to do tonight, but as he'd watched her cross the room towards him, and seen how she turned every man's head, something ugly and primal had clawed through his gut.

She's mine.

He'd discover her truth when she lay in his arms, replete and exhausted. And if she was guilty, he'd deal with her.

No problem.

"Are you in law enforcement?" She continued to scrutinize the menu, as though her question was a casual enquiry and nothing more. What more could it be? Except she'd never shown any interest in what he did when he wasn't with her.

"Something like that." If she'd asked him yesterday, what would he have told her? But she hadn't. She'd asked tonight, and tonight ambiguity shadowed every word she uttered. "I imagine our work runs along similar lines." *Lies.*

He didn't give a shit whether her job entailed espionage or assassination of political opponents. She could be involved in an organized crime syndicate for all he cared.

Anything. So long as she was oblivious of everything connected with Sakarbaal.

She glanced up at him. Tension thrummed in the air between them, as if they balanced on the edge of a precipice and one false word would send them both tumbling into the abyss.

"I hope not." She sounded faintly horrified by the notion.

He leaned across the table, unsure whether he wanted to take her hand and comfort her or grip her throat and throttle the truth from her.

"There's something you should know about me, Rowan." It wasn't his imagination. Wariness cloaked her like a second skin. "Those who cross me don't survive long."

Except Sakarbaal. His proverbial thorn.

The tip of her tongue moistened her lips and the sight mesmerized him.

"Politically or literally?"

He dragged his attention back to her, the woman who had countered his oblique threat with a direct confrontation. But her gaze held no aggression. Only an indefinable aura of sadness that made him want to tear Nico limb from limb for daring to suggest she was anything but an innocent.

"Literally." He couldn't help himself and threaded his fingers through hers. She was warm, vital. *Alive.* "You told me yesterday the world would be a far more dangerous place without you." He smiled, but it was an effort because he wanted to pull her into his arms and hold her until the hard rock lodged in his chest crumbled. "Same here."

Her fingers tightened around his and she leaned towards him until their breaths mingled. "Azrael." Her voice was barely a whisper. He'd never heard anything so seductive in his life. "There are things I need to tell you about my life. Things you need to know about me."

Relief washed through him, loosening the constriction in his chest. If she intended to confide her secrets, then they weren't the ones he suspected.

"Tell me later." He brushed his lips against her knuckles. "Room service?"

Her smile was all the answer he needed, and within moments he'd made the necessary arrangements. As they climbed the worn timber stairs, he wound his arm around her waist. Tonight, after she'd told him of her life, there would be nothing left to discover, and her fascination would dim.

The Tudor theme continued into the bedroom with carved oak furniture and an elaborate four-poster bed. She tossed her coat onto the brocade bed quilt and then turned and flung her arms around his neck.

"I missed you." She rose onto her toes and kissed him, her body molding his in that entrancing way that invaded his dreams. "I'll always miss you."

He laughed against her mouth and pulled back just enough so he could push her bag out of the way. It was a lot larger than the usual ones she carried, a moss green leather monster, but as his fingers closed around it an improbable electrical current jolted his hand.

Instinctively he snatched his hand away. But the aftereffects lingered, like a poisonous echo in his blood. An insistent glimmer of cold, inhuman evil.

"Let me dump this." She untangled her limbs from around his neck and slung her bag onto the floor. Dark energy rippled from the innocuous bag, and dread curled through his gut.

Buried memories clawed through his mind, taking him back to a time of nightmare and horror. When Gabe had lost his sanity over the senseless death of Eleni and become enmeshed within the inhospitable Voids, a labyrinth construct that existed within the vast expanse of Dark Matter. He and fellow archangels Mephisto and Zadkiel had searched that unimaginable hell for Gabe. The hell that was the dominion of the creatures known as the Guardians.

Even after all these millennia he couldn't forget the way the Voids had eaten into the fabric of his being. How it had grasped with acidic greed onto his wings. He'd been in the Voids only a fraction of the time that Gabe had and his injuries, unlike Gabe's, had eventually healed with no lasting physical scars.

But now the psychic lacerations, that until seconds ago had remained latent, sizzled with fiery recognition.

Something in her bag originates from that cursed place.

He pulled away from her and grabbed her bag by its shoulder strap. No reaction. Was he going fucking insane?

"What are you doing?" There was a thread of alarm in her voice as she tried to pull her bag from him. He swung it out of her reach and ripped open the zipper. "Azrael, don't."

He turned it upside down and an astonishing volume of *stuff* tumbled onto the floor. What the fuck had she intended to do when she'd left him tonight, leave the country?

"God, Azrael." She sounded more irritated than alarmed now, as she sank to her knees and began to gather up various items of underwear and toiletries. "Did you have to?"

He crouched beside her. Like a magnet his hand reached out, shoved aside an e-reader and wallet and discovered the source.

A slender tube-shaped medical case.

She made a grab for it, but he beat her to it. Whatever the case contained seeped evil into his palm. His grip tightened. He wouldn't succumb to the overwhelming urge to fling the tube across the room.

It could all be a terrible mistake. She had no idea what she carried. No idea of the effect it had on his archangelic biology.

No clue that she had in her possession a weapon that could, theoretically at least, render him incapable of deflecting *a killing blow.*

Finally, he met her gaze. Anxiety clouded those deceptively innocent eyes and she reached out her hand. "Let me put that away. It's quite fragile."

"What is it?" He flicked open the clasp with his thumb but didn't take his eyes from her.

"It's—medication." She offered him a smile that didn't reach her eyes. She might just as well have prefaced her words with *this is a lie.* "Not mine," she added hastily as if she thought that might improve the situation. "I'm just looking after it for someone."

"Who?" He tipped the phial from its case and his gut knotted at the shimmering dark liquid—gas? —that swirled inside the glass.

His stubborn refusal to face the truth fractured. This had originated in the Voids. And only the Guardians could have procured it.

"The Godfather, remember?" She curled her fingers around his arm, as though she wanted to comfort him rather than kill him.

"This is connected to your family business?"

"Yes." Relief vibrated through that one small word, like he'd offered her an easy way out. "I'm not sure what it is but I think it's some kind of biological pathogen."

For him, the contents of this phial amounted to biochemical warfare. He didn't know for sure what would happen if it was plunged into his bloodstream, but he doubted he'd be able to fight off Sakarbaal.

He might not even be able to teleport. None of them had been able to use any of their normal abilities while in the Voids.

"Ever heard of the Enclave of the Phoenix?"

She recoiled as if he'd physically threatened her. She'd heard of it all right.

"How do you know of it?" Her voice was hushed, and dread licked through every word.

His blood thundered against his temples, filling his head. The erratic hammer of his heart against his ribs jarred every bone in his body. And Rowan's tragic expression was all he could see as she gazed at him as though he had just ripped out her soul.

Against all his survival instincts, he'd trusted her. And she had betrayed him in the worst possible way. To hell with scanning her aura. There was only one way to discover her truth. But even now he couldn't invade the depths of her brain as she deserved, and instead he merely grazed the edge of her mind.

A searing fog of isolation swamped him, threatening to suffocate, to overwhelm. But even as he recoiled, staggered by the depth of darkness that held her in its thrall, the overpowering stench of blood flooded his senses.

The vision smashed through his mind. Sakarbaal, looming. Crimson blood flowing.

Rowan sucking the blood of the most ancient vampire of all.

CHAPTER 20

ROWAN

*R*owan pushed herself to her feet and staggered back until she came up against the wall. Azrael stood too, a savage gleam in his eyes, and all her desperate excuses vanished like sand through a bottomless hourglass.

"Answer my question." There was a deadly lack of emotion in his voice that sent skeletal fingers scraping along her spine. "What do you know of the Enclave?"

A stranger stood before her. There was no hint of the man she'd spent the best two weeks of her life with. No glimmer of the exciting, tender lover she'd lost her head over. His expression could have been carved from marble. Even the gleam in his eyes had died, leaving them eerily blank.

Was this a mask? Or was this the true Azrael? Had she fallen for a cruel façade, for someone who simply didn't exist?

She had the overwhelming urge to run, to hide, but instead she straightened her shoulders and stepped away from the comforting solidarity of the wall.

"I've lived at the Enclave all my life."

A ripple of emotion distorted his carved features and her last shreds of self-delusion crumbled. Revulsion pulsed from him as destructive as sulfuric acid, corroding the air she dragged into her lungs.

He knew what she was. Had always known. And now, when he no longer needed to keep up the pretense, he showed his true feelings. Deep inside, a part of her heart withered and died.

"And you're Sakarbaal's creature."

His contempt was a frigid slap in the face. Never had she thought four words could wield such destructive power. But they thundered in her head. Worse, far worse, than anything she had imagined.

Sakarbaal's creature. Azrael made her sound unclean, foul. And while she hated her tainted blood and up until now had relied on the Enclave for her livelihood she wasn't, and had never been, Sakarbaal's *creature.*

"No." Her voice was strong although she had no idea how. "I'm not his creature, Azrael." What point was there in pretending ignorance? "Angel of Death."

Fury glinted in his eyes, but he didn't ask what the hell she meant, and her last fragile hope fell to dust. Instead he took another step towards her and for the first time a sliver of fear uncoiled.

Sakarbaal had told her Azrael intended to kill her. But even now, even when everything she'd believed about him had been a lie, she couldn't believe he'd end her life.

"How can you be anything else?" His whisper burned her skin. "When you drink his blood like a mindless addict?"

How could he know of that? It had happened only once. Yet he made it sound as if she constantly sucked down the vampire lord's blood.

"I don't—"

"*Dhampir.*"

The rest of her denial lodged in her throat. It was one thing to discover he had always known her secret. But it was nothing compared to hearing him spit the word, like a curse, in her face.

Her battered heart shriveled. She'd never had a future with him. But the bitter truth was—she'd never had anything with him. Everything had existed only in her mind.

Years of training came to her rescue. She couldn't lie with conviction, but she could shove her wounded feelings into a dark corner of her psyche. She might not be able to defeat the angel of death, but she'd rather die trying than die slowly, bit by bit, as he verbally ripped her to shreds.

Nine hundred years ago he had slaughtered unarmed dhampirs in his quest to rid them from the world. That might make him a hunter, but it didn't make him a warrior.

She smothered the memories of the last two weeks. There was no time to mourn their sordid death. They had never been anything but illusions. The truth stood before her, and it was neither noble nor heroic. Maybe he was a demon, after all. Because surely angels weren't evil.

"Murderer." Contempt dripped from every syllable, but she didn't know if the scorn was directed at him, or herself for being so easily used.

He brandished the phial before her eyes. "What does *this* make *you?*"

A fool. That's what it made her. For believing him innocent of Sakarbaal's accusations. But now she knew the truth, would she plunge the unholy poison into Azrael's blood? Could she see him diminish before her eyes, betray what they had shared and offer him up to the vampire lord?

We shared nothing. Yet the thought of immobilizing him for Sakarbaal turned her stomach.

She'd take that tragic knowledge with her to the grave.

"My people deserve vengeance for what you did to them."

He hissed between his teeth, as if she had just tossed the vilest insult in his face. It was surreal. In the past she'd never experienced an emotional connection to those long ago dhampirs who'd been slaughtered without mercy. She'd hardly believed the story in any case. But now, facing the man she'd been stupid enough to lower her guard with, the injustice churned through her like corrosive lava.

They hadn't deserved to die, simply because an angel took exception to their existence.

"And you think you're even remotely capable of exacting such vengeance?" Derision seeped like acid from his words, but she refused to quake before him. "Do you have any idea who you're up against?"

"Yes." She glared at him, trying and failing to ignore the unearthly beauty that radiated from him like a cosmic blast. "Even immortals can die. I've killed enough of them."

He recoiled, a psychic reaction as physically he didn't move an inch. But why would her blunt admission shock him? He must know she hunted vampires. And while she didn't delude herself she could destroy an angel, he was still made of flesh and blood.

And flesh and blood could always be destroyed.

He gripped her throat and shoved her back against the wall, her reflexes helpless against his speed. His fingers bit into her flesh, lifting her onto her toes. Instinctively she clutched at his hand, futilely trying to loosen his grip. Yet for all the loathing in his eyes, he didn't follow through and break her neck.

"I'm no filthy bloodsucker." He hissed the words in her face, his gaze locked with hers. "Look on me, dhampir, and tremble at your conceit."

The room shimmered and she struggled to refocus. She wouldn't give him the satisfaction of passing out. He wasn't going to snap her neck. He was going to slowly cut off her air supply.

But it wasn't lack of oxygen causing her vision to waver. The shimmer was physical, and it surrounded Azrael, but it wasn't a shimmer at all. Desperately she blinked, trying to clear her mind, but still a rainbow hue distorted reality.

Her grip slackened. *They're his wings.* Beautiful, iridescent wings, as if each feather had been created from heaven itself, a breathtaking vision of harmonious perfection.

Mesmerized by the glorious sight, she reached out, desperate to touch. To convince herself they were real, that she was still alive—that this wasn't a mirage brought on by death.

Faster than a heartbeat, he tossed the phial onto the bed and pinned her hand against the wall above her head. His body was only a whisper from hers. His breath fanned her face. And still his glare drilled into her.

It would be horribly easy to drown in his eyes and let this sordid fate take its course. But she wouldn't go down without a fight. All she needed was to distract him for a couple of seconds, so she could pull her stiletto from her boot. Even plunged straight through his heart might not kill him but at least it would make her feel better. For a moment at least, before he decapitated her.

She tried to speak. But only a soundless gasp emerged.

His gaze slid to her lips and his grip on her throat relaxed. She flicked the tip of her tongue over her dry lips, and instantly his fingers tightened around hers, pressing her hand more securely against the wall.

"Do you think to seduce me, even now?" The scorn in his voice flayed her, yet raw lust drenched every word. "You overestimate your charms."

She tried to keep her focus on his face. But his wings filled her vision. How could a creature so cruel possess something of such heartbreaking beauty?

His murderous grasp loosened further, yet he appeared unaware of his concession. Unaware she was no longer on her toes. She hitched in a shallow breath. "I wouldn't seduce you if my life depended on it."

He bared his teeth in a parody of the smile she had once found so irresistible. How easily she'd been deceived. "You weren't so fastidious before."

She still clung onto his hand that clasped her throat, but he was no longer choking her. It was a far from tender touch, but it no longer felt like a prelude to murder.

"I see you now for what you are."

He leaned in closer. So close, his lips all but brushed hers, and his wings enveloped them in a mystical cocoon of iridescence. They might have existed in their own magical world where there was no place for stark reality. A make-believe world where dreams could come true.

A place that didn't exist.

"You always knew what I am."

She'd always thought he was *more*. She'd known he was no vampire and yet he'd reminded her of an immortal. Problem was, she didn't know that many immortals to compare him with.

She didn't have to justify anything to him. He was a bastard, yet her damn treacherous body didn't care.

"You'll never reach your goal through me." With great effort, she managed to loosen her grip from his hand that encircled her throat and slide her fingers over his wrist. Despicable tremors of need danced over her skin and she gritted her teeth. How could she still want him, even now? Why did she have the insane urge to ask him to explain why he'd massacred those long ago dhampirs? Did she really think he could have a plausible excuse?

"I'll reach my goal with or without you." His hand slid from her throat to cradle her face. It wasn't a gesture of tenderness. Unearthly power vibrated in the touch of his fingers, and she knew he could crush her jaw as easily as she could crush spun sugar. "You're expendable."

Pain burned through her heart at his callous words. She was a dhampir. She'd lived her entire life knowing she was expendable. But with Azrael, for a few wonderful days, she'd chosen to forget that.

"Why?" Instead of stealthily reaching for her stiletto she pressed her hand against his heart. Except he didn't have one.

How could he? "Why do you want to wipe us from the face of the Earth?"

He might not have a heart, but the erratic thud beneath her fingers proved his body wanted hers. Maybe not everything over the last two weeks had been a lie.

But nothing else had been real.

"I'll destroy anything that gets in my way when it comes to defeating Sakarbaal." He plunged his fingers through her hair, forcing her head back. "And you put yourself in my way."

The gold flecks in his eyes glittered, and even though her life hung on a thread the phenomenon captivated. How had she not realized he wasn't human before? Was it because she had so desperately *wanted* him to be human that she'd deliberately disregarded the tiny signs?

A mere mortal could never survive the truth of her existence. And although she wouldn't survive Azrael's wrath at least he was a worthy opponent for Sakarbaal.

"So you plan to murder me the way you murdered those dhampirs in Romania?" It was hard to breathe with him towering over her and her senses flooded with the raw, sensual essence of Azrael. She harnessed her focus and injected all the contempt she could into her accusation. *"Coward."*

A dark, dangerous emotion shifted in those gold-flecked eyes. Why was he offended by her comment? He'd made it clear she meant less than nothing to him.

"It was a battle." He growled the words in her face, and she had the strangest sensation he was trying to convince himself as much as her. *Stop making excuses for him.* He had no feelings, no remorse, and he had as good as told her she was next on his hit list. "And you deserve to die for what you are."

CHAPTER 21

ROWAN

"Kill me, then." She glared at him and wrapped her leg around his thigh, bringing her concealed stiletto within reach. Let him think she was hell bent on seducing him, when her only goal was escape. "Look me in the eyes as you murder another unarmed dhampir, Angel of Death."

"Unarmed?" His laugh was derisive and in the split second she drew her stiletto from her boot, he knocked it from her grasp in a move so lightning fast she was stunned. "*Now* you're unarmed, dhampir."

He gripped her throbbing wrist and dragged her arm over her head. Mortification scorched through her that he'd deflected her attack so easily. Had she really imagined she stood a chance against him?

His body melded to hers, as though they were lovers and not the deadliest of enemies. Effortlessly he manacled her wrists with one hand. Her infuriated struggles didn't impede him in the slightest.

"And that's how you like it, isn't it?" It was a pathetic response, but she couldn't stay silent while he meted out his twisted form of justice. She wasn't used to being so defenseless and now her stiletto was gone so too was her last hope of inflicting injury.

"I've no desire for you to stab me in the back twice."

"I wasn't aiming for your back."

"What were you aiming for? Castration?"

His nonexistent heart had been her target. But let him think what he liked. "Give me back my stiletto and I'll show you."

"I have a better idea." His eyes glittered and the breath stalled in her throat. Why did she still crave his touch, when all he wanted was her death? "Dump the pretty façade you've shown me over the last two weeks and fuck me as you really are."

Primal need speared through her. How could her body betray her so brutally? "I'd rather die."

"That can be arranged."

"What are you waiting for?" If he expected her to fall apart in terror, he was going to be disappointed. She wouldn't beg for mercy when he possessed none.

"Don't usually hang around once the target guesses the truth?" He made it sound like a question, instead of a statement. How often did he do this kind of thing? It hadn't crossed her mind he'd made a career of it. Another piece of her broken heart crumbled to dust.

When she'd been a child, she'd day-dreamed of mythical angels because they were so beautiful and pure and *good*. Everything that she wasn't.

How wrong she'd been.

"I suppose that's because they're usually dead by now." She spat the accusation at him. Azrael literally held her life in his hands. She *should* be dead by now. She wasn't that stupid. But he was deliberately keeping her alive because, despite everything, he still lusted for her.

Could she use that to her advantage? Corrupt the one, perfect thing in her life into something cheap and sleazy?

Get real.

It had never been beautiful or special, except inside her imagination. If having sex with Azrael offered a chance of escape, she'd grab it with both hands. To hell with tarnishing her memories.

They were already defiled.

"Necrophilia not to your liking?" He was so close they could kiss. Heady arousal thrummed between them and she stirred restlessly, her body brushing his. *Torture.* He sucked in a harsh breath but didn't pull back. "Doesn't fucking vampires amount to the same thing?"

"I wouldn't know." Her gaze roamed over his face, searching futilely for a chink in his armor. There was none. She turned his accusation back at him. "Does it?"

His wings wrapped around her, obscuring the room in a luminous rainbow hue. The tips of his feathers brushed her naked thighs and caressed her imprisoned arms. She ached to touch his wings, to inhale their evocative, otherworldly scent. Was he attempting to hypnotize her?

"I wouldn't know." His mocking voice echoed her words. "The nearest I've come to screwing the dead is fucking a dhampir."

She flinched. His words shouldn't hurt her, but they did.

"And you couldn't get enough." She arched her back and pressed her breasts against his granite hard chest. He retaliated by crushing her against the wall. Tension swirled, deadly and addictive. "You still can't get enough of me, no matter how much you hate me."

"That makes two of us." His uneven breath meshed with hers. "Admit it. You want me."

Yes. It was a pitiful cry wrenched from the deepest recess of her heart. But she wanted something that had never existed. Here, now, there was nothing but sex and survival at stake.

She had to keep her eye on the prize, no matter how unlikely it might be. *Freedom.*

But she still couldn't lie, even to save her own skin. "You aren't capable of giving me what I want."

He cupped her butt in a possessive gesture and primal need shuddered through her. With a low growl, he ripped off her thong, the delicate material shredding beneath his touch. "I gave you what you wanted for the last two weeks. Tonight is fucking payback."

She brushed her cheek against his and breathed into his ear. "You wish."

His jaw clenched and he inhaled a ragged breath. "Be careful, dhampir."

"Or what?" she said. His stubble grazed her skin and she embraced it. "Your threats mean nothing to me."

His palm trailed over her thigh, a sensual, deceptive caress. She couldn't afford to forget this didn't mean a thing to him. But it was hard to think at all when his finger dipped inside her and then teased her swollen clit.

"I don't make threats."

Desire swirled, clouding her reason. "Prove it."

Conflicting emotion swirled in his eyes, but he didn't rise to her challenge. It was obvious he hated the fact he still desired her. That he wanted her to beg before he surrendered to his lust.

She wouldn't allow him to win this final confrontation between them. Her lips drew back, and she hissed between her teeth. "I dare you."

He wrenched open his pants before gripping her butt and lifting her off the floor. She gasped, desperate for him and not caring that he knew it, and with one savage thrust he invaded her willing body. She slammed against the wall with the force of his possession and for a fleeting moment saw eternity reflected in his eyes.

So many times, she'd fantasized about having sex with him without using protection. But none of them matched the reality.

She could feel every inch of him inside her. Hot, naked flesh. A primitive connection, skin against skin, stretching her so deliciously that she trembled on the edge of pain.

Even now, when her life hung in the balance, it was more than a fuck. She couldn't forget all the good times and laughter she'd shared with him. Even if they'd been nothing more than a lie.

She squeezed her eyes shut, so she didn't have to witness his satisfaction should he realize the truth, and wrapped her legs around his hips in a vise that would crush a mortal man.

She'd take everything she could from him. And keep it locked deep inside.

Azrael

AZRAEL GRITTED his teeth in a futile attempt to regain control. *It's all about control.* For two weeks this fucking dhampir had led him by the cock and driven him beyond anything he'd experienced before. How many others had she driven to the edge? How many others had she fucked before handing over to Sakarbaal?

"Look at me." It was a harsh command and she didn't obey. Frustration ripped through him, but it was more than frustration, more than base lust. And gods, the lust was bad enough. He'd taken countless females without using protection. But it had never felt like this before.

She grasped him so tightly, insanity flickered on the starless horizon. Every tiny tremor caressed his shaft, the sensation of naked flesh a silken condemnation. Her evocative scent invaded, slithering through his senses like a malignant serpent, paralyzing his thirst for vengeance. All he wanted was to fuck her, hard and fast, and then finish her. But all he could do was stand there, impaled in her deceptively desirable body, as though he was the captive at her mercy.

A primitive growl burned his throat and he tightened his grip on her wrists. He should have eliminated her the second she'd admitted her guilt. But he hadn't, because he couldn't. And the only reason he couldn't was because he'd wanted her one last time.

To fuck her while knowing what she really was. The disgust would consume him and obliterate the lingering remnants of desire that still smoldered.

"Dhampir." The word polluted his mind, corroded his soul. He glared at her face and all he could see was her ethereal beauty and the way her lips clamped together in disgust.

She didn't look like a dhampir. Sure as hell didn't smell like one. But it had been nine hundred years since he'd last encountered one. They had evolved beyond anything he might have imagined in his worst nightmares.

The rage pounded through his blood and he rammed into her. Exquisite pleasure spiraled through his cock and splintered low in his groin. Her lips parted, a hellish invitation, and her uneven breath feathered his jaw in seductive temptation.

I'm in control. But beneath the pounding of his heart and the hammering of his blood, it was a hollow affirmation. Because he couldn't control the way she made him feel. Couldn't banish the fury that shredded his pride at the knowledge he'd been so utterly deceived by her façade.

Except it wasn't fury and it was more than his pride. Long ago he'd vowed never to trust again. Never to believe in anyone as he'd once believed in his goddess. Yet Rowan had infiltrated his armor, destroying it from the inside out and he hadn't even known it. She might not have been in his visions where Sakarbaal ravaged the Earth. But he'd been blind to the truth, regardless.

His wings cocooned them, and she looked so innocent, cradled in his iridescent feathers. How many times had he wanted to do this? How many times had he imagined the wonder, the awe on her face when he did?

A harsh laugh flayed his throat. She couldn't even look at him.

His wings meant nothing to her. But even that knowledge did nothing to dampen his lust.

"Angel." It was a whispered curse, yet she still didn't open her eyes. He rocked into her, felt her internal muscles convulse around him, and it was electrifying. Her lips beckoned, and he nearly succumbed.

But he'd never willingly kiss a creature of Sakarbaal's.

"You're wrong." He couldn't help it, and his mouth grazed hers. She was created from darkness, yet she tasted of sunlight. "I'm an archangel. And I don't take prisoners."

CHAPTER 22

AZRAEL

Finally, Rowan looked at him, her eyes dark with a passion he couldn't mistake. Or was this another trick of hers, an attempt to fool him once again? The way she'd fooled him for the last two weeks?

Curse the gods. He knew what she was. What she had done. And he still couldn't trust his own judgement when it came to her.

He had to break free from her dark enchantment. The future of humanity was at stake.

"Archangel." Her voice was unbearably husky. A mockery of every sexy, evocative whisper she'd ever shared with him. "I despise you."

Not nearly as much as he despised himself. "The feeling is mutual."

She hooked her ankles together, crushing their bodies even closer. He slid his hand over her delectable ass, the skin smooth and silken and deliciously curved. Her breath teased his jaw, a delicate echo of something that had never existed, and his searching fingers delved between her spread thighs.

The sensation was exquisite. It was an agony. Sex had never

been so fucking messed up before. Her back arched, propelling her forward and he matched her frenzied thrusts, no longer caring that she knew how desperately he needed this.

Needed her.

The thought whipped through his mind, insubstantial, unimportant. All that mattered was this wild, savage coupling and the primal imperative to possess and conquer. The harsh gasps of arousal and the glazed expression in her bewitching eyes enslaved him, as the last tattered remnants of his control disintegrated.

With a guttural roar he pumped into her. Hard, furious, uninhibited. His seed filled her and despite having done this countless times in the past, it was exhilarating, astonishing. Because it was the first time he'd come, unprotected, inside Rowan.

Panting, he rested his forehead against hers, relishing the shudders that rocked her body and quivered through her as climax claimed her.

But as his frenzied heartbeat slowed, and frantic breathing calmed, the memories crawled back into his mind. And with them came crippling self-disgust at his weakness when it came to her.

He ignored the insidious whisper to remain where he was, to savor the aftermath. One last fuck was all he'd wanted. That didn't include feigned tenderness or insincere affection. Gritting his teeth against the inexplicable urge to ignore this sordid reality, he pulled out of her, and the air was frigid after the wet heat of her body.

She loosened her grip around his hips and staggered as her boots hit the floor. He freed her wrists and she slid to an inelegant heap at his feet.

It was where she belonged.

He shoved his semi-aroused cock back into his pants. He'd taken what he'd wanted from Rowan. She was no use to him now. But instead of liquefying her brain or breaking her neck he continued to glare at her, mesmerized.

She shuffled back until she hit the wall, her hair disheveled, looking vulnerable and fragile.

Looking as if she had just been unforgivably used.

He fisted his hands. She had been used. The way she had used him. They were even, and all that remained was for him to eliminate her for having dared to cross him.

Their gazes clashed. There was no hint of fear in her eyes at her impending fate. Only a faint, unmistakable glimmer of contempt.

Did she have no intention of begging for her life, of attempting to engage his nonexistent sympathy?

"Goodbye, dhampir." His voice was cold, at odds with the inferno blazing through his chest and scorching his blood. She didn't move and when he invaded her with a brutal telepathic blast, a fleeting expression of shock crossed her face before she slumped to the floor.

He exhaled a measured breath and with great difficulty tore his gaze from her. He'd intended to kill her. He should have killed her. But all he'd done was knock her out.

Even now, she corrupted his reason.

With a savage curse in the language of the ancients he crouched and shoved her scattered belongings back into her bag, pausing only to search her wallet. It contained a birth certificate in the name of Abigail Smith. One of her aliases? His jaw tensed.

He slung the bag over his shoulder before picking up the phial from the bed and placing it into his shirt pocket. Then he turned back to her.

If he couldn't destroy her, a fitting punishment would be to wipe her mind and dump her some place where she'd be found by a member of the Enclave. He bent down and scooped her into his arms. For a moment he stared, entranced, at her face. She looked so damned innocent. So damned *human*.

He was still ensnared by her. The sooner he got rid of her the better.

He'd drop her outside the Enclave's HQ in Grosvenor Square. He'd never have to see her again. She would have no idea what had happened, and the members of the Enclave would never imagine that he, an archangel, had returned their spy to them.

But he made no move to wipe her memories. Even unconscious she emanated a lethal lure from her damned DNA. It was outrageous that a vampire could create something that could screw with his senses and yet the evidence was in his arms.

Destroy her now. The demand hammered through his brain, but he was powerless to move. He'd once called her an enchantress, but he'd never imagined how close to the twisted truth he'd been.

The doorknob twisted, a slow, stealthy maneuver, and it smashed him back to the present. Were Rowan's accomplices at the door, ready to investigate why she hadn't yet completed her mission?

It saved him a trip to Grosvenor Square. He'd leave her here for them to find. What fate awaited a dhampir who had failed her master's orders?

Not my problem.

The doorknob twisted back. They'd obviously expected it to be unlocked. Unwilling, he once again swept his gaze over Rowan's face.

There was no line in the sand and he and a dhampir would never be on the same side even if there was. Yet the compulsion to protect her from the wrath of Sakarbaal polluted his reason. As though, despite everything, the line had been drawn millennia ago and he and Rowan stood against the rest of the world.

It reeked of madness. He knew it. Could taste it.

Leave her on the fucking bed.

Instinctively, his grip tightened. A faint *click* echoed through the room, as the lock was picked.

Don't do it.

But he ignored the voice of reason, because there was no way he'd leave her behind to be found by Sakarbaal's minions.

As the door inched open, he teleported, with Rowan still in his arms. To an uncivilized planet hidden in a backwater of Andromeda III.

CHAPTER 23

ROWAN

*R*owan stirred, but the pounding in her brain didn't ease. She forced open one eye. A pale glow illuminated the room, which had massive sofas arranged around a long, low, coffee table. She blinked, trying to clear her vision. Wherever she was, it definitely wasn't the bedroom at the inn. Gingerly she sat up and the world lurched.

Had Azrael knocked her out? She didn't remember him hitting her. In any case, although her head hurt like hell, it was all internal.

Psychic.

A shiver chased over her arms at the implications. The important thing was she was still alive.

Directly ahead, through vast glass doors, a breathtaking panorama of mountains was backlit by the rising sun. The sky was a delicate, rose pink and the scene was so beautiful, so tranquil, that she simply gazed, transfixed.

She wasn't in London anymore. Where had he taken her? How long had she been unconscious?

Her bag was at the end of the sofa and she dragged it towards her. It didn't look like anything was missing, although she was sure he'd gone through everything. She found her phone and peered at the time.

She'd been out of it for less than two hours. How far could an archangel go in two hours? Had he *flown*?

Her mind flooded with the image of his incredible wings. She'd never imagined anything could be so hauntingly exquisite. Had he really taken her in his arms and soared into the heavens? Had she really been carried by the wings of an archangel?

Regret squeezed her heart that she couldn't remember any of it.

Get real. Why would she want to? He'd knocked her out and abducted her.

Focus. It didn't matter how she'd got here. What mattered was finding out where *here* was.

Although her phone appeared to be unharmed, the GPS was dead. Frustrated, she glanced through the wall of glass to the magnificent mountains and tried to place them. Maybe this was his own private island. If so, it was unlikely any inhabitants would be willing to help her get back to civilization.

But that was a secondary problem. First, she had to escape from Azrael himself.

For a treacherous second his smile filled her mind, before she sucked in a sharp breath and pushed the image aside. It was nothing but a lie. Their time together had meant nothing to him.

How wrong she'd been about everything.

Be careful what you wish for.

So many times she'd dreamed of making love with him without using any protection. Well, love had nothing to do with it, but the sex had been mind-blowing. But unlike her foolish dreams, it had been the final death knell.

Slinging her bag over her shoulder she pushed herself from the sofa and gritted her teeth against the pain that rolled through her skull like a noxious wave. At least she didn't have to worry about pregnancy. Dhampirs were sterile. Until now that fact had always gnawed into her soul. The knowledge that it was one more thing that set her apart. One more thing she'd never be able to experience.

But now—now she was glad. *Relieved.* Because she was getting out of this and she was going to start a new life. And the last thing she needed was the fear of conceiving Azrael's offspring.

What chance would a child with such a crazy mixed up heritage have?

Unbidden, the image of a black-haired baby floated through her mind. Dark eyes, flecked with gold, gazed up at her in total trust. Innocence, in a world of foul corruption.

It will never happen. And now wasn't the time to mourn for a future that had never had a chance of existing. Now was the time to focus on survival.

She made her way across the waxed timber floor to the open plan kitchen. The entire place seemed to be open plan, with a wide veranda that wrapped around the property. Only one room at the far end had a door, and even that was flung open as if Azrael had no issues with privacy.

Heart pounding in tandem with her head, she edged inside. It was his bedroom, a magnificent chamber decorated in gold and black, with a vibrant tapestry on one wall and luxurious furnishings that complemented the massive bed. Clearly here was an archangel who appreciated the finer things in life.

Had he really left her alone? It was a tempting notion but how likely was it? She crossed the huge room and entered an equally spacious bathroom. Well, wherever he was she was going to take advantage of the reprieve and scrub her body clean of his touch, his scent.

It was a shame she couldn't do the same thing to her heart.

~

SHE EMERGED from the bathroom ten minutes later, dressed in jeans and tee-shirt that she'd packed in her bag the previous day. Her plans to escape the Enclave and start a new life as Abigail Smith had suffered a setback, but until Azrael terminated her, she still had a chance.

Why hasn't he killed me already?

It wasn't because he harbored any feelings for her. She couldn't afford to indulge that fantasy for even a second. The only reason she was still alive was because he had other plans for her. And none of them involved a happily ever after.

She had to be prepared, if her escape failed. If by some twist of fate she ended up back at the Enclave, she had a perfect excuse for failing in her mission. Azrael had discovered who she really was and abducted her. While Sakarbaal might not consider that a good enough reason and destroy her anyway, there was always the possibility she could get away with it.

The only problem was if the Enclave probed into her private financial affairs and discovered she'd cleaned out her bank accounts yesterday in preparation for her new life. That would be hard to explain away.

So would the six months' supply of amber acid she'd stashed in her car. And that was another reason why she needed to get back to London as soon as possible. It was one thing taking off under her assumed name, but she wouldn't last long without her meds.

She paused in the center of his bedroom and absorbed the silence of the dwelling. There was no trace of vampires in the air. And although he'd been able to approach her without her being aware of it, she was certain he wasn't around.

Slowly she pivoted on her boot heels and looked at a wide door next to the wall tapestry. It probably led to a dressing room. She had no interest in seeing his wardrobe and yet she made her way towards it.

For a moment she hesitated, but the compulsion to push open the door hammered through her blood. It wasn't locked and swung open with ease.

Mesmerized, she stared at the treasures before her. Beautiful, deadly weapons lined the walls. But this was no blockbuster movie gun cache. Azrael's collection showcased antique swords and daggers from long dead civilizations, but they looked in pristine condition. Fascinated she moved closer and ran the tip of her finger over the blade of a sword whose origin she didn't recognize.

Finally, she'd got a break. With weapons, she stood a chance of defending herself against whoever guarded his retreat. Swiftly she weighed up her options and ended up taking a hunting knife and a rondel dagger that would have done a knight proud in the Middle Ages. And then she went over to the glittering crown jewel. An elegant katana displayed on the far wall.

Awe feathered along her spine as she picked it up. Katanas were her weapon of choice and this one was a beauty. It was almost like a lucky sign.

Back in his kitchen she raided his cupboards but found nothing edible. The only bottles he appeared to have were filled with a colorless liquid she assumed was some kind of archangelic alcohol.

Tough. With perverse pleasure she emptied the lot down the sink, before filling them with water and wedging them in her bag.

She pulled out her phone and checked the time. Twenty minutes had passed since she'd first woken up. It was time to leave.

∼

THERE WERE NO GUARDS.

And he hadn't taken her to Europe. Not only was the timing all wrong for sunrise, but it was far too hot for the middle of March, although it was an oddly comforting heat with a welcome breeze. The profuse birdlife was brightly colored with breathtaking plumage, but she didn't recognize any of the species.

She didn't recognize any of the plant life, either.

Azrael obviously had a technologically advanced method of transportation. It wasn't anything to worry about. Maybe he'd taken her as far as Australia.

It still didn't explain why she couldn't pick up a satellite signal.

Except this didn't look anything like Australia. It didn't look like anything on Earth at all, but rather a magnificent fantasy landscape where everything was more vibrant, extraordinary and enchanting.

Or maybe she was suffering delusions from the aftereffects of abduction and lack of food. She glanced over her shoulder. The villa she'd just left was halfway up a mountain, which gave it spectacular views of the surrounding area, including the lush valley below. As far as she could see there were no paths beating a track to the front door. It looked like nothing had been disturbed for decades—centuries, even.

No matter how carefully she wound her way through the wild tangle of greenery, she might just as well leave signs on the trees for him to follow. She needed to find a river to throw him off her trail.

But first she needed to decide what direction to take. She checked her phone compass and frowned at the magnetic interference. Something was wrong. It was pointing due west, but she was heading in the direction of the rising sun.

Frustrated, she shoved her phone back in her pocket and drew the katana. It was sacrilege, but she'd use it to plow her way through and make her journey easier. Let him think she was clueless. A couple of hours later, she finally hit a river and she waded in and then turned and faced the way she'd come.

With a bit of luck, the archangel would assume she'd kept on going in the same direction. It might buy her a bit more time.

~

NIGHT CAME UNUSUALLY EARLY. She refused to consider what that might mean and concentrated on finishing her meal. While she'd learned the basics of hunting and trapping, life in London as a vampire slayer and assassin hadn't exactly honed her skills in that direction. Still, she'd finally caught something and although she wasn't sure what exactly it was, at least after she'd cooked it on her smokeless campfire it was edible.

It wasn't cold but shivers wracked her body, a prelude of the night to come. She finished another bottle of water and tried to ignore the slow burn in the pit of her stomach that had nothing to do with the food she'd just eaten.

Seven years ago, it had taken two days before the chills had started, and another thirty-six hours before the acidic flames had eaten her gut. This time the withdrawal symptoms had started mere hours after she should have taken her last shot of amber acid.

She hugged her knees, her back wedged against a cluster of rocks that provided some shelter from the unknown. She'd been so sure she had at least a couple of days before her body began to fall apart. But what did it matter? Did she really think she'd find a way off this fantasy paradise? She'd walked non-stop and had found no trace of human life. What were the chances that, beyond the *next* mountain, she'd come across civilization?

But what other choice did she have? Crawl back to Azrael and submit to whatever perverse future he had in mind for her?

Shadows lengthened, darkened, then contracted and became more defined. Something was inherently *wrong* with the night and shivers of presentiment scudded over her arms. With a sense of dread inevitability, she looked up at the star-studded night sky. She didn't recognize any of the constellations but that was no surprise. Because dominating the clear, pollution free heavens were a pair of huge, luminous moons.

CHAPTER 24

AZRAEL

*A*zrael hadn't thought the night could get any worse, but he'd been wrong. It appeared to be his MO recently. Because across the crowded floor of the club he'd crashed just moments ago was Nate.

What were the fucking chances that of all the clubs and dives in the universe he'd come across the one archangel he most wanted to avoid? Before he could whip his curdled brain into getting out of there, Nate had not only caught sight of him but was striding towards him.

"What the hell are you doing here?" Nate sounded irritated. "Following a lead?"

"Getting pissed." To underline the point, he tipped the contents of his glass down his throat. The complete lack of reaction as the alcohol hit his stomach reminded him that he'd ended up back on Earth. Why had he teleported to that primitive little planet?

"You won't get hammered drinking that shit." Nate threw an entirely too casual glance around the club before returning his focus to Azrael. "This got anything to do with the dhampir?"

The fact that his current state had everything to do with

Rowan was despicable enough. But for Nate to assume such a thing was intolerable.

"The dhampir has been neutralized." He thought of her lying on his sofa, looking fragile and innocent. The psychic blast he'd given her would keep her unconscious for at least twenty-four hours, but he doubted he'd have a solution as to what to do with her by then.

Even asleep, her toxic siren's call had beckoned him to her side. No female had ever affected him the way she did. He was like an addict, and she was the drug he craved.

But she was trained to seduce. Trained to entice and bewitch and ultimately betray. Gods damn it, she had been genetically engineered to lure Sakarbaal's enemies into her silken web. Even now, when he knew every depraved thing about her, his fascination with her was as destructive as ever.

The fact he should have been able to see through her wiles was irrelevant. He hadn't. And the knowledge was eating him alive.

She should be dead. As far as the rest of the fucking universe was concerned, she *was* dead.

No one would ever discover he'd been unable to carry out such a simple act of retribution.

"Can't believe Sakarbaal thought that plan would work."

The phial Rowan had intended to plunge into his blood was in his coat pocket. If it hadn't been for Nico's warning, would Azrael even now be in Sakarbaal's power?

It galled to be in the arrogant vampire's debt. Twisted his gut to know that Nico was aware of how Azrael had been utterly bedazzled by the dhampir's lure. He was an archangel, and archangels didn't owe others or become blinded by a female's treacherous wiles. That he owed a vampire and had been deluded by a dhampir just made the whole mess that much more contemptible.

"There was never a hope in hell it would work."

Nate shrugged, dismissing the matter. "What brought you here?"

"The search for mindless sex." After leaving Rowan, he'd planned on spending the time in an orgy of sexual depravity so that when he returned, her fatal allure would leave him cold. So far, the closest he'd got was eye contact.

Nate offered him a sardonic grin. "Is there any other kind? Though you might want to give this place a miss." The humor drained from Nate's face. "It's been marked by demons."

The realization that he hadn't taken advantage of any of the offers he'd had tonight because he couldn't get Rowan's scent out of his psyche drilled through his brain. It took more effort than he'd ever admit to drag his attention back to the other archangel and his rabid loathing of demons.

Not that *he* had any love for them, but Nate's hatred boarded on obsession.

In any case, as far as he was aware, demons didn't bother slumming it on Earth. They hadn't since the time their mutual goddess had banished her first Children from her sight, before she'd turned her considerable talents on creating her beloved archangels.

"There's nothing here that interests me anyway." *Because all I want is a woman who possesses green eyes, black hair and the heart of a traitor.*

He shouldn't crave her when she was out of his sight. But raw need burned inside his chest. A need that filled him with both despair and hellish anticipation at the knowledge she was incarcerated in his home.

"In that case," Nate said, "fuck off somewhere else. I'm trying to be inconspicuous here and you're ruining the effect."

"Fine." There was a club in Manhattan he'd yet to try, where off-worlders came to slum it with the oblivious indigenous inhabitants. "Enjoy your demon hunt."

He teleported and found himself standing in his villa.

Rowan was no longer comatose on his sofa.

He cursed violently and the instant flare of fury that his subconscious had smashed what remained of his good sense and taken him home instead of Manhattan vanished.

He'd blasted her with enough power to keep a human under for twenty-four hours. But she wasn't human. She was half vampire. He'd known that but still hadn't compensated for her enhanced abilities.

Because he hadn't wanted to risk damaging her damned brain.

He wheeled round and scanned the villa. It had been eighteen hours since he'd left her. He stalked through the villa until he reached the bathroom and ripped open the door. Her scent lingered in the air, mingling with an intoxicating echo of frenzied sex and unfulfilled lust. It twisted through his groin like a ravenous dragon and his muscles tightened and cock hardened even though she wasn't there.

Where the fuck was she? The villa was halfway up a mountain, surrounded by forest. He'd likely find her out on the veranda, disoriented and confused. Next time he left her alone he'd make sure he immobilized her properly.

As he reached the bedroom doors awareness prickled over his skin. For a second he imagined Rowan was behind him, watching him. He swung around and his gaze caught on the door to his weapons cache.

It was ajar.

Senses red alert, he marched across the room and flung the door open. And came to a crashing halt as he focused on the glaring space where his piece de resistance usually took pride of place.

She took my katana.

He'd psychically knocked her out. He'd been so sure she was completely in his power it hadn't occurred to him that she'd attempt to escape.

But she hadn't merely escaped. She'd armed herself too.

Fury burned through him, but it was directed at himself for not anticipating this. For assuming she would behave in the way he expected her to behave. How could he know how a dhampir would react in any given circumstance? For all he knew she was out there right now waiting to ambush him.

Fists clenched, he glared around at the weapons he'd collected over countless centuries. Every item evoked memories, good or bad. Every piece a cherished part of his long existence.

He could arm himself to the teeth before he went searching for her, but if he couldn't bring down one vengeful dhampir with his bare hands then he might as well plunge that fucking phial in his own neck.

THE TWIN MOONS gave plenty of light to see the way Rowan had gone. She'd hacked through the vegetation like she didn't give a damn if he followed her. The lack of stealth clawed through his nerves.

It was like she taunted him.

She couldn't have gone far. It wouldn't take long to catch up with her and reclaim the weapons she'd stolen.

Reclaim *her*. He shoved the last thought from his mind, disgust curdling his gut. What would it take to annihilate this perverted hold she had over him? There had to be a way he could counteract her poisonous allure.

But first he had to find her. His pride demanded nothing less.

Less than an hour later he reached a river and the blatant trail halted. It would have taken her a good two hours if not longer to have covered the same distance, but she was nowhere in sight.

So much for finding her collapsed and exhausted. The realization that, once again, he'd underestimated her did nothing to improve his mood.

What was he going to do with her when he did find her? He was responsible for bringing her here. He couldn't let her wander freely, when he had no idea what she might do to the peaceful mortals of this planet. So what was the answer? Construct a fortress to hold her prisoner for the rest of her cursed existence?

How long do dhampirs live for anyway? A human lifespan? A vampire's?

Could Rowan be immortal?

The idea was horrifying. She might live for countless centuries. Was he seriously contemplating keeping her captive until she died, no matter how far in the future that event might occur?

Dawn broke on the western horizon and he still couldn't get the notion of Rowan's possible immortality from his mind. Because it wasn't only horror that blazed an acidic trail through his blood. It was a fathomless ache of perverted hope that her tainted blood would keep her alive... indefinitely.

CHAPTER 25

ROWAN

*A*s the sun reached its zenith on this crazy mixed up world, Rowan couldn't hold back the inevitable any longer. Sweat prickled her skin, tremors wracked her body, and with a sick sense of relief she fell to her knees and vomited up her previous night's supper.

The violent gripping pain that twisted her stomach instantly eased, as if the poison eating her gut had been ejected. But she knew better. It wasn't the food that had poisoned her. It was her own body turning against her. Craving its fix of amber acid to keep her primitive urges under control.

She squinted at the sun that rose from the wrong horizon and imagined the phials of medication hidden in her car. But it wasn't the glowing amber fluid that filled her mind's eye. It was the thick, crimson promise of fresh blood flowing over her tongue and sliding down her throat.

Filling her parched body with the sustenance she had so long been denied.

Sakarbaal. It was his fault for filling her veins with his foul blood and polluting her reason. All she should be feeling right now was the agony of withdrawal, the way she had seven years ago. But no matter how much she wanted to believe it she knew it was a lie. Taking Sakarbaal's blood had only brought to the surface the underlying craving she'd lived with her entire life. The need for fresh blood was part of her nature, a part that had been suppressed by the Enclave because everyone knew that dhampirs couldn't be trusted to control their own urges.

Her fingers dug into the earth before she pushed herself upright. *I won't give in to the bloodlust.* Her mother had been human, and she would never forget it. She was only half vampire and she wouldn't let that half rule her.

Gritting her teeth, she pushed forward through the never-ending forests. Mountains soared all around and the river flowed to her left although she no longer waded through it. She had no idea what direction she was heading. But it didn't matter. Because she wasn't on Earth. There was no way she could get off this deceptively beautiful planet by herself, but she'd be damned if she'd return to Azrael's villa and beg for help.

He wanted her dead, even if he hadn't killed her yet. She tried to push him from her mind, but he was a poisoned barb that had hooked itself into the fabric of her being.

His look of revulsion as he threw her heritage in her face haunted her. The disgust in his voice as he called her *dhampir* echoed endlessly around her mind. He wouldn't care about the state of her deteriorating health and that was why she wouldn't bury her pride and appeal to his better nature.

He didn't have one.

But there was a darker truth she didn't want to face. *I don't want him to see me like this.* Despite knowing he'd never felt anything for her, she wanted him to remember her the way she'd been in London.

It was stupid. But the same pride that would never allow her to beg him for mercy refused to allow him to witness her descent into the hell of withdrawal and crazed bloodlust.

His disgust was hard enough to bear. If she was going to die on this unknown planet then she'd rather die with the knowledge she retained at least a tattered shred of self-respect.

It wasn't much. But it was all she had left.

Azrael

As NIGHT FELL, Azrael forcibly acknowledged the fact Rowan had successfully managed to elude him on his own turf. For hours he'd trekked through the forest until the complete lack of trail or scent had finally smashed through his burning anger.

She hadn't continued in the same direction. She'd backtracked along the river.

He'd taken to the skies then, a sure way to expend excess energy but for once it hadn't helped. If anything, it merely fueled his fury that a *fucking dhampir* was playing him for a fool.

Again.

Savagely he kicked the scattered remnants of her campfire. At least now he was on the right track. And from now on he'd tail her like any other enemy. Coldly and efficiently, without letting his personal... *irritation* with her get in the way.

A couple of hours after dawn had broken, he came across a swarm of flies and insects crawling over something rank and unrecognizable. That she no longer bothered to bury the leftovers of her meals irked him on another level. She was deliberately leaving him a breadcrumb trail. Mocking him with the fact she'd managed to out-maneuver him at every turn. Did she really think she could evade him forever? Did she imagine he'd give up the hunt and allow her to roam freely on this world?

She was still alive only because he'd failed in his duty to eliminate her. When he found her, he'd make sure she knew exactly to whom she owed her continuing existence. If the only way to keep her contained was to chain her to a fucking wall, then that's what he'd do. Because no one, least of all a creature who should never have been conceived in the first place, screwed with his head the way she did.

The sun began to dip towards the eastern horizon when he disturbed a few small mammals scavenging the remains of a butchered herbivore. He stared at it, wondering why it snagged his senses, and then it hit him.

She hadn't even cooked this kill. Had she simply hunted it and left it for him to find? A flashing neon sign, pointing him in the right direction?

What was she trying to prove?

A faint, evocative hint of her scent drifted on the breeze. It came from the right, where the forest thickened, and he turned from the river and plunged into the green gloom. His pulse thudded in anticipation of finally hunting her down and showing her that when it came to a contest between them, she would never—*could never*—beat him.

But she wasn't lying in wait for him. Her bag was on the ground, its contents scattered as though she'd feverishly searched for something. But no matter what she'd been looking for, why hadn't she taken her belongings with her? Had he disturbed her before she could repack?

Possibly. It also meant she was close.

The smell of damp earth and ancient trees mingled with another scent. One of bloodied corruption and decay. A foul odor he recalled from nine hundred years ago when he'd slaughtered the spawn of the undead in a medieval forest.

He halted at the edge of a glade. Silver moonlight flooded the clearing, and the black silhouette of the far side of the forest gave a ghostly, eldritch hinterland.

Crouched in the middle of the glade, with her back to him, was Rowan. She slowly pushed herself to her feet, but she was oddly ungainly as though she was drunk.

Her hair was matted with filth and forest debris and an eerie shudder crawled along his arms. But instead of claiming her, he was frozen to the spot, and when she turned to him, his heart slammed against his ribs.

No...

Her unnaturally pale face was streaked with something dark and unnamable. As she stumbled towards him, brandishing his katana in both hands, he was catapulted nine hundred years back in time to that night in Romania.

The crescent moon had thrown the foreboding castle into sharp relief and heightened the foul abominations that shuffled to do their master's bidding. He'd had no compunction in slashing them down, destroying them in order to reach his target.

They were only dhampirs.

He'd done them a mercy, putting them out of their miserable, misbegotten existences.

Rowan was a dhampir, but she was beautiful, intelligent and graceful. He'd never seen the physical connection between her and Sakarbaal's creatures. Even when he'd thrown the word in her face, even though logically he knew what she was, deep in his soul he'd rejected all the connotations.

Not Rowan.

But now, she was nothing like the woman who'd ensnared him in a scented web of lies and seduction. She was unwashed, unkempt, and the closer she came the less he could deny the truth of what stained her lips and teeth.

"Rowan." It was a command to halt, but it was so much more. An agonized entreaty to wipe this nightmare from his vision and return to the woman he knew she truly was.

A spy who had betrayed his trust.

How much easier it would be, then, to treat her the way she so richly deserved.

She didn't even pause. The twin moons bathed the glade in light, too much light, because when he looked into her eyes all he saw was a terrifying blank.

Soulless.

Instinctively, his wings unfurled, and her dead gaze shifted from his face. Instantly he leaped forward and gripped her wrists before knocking his katana from her grasp. She looked back at him and her eyes weren't blank or dead. They were Rowan's eyes, green and glinting and gods help him, but he couldn't—wouldn't —believe she was a condemned, soulless creature of the night.

"What happened?" Raw fury edged his words, but the anger wasn't directed at her. It was directed against Sakarbaal, against Fate, against the cruel irony that the only woman who had ever snared his interest for longer than a moment was a creature he had most despised.

But the only reason she had snared his interest was because Sakarbaal had genetically modified her to do so. *How had he managed it?* What was worse was the knowledge he no longer cared that none of it was real. Rowan was a dhampir and this was her natural state. But he wanted the illusion back.

No matter what the price.

"*Beracid.*" The word was slurred, and her fingers clawed as though she wanted to rip open his face. He had no idea what *beracid* was but now he understood the reason for the dead creature he'd found.

All the times he and Rowan had eaten together had been a façade. It wasn't food that sustained her. It was blood. But, by the state of her, not just any blood.

She needed human blood.

His gut clenched in revulsion. *She isn't a vampire.* She was half human and yet she fed from Sakarbaal, the most ancient vampire of all. Whatever trace of humanity she'd been born with would have been drained from her years ago. He might not like it, but the evidence was in his arms. A travesty of a woman who reeked of fetid blood and internal decay.

How long would a dhampir survive if deprived of fresh blood? By the state of her, not as long as a human could last without food. Another day and she might be dead.

The unnatural hold she maintained over him would die with her. It had to.

But suppose it doesn't?

He'd live with it. But he couldn't live with the knowledge he'd left her here, alone and on a foreign planet, to die. She didn't deserve his compassion, but she had it anyway. For the sake of a few hollow memories, he'd keep her alive, and she would serve as a constant reminder of how he had underestimated Sakarbaal's cunning.

After his goddess' betrayal, he'd sworn to never again be blinded to the truth. Through all the centuries, he'd never lost sight that the vampire was his enemy. But in the end, he'd still been oblivious to the signs.

Still holding her wrists, he forced her to the ground and crouched before her. He wasn't human but his blood was powerful. She would regenerate and when she recovered, he'd work something out. Create a blood bank. One thing was for sure. He wouldn't allow her to feed on him for years without number.

But tonight, there was no other choice. *I won't allow you to die.*

He needed her alive to interrogate her. To discover all she knew of Sakarbaal's plans. It was the primary reason why he'd brought her to this planet.

Keep telling yourself that.

"Take my blood." It was a command as he thrust his wrist against her mouth. His muscles clenched as he waited for her to sink her fangs into his flesh. Fangs he'd never once suspected she might possess.

But all she did was pant erratically, her breath shallow, as if she couldn't draw enough oxygen into her lungs.

"Rowan." He released his grip and wound his arm around her shoulders, pulling her against his body for additional support. It was fucking surreal, went against everything he believed in, but desperation tainted each word. "For gods' sakes take my blood. You're dying."

The tip of her tongue licked feebly over his pulse. He gripped her jaw and forced her to look up at him, but this close all he saw was how the whites of her eyes were a sickly yellow.

She was a liar, a spy and an accessory to his attempted murder. She looked exactly like the dhampirs he had slain in Romania. But despite the filth, and the unforgiving flashbacks to that blood-soaked night, he wrapped one wing around her, protecting her from the outside world.

"Blood." Her broken whisper stabbed through his chest, as visceral as though she'd taken the dagger at her waist and thrust it between his ribs. "Azrael." She dragged out each agony-drenched syllable of his name. But she still didn't sink her fangs into him.

He cursed under his breath before sliding his forefinger between her dry lips. Her teeth were perfectly even. Realization dawned.

How could a vampire's offspring, which required blood to survive, not have fangs?

Rowan was in no state to answer questions. And the question was irrelevant. Without a second's hesitation he took the dagger from her waist, slit open his wrist and offered his archangelic blood to the dying dhampir in his arms.

CHAPTER 26

*A*zrael steeled his nerves as Rowan's lips fastened against his wrist. Reminded himself who—*what*—was sucking the blood from his veins.

It made no difference. Because no matter what she was or how she looked, she was still Rowan. The oddly gentle tug at his wrist was nothing like he'd imagined a vampire's feeding would be. It wasn't a despicable parasite gorging itself. She was Rowan, and she was lapping at his blood with the strength of a newborn kitten.

Pain knotted deep in his chest, but he didn't have time to question it. Because she wasn't feeding fast enough. Already his wound was healing. Carefully he pulled free, intending to reopen his vein. But her head lolled back, her eyes closed, his blood smeared across her parted lips. She hadn't even been able to swallow the little she'd taken.

Panic coiled through him, cold and alien. He'd been so sure this would work. He tightened his grip on her and teleported back to his villa. In his bedroom, he ripped back the covers and gently lowered her onto his bed, before piling up pillows behind her. She lay against them like a broken creature, a jaundiced tinge to her skin. It was starkly obvious her condition had deteriorated in the short time since he'd discovered her.

He was an archangel and possessed healing powers. If she had broken her bones, shredded her flesh or torn her muscles he'd know exactly what to do. But she was dying from the inside because she needed blood, and the only blood available was his.

And she didn't have the strength to take it.

Viciously, he once again opened his wrist. Then tilted her head back, prised open her mouth, and forced his blood down her throat.

Again. *And again.* Times without number through the hellish night. Dawn broke, and Rowan didn't open her eyes, didn't acknowledge him. Just lay against his pillows looking more dead than alive and the truth he'd refused to face for hours thundered through his head.

It isn't working.

She stirred, and desperate hope burned through him. It had taken her body a while to process, but finally his blood was cleansing whatever poison consumed her.

She heaved violently and a noxious black substance, like liquid tar, splattered across his bed. Ice crawled along his spine as she convulsed in obvious agony, the foul emissions still steaming from between her cracked lips.

His blood hadn't helped her. *My blood made her worse.*

All his power, all his immortality, didn't mean a thing.

There was nothing he could do for her.

The hell there wasn't. Just because his blood was poison to her didn't mean he couldn't find her a supply of humans to feed her need. They'd never know. He'd keep them unconscious for the duration. It was only an emergency modification of the blood bank he'd intended to set up for her.

What the fuck am I thinking?

But he knew. He'd known from the moment he'd found her in the forest.

He would sink to any depths to save her.

But what if human blood gave her the same violent reaction? The revolting image of her drinking Sakarbaal's blood flashed through his brain and he recoiled.

No.

But the image refused to fade. Because the answer was Sakarbaal. He was Rowan's Master and without his blood she couldn't survive.

There had to be another way. He cradled her face in his palms, her skin dry and burning with a fever he couldn't control. He had no power over Sakarbaal, no way of contacting any of his elevated brethren in order to extract information from them. Information that could save Rowan's life.

Nico.

He brushed his thumbs across the yellow shadows beneath her eyes. Sakarbaal and Nico had once been like father and son. Was it because, through vampiric blood connection, they *were* father and son?

If Nico had been Made by Sakarbaal then surely his blood could save Rowan.

Was he really considering this outrageous plan? Begging a favor from a fucking *vampire*?

But there was nothing to consider. He was out of options, and Rowan's life was on the line. He contacted Nate.

I need to meet with Nico. Now.

I'm busy. But interest threaded Nate's impatient response as though he'd caught the urgency that thundered through every beat of Azrael's heart.

He didn't give a fuck what Nate or Nico thought. But gods, it was going to crucify him to beg the arrogant vampire for help.

Rowan's dying. She needs the blood of an ancient.

The silence stretched into infinity. Rowan's breath became ever shallower. He pressed his forehead against hers, willing her to hang on. Not give up. To give him some clue as to how he could help pull her through.

The dhampir's still alive? He heard the question in Nate's tone. The question Nate hadn't asked. Because it wasn't a case of her still being alive. It was that he hadn't eliminated her four days ago.

Contact Nico. I'll meet him anywhere. He knew it would take more than that to persuade the vampire. He had to reveal just how deep in Rowan's thrall he had fallen. *His terms.*

Don't hold your breath. I got the impression he thinks as little of the dhampir as he does of you.

It had taken Nico two hundred years to answer his last request. He doubted Rowan had two hours left. He could find a vampire easily enough. But his gut instinct told him a common bloodsucker would harm her as much as he had. He couldn't risk it. Nico was their only chance and if he failed to come through...

She would die. *And I'll be free of her fatal allure.*

"Yo. Az." Nate's voice echoed through the villa and he swung around, a maelstrom of fury and dread colliding in his chest. By the sound of it Nate was at the kitchen door, and then he heard the other archangel's boots stomping across the floor. "Where the fuck are you?"

As Nate entered the room, Azrael pushed himself from the bed and stood in front of Rowan, an instinctive gesture of protection. "What the hell are you doing here? I told you to contact that fucking vampire."

"That *fucking vampire* agreed to meet with you." Nate offered him a ghoulish grin. It was obvious Nico's swift cooperation had astonished him as much as it did Azrael. "His terms are these. You shut down and let me teleport you and the dhampir to the place of his choosing."

Those were his terms? At the very least, he'd expected a contract written in blood, binding him to the vampire for untold centuries. "He trusts me not to track where you take us?"

Nate strolled closer, ignoring the glare he shot his way, and stared down at Rowan. His expression might have been carved from granite. "I might have given the impression that I could negate your ability to track the teleportation, so no. He doesn't trust you. But I do."

∾

WHEN NATE REMOVED the blindfold from around Azrael's eyes— the blindfold being a totally unnecessary precaution purely for the sake of appearances—they were in a spacious living area complete with the latest media technology. Anything less like a vampire's lair he couldn't imagine.

And that was half his problem.

Despite the dozens of vampires he'd hunted throughout Andromeda, his ingrained prejudice against the entire race was based solely on his interaction with Sakarbaal.

"This is something I thought I'd never witness." Nico prowled towards him and instinctively Azrael tightened his hold on Rowan. She weighed next to nothing in his arms, and he smothered the overpowering urge to demand the vampire quit with the score-taking and get the hell on with saving her life. "The Archangel Azrael, slayer of innocents, willing to risk everything in order to save a filthy dhampir."

She's not a filthy dhampir. He wouldn't give the vampire the satisfaction of showing his barbs hit too close for comfort.

"Cut the crap, Nic," Nate said. "Can you neutralize the dhampir's hold over Az or not?"

What the *fuck?*

He rounded on Nate. "That's not the reason we're here. Mind your own fucking business."

"You told me you'd dealt with her. The fact you didn't means only one thing. Sakarbaal's got you well and truly by the balls."

The condemning look from his fellow archangel burned his

soul. Because Nate was right. Sakarbaal did have him by the balls. But he couldn't stomach the thought of letting Rowan die in this horrible, degrading way.

He knew what she was. But even so, she deserved more than this.

"I can fill her arteries with my blood," Nico said, never taking his gaze from Azrael. "And then she would forever be my creature. Just so we're clear on that, archangel."

He'd already guessed as much, but having the fact flung in his face was like acid eating through his soul. "She's already Sakarbaal's *creature*." He spat the last word at the vampire. "But I don't have access to that bastard."

Nico gave a derisive smile. "Sakarbaal doesn't give a shit about his half-breed offspring. He'd sooner decapitate them himself than offer any of them his blood. They're nothing but anomalies of nature, remember?"

It just kept on getting better. Not only had Rowan fed from the ancient vampire, she was his biological daughter as well.

His gut clenched with distaste but he still couldn't drop her to the floor and abandon her to this ignoble fate.

"Are you going to help or not?" Tact be fucked. Nico knew why he was here.

Nico swept an expressionless glance from the tips of Rowan's boots to the top of her tangled hair. It was impersonal yet at the same time deeply invasive and Azrael stiffened with barely repressed offense.

"How swiftly they revert to their most primitive state." Nico looked him directly in the eyes. "Yet still you hold her as if you desire her. How... fitting."

"Fitting?" Despite his best intentions his wings unfurled, each feather vibrating with suppressed rage. There was more to this confrontation than a mutual hatred based on their differing species. At least, there was from Nico. It was like the loathing originated from a personal level.

Nico bared his teeth in a feral mockery of a smile. "Why do you think I told you Sakarbaal had set his assassin on you? Because I gave a shit about your existence?" He flicked Rowan a derisive glance. "No. It was because I sensed your attraction to the dhampir. I wanted you to know what manner of creature you had fallen for. Wanted you to face the choice of allowing her to live—or killing her in cold blood."

Ice prickled along his arms. *It is personal.* And if he couldn't find a way to get through to the vampire, Rowan would die.

Rowan

AN ACIDIC BURN ate through Rowan's gut and scorched her blood as her body disintegrated from the inside out. But buried deep in a hidden corner of her psyche, a tiny core of sanity glowed, and she clung to it, relentlessly.

"Beracid." She heard the words in what remained of her sane mind, felt a disconnected movement of what could have once been her lips as they formed the desperate plea. But had he heard her? Had anyone heard her? Did the vampire who sounded so cold and condemning know of the medication she needed to survive?

"Rowan." Azrael's voice penetrated the fog that threatened to suck her down into eternal oblivion. "It's going to be okay. Don't give up."

He sounded like he really cared. As if everything that had happened in the Tudor inn had been nothing more than a nightmarish fantasy. *Had* that really happened? Or was it another twisted memory corrupted by her feverish mind?

"Give her to me." The commanding voice of the vampire tore through her unraveling thoughts. Azrael's arms tightened around her but she was disconnected from him, floating beside her physical body, and his touch was oddly insubstantial.

"Do what you have to do here." He no longer sounded as if he cared. He sounded feral.

"If you want her to live, give her to me. And know that you'll be forever in my debt."

This was wrong. She couldn't let Azrael, her beautiful archangel, sink into the vampire's clutches because of her. But even as she struggled to reclaim the use of her limbs her body was handed over, and unfamiliar arms wrapped around her.

A distant sense of panic washed through her, recognizable but not wholly understood. With Azrael she felt safe, even if she was dying. But with this vampire there was no guarantee of anything, and she wanted to be back in her archangel's arms.

"Be still." It was an autocratic demand, yet there was no derision in the vampire's tone or undercurrent of the loathing she'd subconsciously absorbed earlier. "I won't harm you."

How easy it would be to sink into the crimson oblivion that beckoned. Finally, she'd be free of the pain that wracked her body. But still she fought against the encroaching abyss, the way she'd fought it from the moment the withdrawal had kicked in.

There was no way of knowing what he intended to do with her. But she'd rather be conscious, if incapable, than comatose and unaware of her fate.

She heard another door kick open and he carried her through.

"*Mon dieu*," a familiar voice exclaimed.

Meg? *Where am I?*

"All it took was three days." Suppressed fury heated the vampire's voice as he lowered her onto what felt like a bed. "Four at most. And you have the nerve to call *us* barbarians."

"What did the demon do to her?" Meg's unique scent drifted through her senses and she struggled to open her eyes and shove the vampire away. But instead she lay there, immobile, while Meg examined her as if she were nothing but a piece of meat. Dimly she was aware of another pair of feminine hands taking blood from her veins, hair from her head and swabbing the inside of her mouth.

"Damned his pride to bring her to me." There was no satisfaction in the vampire's voice. "He is entirely in this dhampir's thrall. It's as well Sakarbaal thinks she's dead. If he knew how utterly his methods had brought an archangel to his knees, then none of us would be safe."

Something cool pressed against her throat, a familiar pressure hissed through her skin and amber acid sizzled through her depleted arteries. Meg had given her what she so desperately needed. Liquid fire flooded through her mind, jolting her back to full awareness. Memories clarified, the suffocating fog receded, and her body embraced the cursed drug that not only curbed her vampiric cravings but allowed her to keep her fragile façade of humanity.

"Sakarbaal's methods?" Scorn scorched Meg's voice. "I told you Rowan is not one of his whores. She fell at the first test and even if she hadn't, I would have ensured she failed his final criteria."

Finally, her eyelids flickered opened. Above her, glaring at each other, stood Meg and a tall, lean vampire. The iron bands crushing her chest eased, and the fog in her brain faded with every passing second.

Meg wasn't behaving like she'd betrayed Rowan's secret to Sakarbaal. So who had told him about her meetings with Azrael?

"Meg." Her throat ached with the effort of articulating, and her voice sounded weak and insignificant. But both vampires instantly stared down at her, as though she had suddenly grown a magnificent pair of iridescent wings. *Is Azrael still waiting for me?* "What are you doing here?"

Meg sank onto the bed and clasped her hand, apparently oblivious to the dried blood and filth that clung to her like a second, foul skin. "How are you feeling, *cheri?*" Concern filled her beautiful blue eyes. "I feared the demon had murdered you when they brought back your car. Sakarbaal left London, and no one else at the Enclave truly knows what is going on." She paused and gave the vampire on the other side of the bed a swift glance. "That is why I approached the Strigoi for information, with an offer they couldn't refuse."

CHAPTER 27

ROWAN

"The Strigoi?" Rowan attempted to push herself upright, but it was too much of an effort. Instead she stared at the unknown vampire and a strange sensation of familiarity rippled through her.

The members of the Enclave and the Echelon had been enemies for centuries. The Elector High Council of the Enclave might despise dhampirs but at least they allowed them to live. It was common knowledge the Echelon elite wanted them all dead.

They had been taught their history as children, but it was a history taught by vampires of the Enclave. There was no corroborative evidence in human libraries, no way to double check online resources. Unlike her friend Belinda she had never been given a Strigoi target and as far as she knew hadn't, until now, even met one.

I'm sick of the lies Brad had told her. And so was she. But as the searing withdrawal symptoms receded and her numbed instincts sharpened an absolute certainty gripped her.

She had encountered this vampire before.

Yet she couldn't detect his presence in the way she could detect any other vampire. It was only a faint, elusive glimmer, as if he was on the very peripheral of her psychic vision and if she turned too swiftly, he would vanish without trace.

Vanish without trace. Memories collided and in that moment she knew, without doubt, why he was so oddly familiar.

"You were standing across the road from *Estella's* when I left with Azrael," Rowan said. It wasn't a question. It wasn't even an accusation. It simply was.

His expression didn't alter. "I suspected you'd become aware of me. But I had the information I needed."

Information he'd used against Azrael. She recalled the disjointed segments of conversation she'd overheard when Azrael had brought her here, the repressed violence simmering beneath every word the vampire spoke. She could detect none of that violence in him now, but that didn't mean anything. Not when she could barely detect he even *was* a vampire.

"How could you disappear like that?" Rowan asked. It shouldn't be possible. Even though she might not be able to defeat an ancient in combat, she should still have been able to track his movements.

He didn't answer right away. She had the oddest conviction her question had told him something that until now he'd merely suspected.

"We share the blood of Sakarbaal." Distaste colored his words, and she wanted to take issue with his statement because she didn't share Sakarbaal's blood. She had taken such a small amount from the vampire it couldn't possibly count. *Even if his blood instantly healed my injuries and showed me ancient memories.* She shoved those thoughts aside. In any case, that had happened after the incident at *Estella's.*

But clearly the vampire hadn't finished. "He Made me over two thousand years ago, and as far as I'm aware, I am the last of the few he took for his own. As for you," he paused, apparently considering whether to continue or not. A butterfly touch of foreboding whispered along the back of her neck. *I don't want to know.* "As his biological daughter it seems you're unable to track your own bloodline."

I'm not Sakarbaal's biological daughter.

The denial screamed through her mind, and her abused stomach knotted in distress. It was horrible enough knowing that her father had raped her mother and left her for dead. But for that vampire to be Sakarbaal, the vampire whose ancient order had rescued her mother and then nurtured the offspring, was horrifying.

When she'd hacked the medical records, the similarities between the victims of vampiric rape had haunted her. She might not want to believe the vampire's accusation, but deep inside a sick acceptance stirred. Another twisted thread scraped through her heart. If Sakarbaal was her father wasn't it also possible he had sired all the dhampirs the Enclave had *rescued* over the last fifty years?

"Sakarbaal is not Rowan's father." Meg sounded horrified. At least not everyone within the Enclave was party to the disgusting origins of its dhampirs.

"None of the victims were random, Meg." Despite the over-powering need to close her eyes and drift into blissful sleep, she didn't take her gaze from the Strigoi. The vampire who had been Made by Sakarbaal. "They were chosen by Sakarbaal. Why else were they all AB Negative? That's my blood type, too. And Brad's." She tore her gaze from the hypnotic eyes of the vampire and looked at Meg's shocked face. "It's the blood type of every victim and dhampir they gave birth to over the last fifty years." *And those innocent embryos whose blood hadn't ticked the right box had been disposed of.* "What's the betting it's also Sakarbaal's original blood type as well?"

"I do not believe it." Meg's voice shook. "The Enclave gives sanctuary to dhampirs. The vampires responsible for the rapes are feral—uncivilized. Why would Sakarbaal resort to such barbarity?"

"Sakarbaal," the Strigoi said, "will do anything in order to achieve his goal."

"What is his goal?" Meg sounded like the aristocrat she had once been.

"I have my suspicions. The dhampir medication you gave us should reveal some answers very soon."

The vampire's words pierced the fog of exhaustion that threatened to take her under and she shot Meg a probing look. "That was the offer they couldn't refuse? You gave them amber acid in exchange for information... on *me?*"

"The Strigoi are arrogant and proud, but also powerful. Plus, one of their ancients resides here in London. If anyone could help find out what had happened to you, Rowan, Nico could. But naturally, an incentive to assist was required."

"An incentive might not have been required," the vampire—Nico?—said. "But it will be interesting to see how Sakarbaal has refined his methods after a thousand years."

"His methods?" Had Sakarbaal sired dhampirs in this revolting manner a thousand years ago? Taken them in under the pretext of sanctuary?

Got them hooked on a primitive version of amber acid?

Were they the dhampirs of nine hundred years ago, whom Azrael had slain without mercy?

Nico regarded her, as if she was an interesting insect he had captured and intended to vivisect. She refused to drop her gaze, despite how desperately hard it was to keep her eyes open. Somehow, she knew Nico would interpret that as a sign of weakness, and any respect he might harbor for her would vanish.

A Strigoi respect a dhampir? What was she thinking? Yet still she held his unblinking gaze.

His unspoken challenge.

He gave an almost imperceptible smile, as though he knew her thoughts and they amused him. "Your amber acid, whatever it truly is, is certainly remarkable. It's hard to imagine that moments ago you were close to death."

My name is Rowan Moreton, and I am an addict. But what exactly was she addicted to? Could the Strigoi really unearth the hidden truths of amber acid? Or was it merely what they had all been told it was—a sanitized medicated substitute for fresh blood? Not just because as a dhampir she was incapable of mastering her primal urges, but because her corrupted immune system couldn't cope with the real thing?

She'd discovered to her cost that at least that wasn't a lie. She couldn't stomach raw animal blood and she hadn't even been able to tolerate Azrael's blood. And if she couldn't process the blood of an archangel, what were the chances her body could accept a mere human's?

How she hoped there was more to the amber acid than they had all been told.

Nico moved closer. "But if you want to regain your strength instantly, then you require my blood."

She recoiled, but it wasn't the thought of taking the Strigoi's blood that caused the panicky flutter in her gut. It was the primitive, desperate urge to take what he offered. Because his blood was of Sakarbaal, her sire, and his blood wouldn't poison her.

Tendrils of fatigue slid through her veins and wrapped around her mind. Reminding her that, despite the fact she was no longer at the mercy of the amber acid's brutal withdrawal symptoms, she was still far from full health. It would take her body at least a couple of days to recover. A couple of days while she felt like shit and would be unable to do anything more vigorous than converse from her bed. It would be so easy to acquiesce to Nico's... command.

"No." Her body screamed in protest, but she wouldn't be a slave to her primal urges. Not when now, unlike the last few days, she was in control of her base instincts. "I won't let you use me to hold any form of power over Azrael."

For a fleeting second, she saw admiration glow in the ancient vampire's eyes. As though her refusal had somehow elevated her status. The fact she was a dhampir didn't appear to register in his appraisal at all.

Had all she'd learned of the Strigoi Echelon's universal loathing of dhampirs been nothing but an elaborate lie?

"Then accept my blood as a gift." His voice was persuasive, a smoky promise. "I care nothing for the archangel, but you," he paused, to allow his words to fully penetrate her exhausted brain. "*You* I would have understand."

She had no idea what he meant, and she didn't much care. Only one thing mattered. "If I take your blood the only one beholden to you will be me. Azrael owes you nothing."

Nico offered her a smile that didn't reach his eyes. "Agreed." He sank his fangs into his wrist and despite herself she watched, mesmerized, as his crimson blood filled her vision. He raised his head and pressed his wrist against her parched lips. "Drink, Rowan, and discover the bonds that connect us together."

She closed her eyes and sucked down the luscious fluid, uncaring of how her frail human sensibilities trembled in despair. Already she could feel the strength flowing through her, but as she drank deeper Nico opened his mind to hers and his memories flooded through.

Unease crawled over her flesh, but she couldn't let go, couldn't push his arm away. All she could do was take what he offered, his blood and his memory intertwined.

Nico, on his knees before the castle in the aftermath of the slaughter, the ravaged grounds soaked with the blood of the slain. Grief and fury, even now, after all these centuries, raging through him, tainting everything he touched, as he clasped a fallen young dhampir in his arms, her eyes the same molten gold as Nico's. The greatest betrayal.

And she understood.

CHAPTER 28

*W*hat *the fuck was the vampire doing to her?* Azrael glowered at the door and only just fought back the primal instinct to storm through this cursed place until he found her. It burned his gut that Nico, that fucking arrogant bastard, could heal Rowan while he, an archangel, could not.

"For fuck's sake." Nate's violent hiss slashed through the fraught silence. "It's only sex, Az. You can get that anywhere. Go screw a few mortal females and get this one out of your system before she destroys you."

Would Nico's blood flowing through Rowan's veins be enough to eliminate whatever Sakarbaal had done to ensure she was so irresistible? When he next saw her would this unnatural ache in his chest ease? Would he look at her and feel nothing but mild compassion for her plight?

"She won't destroy me." He didn't deign to look at the other archangel. "Whatever she's done, she is as much a victim of Sakarbaal as the phoenix he captured a thousand years ago."

Nate swore in the language of the ancients. Clearly, he didn't feel the same way. "She looks like shit and she's still leading you by the cock. Nic had better find a way to scrub her clean before he brings her back."

Azrael gritted his teeth. The only reason he was so concerned for her welfare was because she had been genetically engineered specifically for that purpose.

How Sakarbaal had managed it he couldn't begin to imagine. But as a weapon it was phenomenal. How many others had fallen, unaware, beneath its insidious power?

The door opened and Rowan entered the room. She was still covered in filth and grime. Her hair was tangled but her eyes were focused, filled with keen intelligence, and her skin was no longer a deathly pallor.

He had never seen a more beautiful sight in his life.

"Azrael." Her voice was husky but otherwise just as he remembered. He remained rooted to the spot, unable to respond, because what he wanted to do, what he wanted to say, would only confirm, irrevocably, that her unholy hold over him hadn't diminished at all.

"Back as promised," Nico said, following her into the room. "As good as new."

"Nico." Rowan didn't raise her voice, didn't take her gaze from him, but Nico shrugged and leaned against the architrave as though she had given him an obscure warning. "Thank you for saving my life, Azrael. I would have died out there in the forest if you hadn't found me."

He glared at her, and hoped it disguised the way he wanted to drag her into his arms and take her back to his villa. He was still in her thrall, but he'd be damned if he'd let everyone know it.

"It wasn't Azrael who saved your sorry ass." Contempt dripped from every word Nate uttered. "It was Nico. Save your false gratitude for those who earned it."

Her gaze didn't waver from him. Gods, her eyes were beautiful. He could almost believe she hadn't the first inkling of the evil that lurked in the darkest crevices of creation.

"I accepted Nico's offer of blood in order to regain my strength more quickly. But it wasn't his blood that saved my life." The tip of her tongue moistened the seam of her lips and with a jolt he realized she wasn't nearly as calm as she appeared. "The truth is—I've been on medication since the moment I was born. I suppose you could say I'm addicted to it and that's why I nearly died. Because I can't live without my drugs."

She was a drug addict? Was it some kind of preternatural pheromone? Was that the secret to her fatal allure?

The full force of her confession slammed through him. If the drug was the reason why he couldn't let her go, it was also the reason she was still alive. For him to be free of her, she would have to die.

"What is the drug?"

"I don't know." Distress threaded through her confession but was that just another facet of her façade? "All dhampirs take it as a substitute food source. We can't tolerate untreated blood." She glanced at an oddly familiar blonde woman by her side. "But there's more to it than that. There's got to be."

"The Strigoi will discover what we need to know." The blonde spoke with a French accent and he recalled that she'd been with Rowan at the club the night they'd first met. "Their scientists are not hampered by centuries of Sakarbaal's edicts."

He dragged his gaze from Rowan and looked at Nico. The vampire's blood polluted Rowan's veins now, but he hadn't saved her life. Yet Azrael was in his debt. "When will you have the results?"

Nico shrugged one shoulder in an attitude of nonchalance that irritated the shit out of him. "Tomorrow night."

He returned his attention to Rowan. "You will return with me. I've questions that you will answer."

"Rowan will go nowhere with you." The blonde vampire sounded outraged and stepped in front of Rowan like that would protect her. "She nearly died when you abducted her before."

"It's all right, Meg," Rowan said, moving so that the vampire no longer stood between them. "Azrael deserves some answers." She looked at him. "And so do I."

She deserved answers? From *him*?

"Come here." Damned if he would go to her. It was bad enough he couldn't simply teleport back to his villa but for appearances sake he had to allow Nate to take them back.

She walked towards him, and he waited until she was right in front of him. Then he wrapped his arm around her shoulders and jerked her roughly against him.

"Nate." It wasn't a question and although he could feel the impotent fury rolling from the other archangel like an open furnace to hell, all Nate did was grip his biceps and get them out of there.

ROWAN HAD BEEN in his bathroom for almost an hour, and Azrael prowled the length of his bedroom trying without success to ignore the seductive, feminine fragrance that drifted beneath the bathroom door.

After they'd arrived Nate hadn't said a word, and after one condemning look had left them to it. Azrael had retrieved Rowan's bag and his katana from the forest and then she'd disappeared to clean up.

She'd look less vulnerable when she didn't remind him of how close she had been to dying. Then he'd be able to question her. Discover just how much she knew.

He couldn't think beyond that. Because no matter which way he looked at it, the whole thing was an unholy mess.

The bathroom door opened, and she came into the room. She wore a sleeveless tee-shirt and black jeans, and her feet were bare. The sight of her naked toes caused his chest to constrict. They gave her an air of vulnerability.

But nothing else about her screamed vulnerable, despite the way her damp hair framed her face and curled over her shoulders. She looked ethereal, in the way an ancient water goddess presented a deceptive air of fragility that hid a core of steel.

Rowan was no goddess. But she wasn't fully human, either. Yet even knowing what she was, even with the vivid memory of the last day etched forever in his mind, when he looked at her he didn't see the filthy, primitive dhampir she had devolved into.

That wasn't the true Rowan. The real one stood before him, looking at him with a steady, unblinking gaze, waiting for him to say something.

Except that's a lie. This Rowan was the façade. Without her drugs she reverted to her true nature. It didn't matter if that repelled the essence of his being. It didn't change the facts. The Rowan he'd known during the last two weeks was an illusion.

How desperately he craved to crawl back into that illusion and to hell with reality.

"How did you know where I would be that night we met?" He kept his voice dispassionate because there was no way he'd allow her to guess that she still retained such an unnatural hold over him.

"I didn't. Meg and I were celebrating my birthday."

Her birthday? Dhampirs had birthdays? That had never occurred to him before. *How old is she?*

"How did you plan on finding me?" There must have been a plan in place. Sakarbaal wouldn't have gone to so much trouble with her if he hadn't also masterminded a way for her to cross Azrael's path.

"Azrael, I didn't even know you existed until I saw you that night in the club." She didn't sound defensive. Was she as innocent as he wanted to believe, or was she the universe's greatest actress? The nauseating vision of her sucking Sakarbaal's blood pulsated through his mind, a noxious reminder she was not all she claimed to be.

"When did Sakarbaal tell you about me?"

She flinched. Finally, his words elicited a reaction, but it didn't give him any satisfaction. He might just as well have thrust his dagger into his own gut.

"It was the day you and I had spent together in London. He caught me that night. I'd just got back after an assignment and was injured." A shudder rippled over her. It was obvious the memory unnerved her, and he throttled the urge to pull her into his arms and to hell with the truth.

He needed the truth. No matter what.

"Yes?" The word was harsh but instead of intimidating her— not that he wanted her cowering before him—she straightened her shoulders and returned his fierce glare.

"He forced me to take his blood. It was the first time. And as his blood healed my injuries," her eyes blazed with accusation, "he showed me the great massacre that took place in Romania nine hundred years ago."

CHAPTER 29

ROWAN

*A*zrael returned her glare, unblinking. The slender thread of hope that he hadn't been the one who had slain those ancient dhampirs in cold blood irrevocably unraveled.

"You haven't answered my question." His voice was arctic.

They might have been back in the Tudor inn, with the disdainful gleam in his eyes. But that was a lifetime ago and it didn't matter how he glared at her, or how his magnificent wings unfurled in unspoken threat. She'd heard fragments of his whispered words while she'd been struggling in the void between reality and oblivion. If he truly despised her the way she had once feared, he would never have begged her to fight for her survival. And he certainly wouldn't have injured his pride by approaching Nico to try and save her life.

The Archangel Azrael might never want to share her bed again. But he wasn't intent on murdering her either.

For years, she'd fantasized about finding someone who would accept the sordid reality of her life. How fate loved to twist things. Instead of a vulnerable human, she'd fallen for Azrael, an immortal who not only knew what darkness seethed beneath the brittle surface of humanity but had pledged to rid her kind from the face of the Earth. And yet he was the one she trusted above everyone else she knew.

"Sakarbaal told me about you that night. Said you were only using me to get close to him." She hadn't believed a word at the time. But considering the facts she now had in her possession that possibility was looking more like the unpalatable truth by the second.

After all, Azrael had approached her in the club. He had been the one to suggest they meet again. Maybe he'd grown to like her over the time they'd spent together and maybe his plan had been to eliminate her when his assignment was finished.

So many maybes. Only one thing was clear. If he felt nothing at all for her, he would have killed her that night in the inn when, presumably, his plans had disintegrated.

"And you believed him." It wasn't a question. And he sounded pissed off, as if he thought her contemptibly naïve to believe such a thing. Or was that just her sense of self-preservation kicking in, so she wouldn't dissolve into a puddle of ignoble humiliation?

"No." She resisted the urge to wipe her sweaty hands on her jeans. She couldn't let him see any weakness, any uncertainty. "I didn't. I had no idea what his real plan was, but I decided I'd had enough. I was going to make a new life for myself away from the Enclave. That night at the inn—I thought it would be our last night together. And I wanted to warn you about Sakarbaal."

"And you just happened to have a phial of the Guardians' lethal atmosphere in your possession."

The Guardians? Who were they? "I don't know what was in it." She frowned, as the strangeness of his accusation penetrated. "Atmosphere? What do you mean by that?"

"That you were going to plunge into my bloodstream," he said, ignoring her question, "in the hope it would incapacitate me for your master."

She folded her arms, and irritation flared. He was so very

217

quick to judge. So very sure that it was her who was in the wrong.

"That was Sakarbaal's plan." She didn't bother trying to hide the edge of impatience in her voice. "I had no intention of following through. I've spent the last two weeks thinking you were a human man who needed *protecting* from the dangers of my life." What a joke that had been.

He didn't answer right away, as though her response had been unexpected. His wings, which she constantly battled not to gaze at in reverential awe, folded back and his stance became subliminally less aggressive. She didn't want to read too much into it, because his expression gave nothing away, but it seemed he was genuinely considering everything she'd just told him.

"You're telling me Sakarbaal knew nothing about you meeting me before that night you sucked his blood?"

He made it sound so vulgar. *Depraved.* Like he imagined she had enjoyed taking Sakarbaal's blood. That she'd been given a choice.

She hadn't any choice. But the stark truth remained. She'd relished every drop of his cursed blood.

"I don't know how he knew about you." She still had no idea how he'd discovered her illicit liaison. It certainly hadn't been from Meg. Because Meg had put her existence on the line by going to the Strigoi and offering them amber acid in exchange for information about Rowan.

She might love Meg in a strange, hybrid mother/sister way but until now it had never occurred to her that the love might be just as strong from Meg.

Vampires won't turn against their own for us, Brad had said. But he had been wrong.

Azrael's feathers undulated in a beautiful, distracting shimmer of color. "Why was he following you the night we went to *Estella's*?"

She tore her fascinated gaze from his mesmerizing wings and

stared into his gold-flecked eyes. Would he ever again look at her with warmth and desire?

"I didn't know he was." A shudder inched along her spine at the thought of Sakarbaal tailing her.

Another thought struck her. Was it really her he had been following? Or had it been Nico?

Or had both vampires been tracking Azrael?

"I find it hard to believe he waited so long before giving you your orders."

She thought she'd been so clever. Thought nobody had guessed her secret. But Brad had. So had Lily. And so had Sakarbaal from virtually the moment he'd returned to London.

He had known she was involved not just with any archangel but *the* archangel he'd crossed swords with in the past. He'd bided his time, waiting to see if the liaison continued. And only then had he made his move.

No wonder she hadn't faced any repercussions from that night. Her role in the vampire's victim's outburst in *Estella's* had been tolerated, because she'd been with Azrael.

She unfolded her arms. She'd answered his questions, told him the truth and still he accused her of things that were beyond her control.

She had accusations of her own.

"And I find it hard to believe that you could annihilate a thousand defenseless dhampirs, just because they offended your—" For a second words failed her, as blood-soaked memories— memories that weren't hers— from that terrible night flashed through her mind. She hitched in a jagged breath. "*Sensibilities.*"

"We're not here to discuss my past." He took a step towards her, the breathtaking iridescence of his wings threatening to ensnare her. "We're here so I can decide whether or not you deserve to live."

"Why? Because you're the fabled Archangel of Death?" Not a fable though, was he?

"No." Irritation flashed across his face. "Because I never allow my would-be assassins to survive."

"Do you honestly believe I would've attempted to kill you that night?"

"No, I don't." He growled the confession, as though it corroded a part of his soul to utter the words. She stared at him, shocked he'd admitted such a thing when he seemed so hell bent on proving her guilt.

"Well, good." How lame did she sound? She'd expected more of a fight to prove her innocence and his sudden acceptance threw her into a spin. But no matter how he'd so easily disarmed her she still intended to ask questions of her own.

But he'd already answered one without even knowing it. He hadn't been aware she was a dhampir that night in the club. He hadn't picked her up solely because of her connection to Sakarbaal. Their time together hadn't been a cruel fabrication after all.

"Sakarbaal didn't send you to seduce me." It wasn't a question. It was like he stated a revolutionary fact. One he found devastating.

That didn't make sense. Why would he rather believe she was one of Sakarbaal's undercover spies who included sex in their lethal arsenal?

It was a mystery and one she'd return to later, but right now she had more important things to discuss with him. "I've answered all your questions. I think I deserve some answers in return."

He looked at her for a long moment. It was obvious the thought of answering her questions filled him with despair. "You'll remain here. I'll ensure a supply of your medication is always available. You'll be safe from Sakarbaal's wrath while you remain under my protection."

For a moment his bizarre comments made no sense. And then she realized, he thought he had just answered her concerns.

She wasn't sure whether she was touched or exasperated by his presumption.

"Thanks for the offer, but we can discuss that later." She didn't miss the disbelief that flashed over his face at her words, as though he wasn't used to having his benevolence swept to one side. "I've spent my whole life wishing I was fully human. But I'm not. I never can be." The words lodged in her throat, but she pushed them out regardless. "I'm a dhampir."

"I know that." His voice was as expressionless as his face. It didn't inspire her with confidence but at least it was better than seeing disgust in his eyes.

"And nine hundred years ago, you decimated my race."

Silence screamed between them as primal rage pulsed from him and battered her with relentless psychic waves. But it was somehow off-kilter. The rage wasn't directed at her or those ancient dhampirs but beyond them.

Sakarbaal.

That was no great surprise. Of course Sakarbaal was the reason behind that massacre. But she wanted to know Azrael's part in it. Because unlike Sakarbaal and his potentially corrupted memories, she trusted Azrael to tell her the truth.

The way I trust Nico's memories? She shoved the thought aside. She couldn't deal with that, not yet. *One thing at a time.*

"Tell me the name of the order of vampires you've served all your life."

"What?" She frowned at him, and disappointment surged through her. He had no intention of discussing it with her. "I don't think I'm being unreasonable in wanting to know—"

He leaned towards her, and his wings unfurled in a magical, shimmering haze around her.

"Tell me." It was a command.

She let out an impatient sigh, mainly in a vain attempt to hide just how much his wings fascinated her.

"The Enclave of the Phoenix. But you know that already." He'd thrown it in her face back at the Tudor inn.

"Yes, I know." There was a bitter note in his voice. "But do you know why Sakarbaal chose *phoenix*, Rowan?"

Shivers crawled along her arms although she wasn't sure why. And although she had no idea where he was going with this, it was obviously important.

"It's our mascot. It's been our mascot for centuries." The image of the phoenix was carved into balustrades, worked into tapestries and featured in many of the priceless paintings that adorned the interiors of the Enclave's numerous properties. The legendary phoenix died, only to be reborn from its ashes. Her earliest memories were of being told it was a metaphor for how the superior vampire race arose from the embers of humanity. It was such an intrinsic element of her life she'd never really taken the time to think about it.

"Let me tell you why." A thread of contempt scorched the words, as though her answer had been meaningless. "Nine hundred years ago I freed a phoenix Sakarbaal had kept captive. The dhampirs were guarding his castle."

Phoenixes were creatures of myth. They weren't real.

But how many humans believed in the existence of dhampirs? Of *archangels*?

She wanted to dispute his accusation but no matter how fantastical it sounded, she believed him. "What was he doing with it?"

"I don't know." Frustration seethed beneath the words. "But somehow he was manipulating its essence and distorting the astral planes."

She didn't have a clue what he meant. "Its essence? You mean its soul?"

"It took years to trace the elusive fragments back to the source of entry from the physical plane," he said, as if that was a perfectly logical response to her question. "I finally hunted him down to his lair in Romania. His vampires fled, leaving only their mindless dhampirs between me and my quarry."

Unwanted images from Sakarbaal's memories of that time pounded through her mind. She wanted to believe they were untrue, distorted. That the dhampirs in question had been highly trained warriors who stood at least a whisper of a chance against an avenging archangel.

But superimposed on Sakarbaal's bloodied carnage were Nico's memories. A different perspective to that of their mutual lord but one thing remained harrowingly similar.

The indisputable fact that the dhampirs were woefully inadequate to fight anyone, let alone an immortal.

"Dhampirs aren't mindless, Azrael." But even as she defended her race the devastating reality ate through her heart. Without her medication it took barely a day before she reverted to a dhampir's base instincts. And while a tiny section of her mind had screamed in futile agony, it hadn't stopped primal need from dictating her decaying body.

His gaze sharpened on her. "They were nothing like you." His voice was harsh, as though he guessed her thoughts and refuted them utterly. But how could he, when he'd seen her at her worst? "Their only imperative was to obey their master and keep me from entering his lair."

Sakarbaal's half-truths and manipulated images faded, until all that filled her mind's eye were the memories of Nico.

She knew Nico was just as capable as Sakarbaal of concealing the truth from her. Of letting her see only what he wished her to see. She knew full well he hadn't revealed everything to her. But what he'd shared had been underpinned with a raw, primeval grief.

Azrael had to answer for what he'd done. Her gaze didn't waver. "But did they all deserve to die by your hand that night?"

His wings unfurled in a blatant gesture of arrogant intimidation, but instead of cowering before the Archangel of Death, she struggled against simply embracing the glorious, heavenly sight of his iridescent feathers.

"Do you dare to question *me?*" He sounded like a god from Olympus and the leashed fury in his voice flayed her senses. But was the fury directed at her?

It didn't matter. She was a dhampir whether she liked it or not. And someone had to speak up for the dhampirs of the past. To vindicate their pitiful lives and inherent inability to make their own choices in their fate.

"Yes." She took a step towards him. They were close enough to embrace. Close enough to kiss. "I dare to challenge your choices that night, Azrael. You're an archangel. You didn't need to face the dhampirs. You could have teleported directly to Sakarbaal himself."

CHAPTER 30

AZRAEL

*N*o one challenges my word.

He focused on that truth and whipped up a futile rage at her nerve. Who was she to question him? The Archangel Azrael, who answered to no one?

But his fury was hollow, without fire or direction, because it was nothing but a brittle lithosphere that hid a seething mantle of denial.

The stark, unvarnished fact was Sakarbaal had not sent Rowan to seduce him.

He'd misunderstood Nico when they'd confronted each other in the club and taken Nate's careless comment as fact. But Rowan hadn't been genetically engineered specifically to entrap him. Sakarbaal hadn't enhanced her with any preternatural pheromone designed to enslave Azrael's libido or blind his judgment.

The genetic modification the vampire had wrought was by selectively breeding only the beautiful and intelligent. *That's all Nico had said.*

There were no intangible threads binding him to her side. He should have been able to dispose of her without a second thought in the Tudor inn that night. Should have eliminated her with detached compassion when he'd discovered her wretched state in the forest.

There was no ungodly reason why he should have flayed his pride by seeking Nico's help.

So why the fuck had he?

An answer hovered on the far horizon, hazy, insubstantial. *Terrifying.*

"Azrael?" Her voice pierced his mind and she looked so damned innocent, freshly scrubbed from her shower, that he could scarcely comprehend she was the same woman he'd taken, in rank desperation, to the vampire.

"I don't need to explain myself to you." Deep in his gut a knot twisted, similar to the panic that had gripped him when he'd thought her about to die. But she was nowhere near death now. Yet his muscles tightened with a dread he couldn't name.

She didn't flinch at his autocratic tone or the blazing glare he arrowed her way. Instead she gave a faint frown, as though she saw through his façade to the turmoil beneath. *Damn her.* Why did she never behave the way any other mortal would?

Because she isn't any other mortal. She wasn't even fully mortal. *She's Rowan.*

It seemed time slowed as she reached for him. He should move back, knock her arm aside *enter her mind and render her unconscious.*

With infinite tenderness she pressed the palm of her hand over his heart. *She has no hold over me.* There was no reason why he should want, more than anything, to cover her hand with his. To pull her close and lose himself once again in her wondrous, welcoming body.

"Yes." Her voice was gentle like she soothed a child, not contradicted an archangel. "You do need to explain yourself to me."

Awe collided with the denial and the maelstrom of emotions that broiled in his chest and sizzled through his veins.

"Do you, a dhampir, set yourself up as my judge?" But there was no rancor in the words. She was a dhampir. If she was not, then she wouldn't be Rowan.

"I only want to understand."

The last thing he wanted was to relive that night of savage butchery. But against his will the stench of rotting humanity flooded his senses and he recalled, as though it had been mere moments ago instead of almost a millennium, how he'd believed their destruction was a mercy. A release from their pitiful existence.

Yet he hadn't felt that way when he'd discovered Rowan in the forest.

The vampires had fought back, until they realized he was no ordinary hunter. And then they had fled, leaving their ill-equipped offspring behind. But had all those dhampirs been sired by Sakarbaal? Had he slaughtered Rowan's half-blood siblings?

His soul recoiled from the possibility, but that didn't mean it wasn't true. He answered to no one. But it was a hollow assertion. Because Rowan wasn't *no one*, and gods damn him, he couldn't lie to her. Even by omission.

"I could have left the dhampirs alive." The admission seared his soul. He'd never before acknowledged there had been any other choice that night. "But I destroyed them. Without their master what would they have done? How would they have survived? Would they have swarmed into the surrounding villages? Caused more carnage and hysteria among the superstitious humans?"

She was silent as if she, too, was reliving that long-ago night. And then she spoke.

"So what you did, you did out of a sense of mercy?"

He heard the thread of hope in her voice. How easy it would

be to simply say *yes*. She had given him an out. He could take it and she'd forgive him.

He, an archangel, craved the forgiveness of a dhampir. The universe truly was a fucked-up bitch.

Her beautiful green eyes stared at him, unblinking. If he told her his actions had been driven by nothing but compassion, she'd believe him without question.

She would be his and willingly remain with him for the rest of her life. If he admitted the truth, the hope in her eyes would die and she'd demand her freedom.

And he had no intention of ever letting her go.

He'd already crushed his pride into the mud to save her life. How could he risk sharing the truth, when he knew it would forever tear them apart?

But in the end, there was no choice.

"No." The word tore from his throat, a bitter denial and with it went every hope that Rowan would ever again look at him the way she did now. "I knew what they might do if left to fend for themselves, but that wasn't the only reason why I cut them down that night."

She didn't move but tension vibrated through her and he imagined her fingers, pressed against his chest, closing around his heart and squeezing without mercy.

"Then why?" It was a whisper and there was no censure in her voice. No underlying contempt or disgust. How low had he sunk that he could find cold comfort in such self-delusion?

"Because they should never have been conceived." His voice was harsh, and he waited for her to recoil but she remained immobile. "They were loathed and feared by humans and despised by vampires." He remembered her earlier accusation and the words ate into his heart. "Most of all they offended my *sensibilities*."

This time the silence slashed through him like the blade of his katana. The katana he had used to slay those long-ago dhampirs.

"Yes," she whispered. As if he had just confirmed something she had known, something she'd been unsure as to whether he would admit. *What the fuck am I thinking?* She could know no such thing. Yet she didn't retreat and before he could stop himself he wrapped his wings around her, imprisoning her.

Still she didn't move.

"Dhampirs have always been on the outside," she said. Did she think she was telling him something he didn't know? Had she not yet processed the fact he had slain her kind in cold blood because of what they were? "I always believed we could never truly fit in with vampires or humans." She hesitated, before taking a deep breath. "I was wrong. Meg risked everything to try and find me and I've discovered that some vampires do love their half-blood offspring."

A chill crawled over his arms. Gods, surely she wasn't deluding herself that Sakarbaal cared about her? How could she imagine that, when the evil bastard had sent her on what would have been in any other circumstances, a suicide mission?

"Sakarbaal is incapable of love."

Rowan frowned. But she didn't pull her hand from his chest, and her fingers branded his flesh with the condemnation she still hadn't flung in his face.

"I'm talking about Nico," she said, and he stared at her, incomprehension thudding through his brain. Why the fuck were they talking of Nico? "When I accepted his offer of blood, he showed me his memories from that time. He had a child with a human—a human he cared for. He wanted their child." Awe threaded through her words, as if she had never imagined such a thing could be possible. She wasn't the only one.

Nico had sired a dhampir? That he had *wanted*?

His ironclad perception of the hierarchy of creation cracked. Not all dhampirs were conceived in hate.

Dread gripped him. He'd been right about one thing. The loathing emanating from the vampire had been more than the antipathy of two different species' inherent distrust of each other.

It had been personal.

"He hates me because I killed his—" The words locked in his throat. Dhampir? Offspring? "Child that night." But if Nico had loved his child why had he allowed it to become feral? Was that the fate of every dhampir since the beginning of time? Was Rowan's mysterious amber acid the only magic elixir that could change the destiny of her race?

"He does hate you," she said, regret weaving through the words although he couldn't imagine why. "But not as much as he hates Sakarbaal. He told Nico his human and dhampir had died in childbirth. It was only years later, when Nico returned to Romania on the night you faced Sakarbaal, that he discovered the truth. You let Sakarbaal escape, and it destroyed Nico's revenge." She shuddered, and instinctively he took her hand. She didn't push him aside. "He saw firsthand how his beloved lord would use anyone in any way to further his plans, no matter what the cost."

No wonder the two ancients had parted ways almost a millennium ago. Deep inside, unwelcome empathy for Nico unfurled.

What a fucking mess.

Rowan's scent weaved a seductive trail through his senses. The skin of her hand was silky-soft beneath his fingers. He dragged in a deep breath to clear his head and instead her irresistible fragrance invaded and conquered.

She wove no spell, yet he was bewitched. There was nothing he could do to escape, but he wouldn't name the reason why.

Not now. Not ever. Maybe then, the acidic fear eating him alive would simply... die.

"What were Sakarbaal's plans?" Why wasn't she glaring at him with contempt or worse? Didn't she understand what he'd told her? The reason why he'd slaughtered those dhampirs in the past?

"Nico didn't show me."

He'd discuss it with the vampire tomorrow, when he returned —with Nate's assistance—to find out what the Echelon had discovered about the amber acid.

But that was tomorrow. He still had to get through tonight. With Rowan.

CHAPTER 31

ROWAN

*A*zrael's heartbeat beneath Rowan's palm was a strangely comforting tattoo, and his wings surrounded her in a mystical shimmer. But despite how his fingers entwined with hers, and the way he looked at her as if he never wanted this moment to end, she had the certain conviction he'd shut himself off from her.

A part of her—a tiny part—wanted to shove him away. Wanted to condemn him for the part he'd played in the massacre so many centuries ago. But it was a faint, insubstantial desire. Because he had told her the truth.

He needn't have. She would have believed him if he'd told her he'd killed the dhampirs purely as an act of mercy, no matter how the whispering voices in her head mocked her.

The creatures she'd seen from both Sakarbaal and Nico's memories were nothing like the dhampirs she knew. God, she might have slaughtered them herself to end their suffering, even if the act tore her heart to shreds.

For one heart-stopping moment, raw vulnerability had glowed in Azrael's eyes. And she'd known. It didn't matter what he told her. Nothing could change the way she felt about him.

But he hadn't lied to her. For that alone she might have loved him.

If she didn't already.

"I'll find out," he said, and it took her a second to remember they'd been talking about Sakarbaal's plans. His fingers slid along the back of her hand, a light, barely there touch. A touch that branded her his for all time. "I believe he's captured another phoenix. Whatever he's planning, I'll stop him, Rowan."

She cupped his jaw. His five o'clock shadow grazed her palm and for the first time she saw just how exhausted he looked. As though he hadn't slept in days. And he hadn't, because he'd been hunting her.

Before he saved her life.

A strange pain compressed her heart. Did Azrael, Archangel of Death, even realize how much his actions gave away?

"*We'll* stop him." Her emphasis was slight but firm. All her life she had lived in the shadow of the vampire lord, the oldest of the Ancients. It had been an unspoken fact that if not for him, she would've died in the gutter. All her life she'd harbored a deep hatred of the unknown father whose tainted blood she shared. It turned her stomach to know the truth of her conception but now she did she owed it to her mother—to Lily—*to all Sakarbaal's victims*—to exact vengeance.

She had no doubts the order to murder Steven had come direct from the vampire lord. Had he carried out the assassination himself? The blood-soaked memory flashed through her mind, and a shudder slithered along her spine. Steven would be avenged.

Azrael's fingers gripped hers. "I'm sorry." The words tore from him, tortured slivers of his soul. "For all of it, Rowan."

He'd never know how much his regret meant to her. But although he'd played his part, he wasn't to blame for everything that had happened. Maybe it was time to share her own guilt.

"This is Sakarbaal's doing." Her voice was hoarse, and her

throat ached with unshed tears. "All of it rests on his shoulders." She hitched in a ragged breath. Azrael deserved to know the whole truth. "Dhampirs were forbidden to become involved with humans. But it didn't stop me. I thought we were invincible."

His gaze sharpened. "You fell in love?"

"I was sixteen. Steven was a student, working part time at a café I used to go to. He made me feel like a *human*."

Azrael's jaw tensed. "Sakarbaal killed him."

"Because I wanted a normal life. Because he was with *me*."

"No." Azrael's harsh denial cut through the guilt twisting through her. "Sakarbaal murdered Steven to consolidate his power over you. You're not responsible for his actions."

"I know that, but—"

"You just told me this was Sakarbaal's doing. That it all rests on his shoulders. It doesn't absolve me from my actions, Rowan, but you didn't do anything wrong. All you did was love. Don't let that vampire tarnish those memories."

For seven years she'd lived with the knowledge that Steven would still be alive if not for her. But although she'd never get over the grief of his untimely death, Azrael was right.

She wasn't the one who had Steven's blood on her hands.

But she would still avenge his murder.

Azrael's breathtaking wings drifted across her bare arms. "You need to rest."

Each glorious, individual feather caressed her skin as he slowly folded his wings, shattering the iridescent cocoon that had shut out the rest of the world. His fingers trailed the length of her arm and somehow she knew that once he stepped back from her, he would never again return.

"No, I don't." Just hours ago, she'd been hovering on the brink of death. But with the potent cocktail of amber acid and Nico's powerful blood sizzling through her veins the last thing she wanted to do right now was sleep.

Unless it was with Azrael.

"Rowan." There was a hint of warning in his voice. But she heard the desperation beneath. His iron-clad control was in danger of collapsing if he didn't put distance between them.

He still wanted her. He cared for her. But how deeply did he resent those facts? Was that the reason he pulled back? Or was it because he genuinely thought that she *needed to rest?*

She had no more secrets from him. He knew the worst and he hadn't struck her down. What did she have to lose if she probed a little deeper, forced him to face the consequences of what he'd done?

"You could have left me to die in the forest." She cupped his jaw, her thumb gently caressing the rough texture of his skin. He didn't respond, not verbally, but his jaw clenched beneath her palm and the golden flecks in his eyes glittered. She gazed, transfixed by the phenomenon, until she realized his hand had fallen from her arm and he was no longer touching her. "Why did you save my life?"

The tips of his wings brushed against her arms, a soft, sensuous caress yet unimaginable power vibrated through each shimmering feather. It reinforced the knowledge that when it came to Azrael, her preternatural powers meant nothing.

"Sakarbaal used you for his own ends." There was a harsh undertow to his words. "Whether you were in league with him or not, you didn't deserve that fate. Besides, I prefer to mete out my own brand of justice on my enemies."

"I'm not your enemy." She trailed the tips of her fingers over his breathtaking wings. They were magnificent, incredible, and she'd wanted to touch them from the moment he'd first displayed them to her.

His feathers rippled in a sensual response, causing tremors to lick over her fingers and along her arm. She knew she should tear her gaze from the shimmering iridescence, that she owed him the courtesy of holding his gaze, but it was no good.

His wings mesmerized. And she was helpless beneath their mystical thrall.

"No." There was a hollow note to the word, as if the knowledge she wasn't his enemy was somehow worse than if she had been. The despair in his voice was enough to break her besotted enchantment and she looked at him. He was staring down at her and for one heart stopping second, she saw the promise of eternity in his eyes.

It vanished instantly. But it was enough. Whatever internal battle he fought couldn't disguise one thing.

She meant more to him than he was willing to face.

There were so many things they needed to talk about. But they could talk forever, and he would never tell her what she really wanted to hear. And although nothing could change the way she felt about him she couldn't find the nerve to tell him.

But she could show him.

Slowly she began to unbutton his shirt. His eyes darkened and one hand covered hers. "Don't."

She offered him a small smile. "You don't mean that."

His fingers curled around her wrist. But instead of wrenching her from him he merely held her in a loose embrace, and his thumb skimmed her pulse in a provocative caress.

"You nearly died."

"I know." She rose onto her toes to slide his shirt from his shoulders. His wings prevented her and for a second she forgot what she'd been saying as their beauty once again enchanted her. "But I'm not dying now."

"Rowan," he said her name again, and the anguish in his voice pierced her heart. She tore her fascinated gaze from his wings and silenced him with a fleeting kiss on his lips.

"If you're going to tell me to stop, then don't say anything at all."

"When have you ever done anything I've told you?" Finally, there was a hint of amusement in his voice and the knot of anxiety deep in her chest eased. He wasn't going to fight her. He wasn't going to push her aside. He was willing to take what she wanted to offer.

She attempted to wrench his shirt off once again and failed. Frowning she curved her hands over his shoulders and tilted her head to one side as she contemplated her obstacle.

"Why did I never have trouble with your clothes before? I mean your wings have always been there, haven't they? Even when they were invisible." And not just invisible. She'd explored every inch of his body on countless occasions and she was damn sure she would've noticed touching a pair of invisible wings.

He flashed her a grin and her heart melted. He looked so irresistibly gorgeous when he smiled like that.

"They were never just invisible." He unfurled them to their full, incredible width, and she only just managed not to gape in reverential awe at their majesty. "They were cloaked by an archangelic glamour. Universe of difference, Rowan. As far as mortals were concerned, I didn't have wings. Therefore—I didn't have wings." His grin turned smug.

She allowed him his moment of superiority. Because surely there had never been a more beautiful sight in the universe than the splendor of Azrael's extended wingspan.

"All right." Her voice was husky, but she didn't care that he knew how much she wanted him. "That's a cool party trick. But how am I supposed to strip you naked for my perverted pleasure now?"

"Watch." He folded his wings, tore his shirt over his shoulders —and it slid with unnatural grace along the length of his feathers and fell to the floor.

How could he do that? But it didn't change the truth.

He could pull clothes off his back as if his wings were scarcely there.

"That's..." She glanced at his shirt, crumpled on the floor. "That's..." She tried again but it was no use. For the life of her she couldn't string more than a couple of words together, and neither of them made much sense in any case.

"Impressive?" He unfurled his wings once again, clearly preening before her.

"Yes." She pressed her palms against his sculpted chest, and silently embraced the steady thud of his heart beneath her fingers. *Impossible* was the word that hummed through her mind but since only days ago she'd not believed archangels existed, it was all relative. "You *are* impressive. And I'm not just talking about your ego here, either."

He cradled her face between his hands and the smile slid from his face. He stared at her as if he had never seen her before. As though he was memorizing every tiny detail. He didn't say a word, but he didn't have to, because for an eternal moment raw grief glowed in his eyes and tightened his jaw.

Azrael would never say *I love you.* He was an archangel, and she was merely a dhampir. No matter how many times in his long life he had fallen in love she knew, in her heart, the other women's heritages hadn't been polluted the way hers was.

He might love her. But he didn't love her the way he'd loved those other women in his past. Because, at his core, he would never be able to forget she was the half-breed offspring of his deadliest enemy.

Bittersweet sorrow squeezed her heart for all that she had— and all that she could never have. He might never be able to admit how he felt about her, but this strange twilight love they shared was so much more than she'd ever dreamed could be hers.

She trailed her fingers over his rock-hard pecs and then lower to mold his perfectly chiseled abs. His body was faultless. *Impressive.* She'd always thought it, and now she knew why.

Because he shared the blood of ancient immortals.

She unbuttoned his pants and slid her hands over his lean hips and taut butt. Still he didn't say anything. His mesmeric gaze ensnared her, as if he believed she might vanish if he so much as blinked.

"I'm not going anywhere," she whispered. Not tonight, anyway. Tomorrow was soon enough to make plans for the future. Plans that didn't involve staying here on his beautiful, fantasy planet for the rest of her life as he appeared to imagine.

"I know." His words were low, smoky and seductive. But beneath that, steely resolve vibrated, and she knew her suspicions were right. It wouldn't be easy to convince him to let her leave. But right now, all she had to convince him of was just how much she wanted him.

She tugged his pants over his hips and shoved them roughly down his thighs. But he didn't respond by ripping her tee-shirt over her head or tearing her jeans from her legs. He remained exactly where he was, cradling her face and gazing into her eyes with a fierce intensity that caused ripples of desire to cascade over her exposed skin.

Finally, he lowered his head. Time slowed and she noticed every little detail in vivid relief. The way his dark hair framed his face, the bewitching golden flecks in his eyes, the tense set of his jaw as though he contained his emotions by sheer force of will.

She didn't want him contained. Her nails dug into his hips and scored his flesh as she dragged her fingers along his ribcage. He reared beneath her hands but didn't pull her into his arms as their lips met.

It was like they had never touched before. He kissed her as though she was a reluctant virgin, a fragile human, a creature who knew nothing of the heights of passion.

So gentle, so tender, his lips barely brushed hers in a chaste caress. It was the most erotic touch she'd ever experienced. He didn't try to penetrate or conquer. Yet exquisite sensation flickered over her sensitized skin, like pinpricks of flame, elusive and addictive.

She clutched his back, felt his wings tease her knuckles. His eyes darkened but instead of invading her willing mouth he nibbled a delicate trail along the outline of her swollen lips.

His hands slid from her face and his fingertips teased the column of her throat, skimming with seductive promise over her hammering pulse. He tugged her tee-shirt upwards, way too slowly, and with a strangled groan she gripped the hem and yanked it up.

"Get it off me," she panted and for once he obeyed without question. She hadn't worn a bra and for a moment his gaze snagged on her naked breasts. Just the knowledge that he was looking at her was enough to cause molten lust to surge between her thighs in primitive need. She reached for him, wanting to spear her fingers through his glorious hair.

He caught her wrists. But his grip was loose. She could easily escape if she wanted to, but why would she want to escape when he pressed her arms to her sides and stepped towards her, closing the distance between them?

He pressed his mouth against her throat. But he didn't bite, didn't claim. Instead she felt the tip of his tongue taste her flesh. His heat grazed her skin and then he drew in a deep breath and inhaled the essence of who she was.

Prickles of raw desire radiated along her throat, over her breasts and aching nipples. She fisted her hands but didn't try to pull free. If he wanted to torture her then she was his willing captive.

He trailed kisses along her shoulder and skimmed his fingers over her hands and wrists. The lightest of touches, as though she was made of the finest porcelain and somewhere deep inside the thunder of her mind discordance stirred.

His dark head nestled against her, as his mouth worshipped her sensitized breast. His touch drove her crazy and she loved how he made her feel. But was this foreplay because he wanted to go slow and tender and drive her out of her mind—or because he couldn't forget what she really was?

"I won't break, Azrael." Her voice was uneven, but a thread of desperation weaved through the words. She tried to smother the flicker of hurt, but it was impossible. Would he always now wrap his desire for her in this odd cloak of restraint?

His fingers tensed against her arms. "You did break."

She stared at the back of his head as his tortured words echoed through her brain. He was treating her like glass because he thought she might *shatter*?

A deep ache filled her chest, making it hard to breathe. She raked her fingers through his hair and pulled him upright. Dark desire filled his eyes, leaving her in no doubt that he wanted her. Whatever he might feel about her tainted heritage had nothing to do with *this*.

"It won't happen again." Not now she knew her limitations.

"You nearly died." Raw savagery spiked each word. "You *could* have died." The accusation thudded between them, a personal insult that she'd had the nerve to *almost die* when he hadn't decreed it should be so.

"Yes." She gripped his hair. "But I didn't die, Azrael. I'm alive and I'm here with you. And I want to prove with you just how far from death I am."

CHAPTER 32

AZRAEL

*I*t didn't matter how hard Azrael searched her face, he couldn't see a trace of recrimination. Her beautiful green eyes held no condemnation. By hearing his confession, she had absolved him from sin.

Guilt clawed through him, regardless. Guilt and lust and another powerful emotion he couldn't face, but one that left a searing sensation of cold terror in its wake.

He had almost been too late to save her in the forest. Nico might have refused to help. The thoughts were crazy, redundant, because he had found her, and Nico had helped. But the alien fear dug poisoned talons deeper into the core of his soul. Logic had no part of its twisted trajectory.

When he'd thought her a frail human, he'd barely reined in his lust for her. When he'd imagined she was his enemy he'd taken all she offered him. And now he knew everything about her, he was afraid to touch her at all.

Her existence rocked the foundations of every truth he'd built his life on. As a direct descendant of Sakarbaal she was a risk he couldn't afford to take. From the moment he'd met her, his judgement had been compromised. He couldn't chance being distracted from his mission, but her presence was always with him, whether he wanted it or not.

But none of it was the reason why now, when she offered him all that he craved, he remained immobile as a deeper truth, one that threatened to splinter the core of his being, thundered through his heart.

She was a dhampir, but she was also mortal and… *she could die.*

She stepped back from him and slid her jeans down her legs. Desire and need collided low in his groin, an agonizing reminder that no matter how noble his intentions when it came to Rowan, he only had to look at her—only had to think of her—and he wanted her naked in his arms.

She kicked her jeans aside then came to him and tugged his pants to his ankles. Her warm breath feathered the inside of his thighs, a tantalizing caress filled with endless promise and unfathomable despair.

Before he could stop himself, he raked his fingers through her gorgeous hair. So soft and tempting, and her evocative scent drifted on the air like an elusive embrace. She pulled off his shoes and he kicked off his pants and despite the fire in his blood the knot of terror in the center of his chest refused to die.

She knelt at his feet, her hands clasped around his ankles, and looked up at him through her long black lashes. Again, she reminded him of an ancient goddess and why wouldn't she? Immortal blood did flow through her veins. It just wasn't the same immortal blood that he'd once fantasized.

Her nails scraped along the back of his calves. She was a mesmerizing vision of innocence and seductress, with her dark hair tumbling over her naked shoulders. Her bewitching eyes ensnared him once again, but instantly the thought crumbled. Because he'd never escaped the enchantment of her eyes since the moment they'd met.

She smiled. How could something so simple cause his chest to constrict? But he knew why. It was because only hours ago he would have given anything—*everything*—for her to once again look at him the way she was now.

Fate had heard his desperate plea. And that twisted bitch had taken his offering and granted his wish.

He tangled her hair through his fingers as she knelt before him. Her arms imprisoned his thighs and she gripped his ass as she slowly, provocatively, licked the tip of his cock.

Sensation sizzled through his blood and pounded along his erection. Need engulfed him, so primal that it vanquished the fear and conquered the despair. In a diminishing sane corner of his mind he knew it was only a temporary respite, but it was one he craved with everything he was.

Gods, she felt so good. Hot and wet and her breath drifted across his slit with tantalizing promise.

Slowly she stood up, her erect nipples burning a trail of fire across his thigh and abdomen. Then she looked into his eyes and the fear, the despair, and the overwhelming need and desire meshed, became indistinguishable. The sensation arrowed through his soul, splintered through his mind and captivated the essence of his being.

This one perfect moment as Rowan entwined her fingers through his and pressed his palm against her heart. A moment he would remember for the rest of his immortal life.

"Would you do something for me?" Her whisper threaded through his thoughts and it was an effort not to tell her that he would do anything for her. Because the knowledge all but paralyzed him.

"Sure." He aimed for nonchalance and failed with spectacular honors. She would have to be dead not to know she meant more to him than anyone he'd ever encountered.

And she isn't dead.

She smiled again, but this time there was an indefinable aura of sadness in her smile as though his answer had somehow wounded her. But instead of telling him what she wanted she gently tugged at his hands and led him towards the glass doors that opened onto the veranda.

"You want me to…" *Fuck, screw, shag.* The words hammered in his head, trying to drown out what he wanted to say to her. *Make love to you.* He'd said those words a thousand times in the past. But never in the past had they stabbed through his heart with such devastating implication. He abandoned the struggle. "Outside?"

She opened the door, pulled him across the threshold and then wrapped her arms around his waist. Her body molded to his. Warm, vital. *Alive.*

"Is this your private planet?" Her fingernails teased him in an erotic dance across his flesh. He cradled her delectable ass, pulled her closer, and the feel of his cock entrapped against her belly was indescribable torture.

"It's not my planet. I found it a while back, decided to make it my base. The indigenous humans are similar to those on Earth from about a hundred and fifty thousand years ago." He breathed in deep, savoring the fresh, clean scent of her hair. "Except they appear to be missing the war gene."

She snuggled closer, and the tips of her fingers caressed his feathers. Ripples of desire radiated outwards and instinctively he unfurled his wings in sensual pleasure. He'd long wanted her to admire his wings. And this time he planned on enjoying her rapture. Maybe one day he'd even be able to erase the sordid encounter in the Tudor inn from both their memories.

The back of her hands glided across the underside of his feathers and the green of her eyes all but vanished as her pupils dilated.

"In that case, I want to take you… up there." Her gaze drifted to the skies, and despite everything an unexpected laugh rasped along his throat.

"You want me to fly through the heavens as we make love?"

The words came easily, and his heart didn't shatter in his chest, and the universe didn't tumble into ash around his shoulders. Instead, raw lust gripped him, and the vision of Rowan as she climaxed in his arms all but incinerated the black fear that still held him in its lethal claw. "You'd better hold on tight. It could be a rough ride."

CHAPTER 33

ROWAN

*R*owan wound her arms around Azrael's neck, and he tightened his grip on her bottom and hoisted her up. She laughed at the sheer decadent evil on his face and wrapped her legs around his waist. There was no need to worry she might accidentally crush his ribs. She could grip him as tightly as she liked, as brutally as she needed, and there was never any danger he'd end up in the hospital.

He drew back his magnificent wings and she gazed, spellbound, as his feathers undulated in iridescent splendor. The mountainous backdrop faded and the mid-afternoon sun dimmed.

The villa fell away as his powerful wings brushed against her in a mesmeric wave. Terror and exhilaration pounded through her blood as she held him in a death grip and craned her neck to see how high they were.

But all she could see was the endless azure sky, his incredible wingspan, and irresistible grin of self-satisfaction at her awe. It didn't matter what planet they were on or where in the universe he'd taken her. Because she was in Azrael's arms and he...

He really is flying.

One false move and she'd plunge to her death. Except he would never let her go. Never put her in any danger. She'd once told him her most outrageous fantasy was to completely trust her partner. At the time she'd meant to trust him enough to share the dark secrets of her life.

He already knew more about her than she'd guessed back then.

She trusted him. Completely. And she wanted him to know. Slowly she unhooked one arm from around his neck and speared her fingers through his windswept hair. He held her as securely as if they both stood on solid ground.

"Don't let me fall."

"Never." He was no longer laughing, and his intense gaze stoked the desire curling through her. His fingers skated up her back and shock pulsed through her at the knowledge he could hold her so easily with just one arm.

She had no idea how fast they were traveling, but the wind whipped her naked body in an erotic touch that bordered on pain. She captured his lips and this time he wasn't gentle, didn't hold back, or behave as though she might splinter beneath his onslaught.

This time he kissed her as if she was the reason for his existence.

Open mouthed she drew him inside, delighting in the sensation of him invading and exploring. He was frenzied, plundering, as though he wanted to brand her for the world—*the universe* —to see.

She slid her tongue against his and although she pushed against his dominance, she embraced it. His hand clamped the back of her head, holding her still, holding her close, and his teeth tore her lips and her blood bound them both.

His body was a furnace and his heat scorched through her. It seemed he created a cocoon around her as the wind no longer chilled her back. Feverishly she lifted her hips, desperate to feel him inside her once again. The head of his cock nudged her sensitized clit and her choked moan echoed in her mind and vibrated through her blood.

He swore inside her mouth. Something hot and foreign and unimaginably arousing. She didn't need to understand the words to understand their meaning and she laughed without breaking lip-contact.

"You'll have to oversee the docking procedure this time." She gripped his hair harder, tightened her thigh muscles and dug her nails into the side of his throat. "If I move, I might lose my balance."

The rush of the wind—or maybe it was the sound of his heavenly wings—thundered in her mind, a thrilling counterpoint to the erratic thud of her heart. A rumble of laughter shook his body, sending ripples of raw need spiraling over her skin. Their bodies meshed, her breasts crushed against his chest, and then he roughly hoisted her upwards.

"Docking procedure initiated." His words grazed her lips, as tantalizing and erotic as the feel of his cock teasing her. Laughter threaded through his words, an exhilarating aphrodisiac. "Request permission to enter."

A groan of frustration tore from her throat. "Granted."

And then, in case he had any more twisted ideas about prolonging her torture, she released her death grip around his neck and sank onto his rigid shaft.

So good. So right. For a lingering moment she savored the sensation of being impaled, filled, *possessed.* Her hands gripped his shoulders, but it was pure reflex. She knew she was safe. Knew he would never let her fall.

But she clung onto his shoulders, and every powerful flex and contraction of his muscles sent delicious thrills tingling along her flesh. The incredible, magical colors of his feathers filled her vision, a heavenly visage haloed with sunlight. How could he be a harbinger of death? He was her Archangel of life, of light. The Archangel who had shown her the meaning of love.

His breath rasped against her mouth and his hands palmed her butt, crushing her against his hard body. With every sweep of his wings the friction increased as he shoved her down his erection, and then dragged her up again.

"Gods, Rowan." The words were jagged. His eyes were a breathtaking glitter of black and gold and she nipped his lip, savoring his taste, a wordless encouragement. He gave a strangled groan in the back of his throat. "You push me to my limits. *Every time.*"

"Yes." She uncurled her fingers from his shoulders. "Every time, Azrael."

She slowly raised her arms from the security of his strong body and flattened her palms against the living panorama of his wingspan. Her life was in his hands. And his wings were in hers.

Awe collided with lust and love and desire, became one and became everything. His grip around her tightened and a hint of madness glinted in his eyes. And then, without warning, he teleported, the sensation disorienting her as it had when they'd returned from Nico's.

She clung onto his biceps as her mind scrambled to adjust. Azrael was still flying, but it was no longer midday. The sky was a delicate shade of pink and as he turned, she saw the breathtaking sight as dawn broke on the far horizon of a peach-tinted ocean.

"Beautiful." The word was uneven, all she could manage. His thrusts became frenzied, slamming into her, and only his hands locking her in place stopped her from splintering across the heavens.

"You." He ground the word between his teeth, and she had to struggle to hear him, struggle to focus. "Are my dawn, Rowan."

His tortured confession shattered through her, as potent as if he'd laid bare his soul and said the words she knew he could never admit. *I love you*. Because, in a way she'd never imagined, he just had.

She forgot about the beauty of the sunrise, forgot about their fragile future and her sordid past. Time ceased to exist. This magical moment that balanced night and day, darkness and light, encompassed her world. And his agonized roar of release as he filled her quivering body filled the aching chasm in her soul.

With shaky hands she cupped his jaw and stroked her thumbs over his five o'clock shadow. Already night gave way to day, the pale yellow sky heralding that reality crouched just beyond the horizon. But right now, her reality didn't matter.

Nothing mattered but the archangel in her arms, who looked at her as if she was his salvation.

CHAPTER 34

AZRAEL

*G*abe yanked open the door of his farmhouse and squinted at him. "It's one in the morning. This had better be good."

No, it wasn't good, but Azrael knew damn well it would be of interest. That's why he'd left Rowan sleeping and turned up on his friend's doorstep. From his shirt pocket he pulled out the phial he'd taken from Rowan just days ago.

"What do you make of this?" He held the phial up and its contents shimmered with tangible menace. Gabe stopped scowling and stared at the phial, disbelief clouding his eyes.

"Is that—?" He didn't need to finish. Because it was obvious he could feel the eerie pull of the Guardians' Voids from where the swirling black contents originated.

He shoved the phial back in his pocket and stepped into the hall. "The question is, what is a three-thousand-year-old vampire doing with it?"

No need to tell Gabe about Rowan's part in all this. She'd been an innocent pawn.

He hadn't meant to think of her. Not here, not now. But gods, it was hard not to, when she was constantly in his mind. As necessary to his survival as the air he breathed.

"Sakarbaal? You've found him again?" Gabe pushed the door shut.

"I've picked up his trail."

"How did you get hold of that phial?"

"I acquired it from one of his operatives," he said in a cool voice.

Last summer, when he'd detected unprecedented disturbances on the astral planes, he'd traced them to Gabe. To the woman—to Aurora— that Gabe had rescued from the Guardians' clutches. And Gabe had looked at him in the same way that Azrael was glaring at him right now.

Say what you like to me. But leave my woman out of it.

Azrael wasn't human, was far from primitive and had no desire for a mate. Yet when it came to Rowan his instincts were nothing less than primal.

Gabe appeared to realize he had no intention of elaborating on who this mysterious operative was. "Why are you here?"

"Sakarbaal intended to target me with this stuff. How the hell would he get his hands on something that doesn't exist outside of the Guardians' Voids unless he's in league with them?" No need to state the obvious—that Sakarbaal also appeared to know that archangels were vulnerable to the Guardians' atmosphere. Why else would the vampire have intended it as a weapon?"

"You should speak to Mephisto."

He hadn't expected that response. Why would Mephisto, the biggest party whore in existence, be interested in something like this?

"There must be a way of neutralizing the affects the Voids have on us. Aurora can analyze this sample in one of the research facilities you're funding." She could also analyze Rowan's amber acid. He'd trust her findings above anything the vampires chose to tell him.

"Mephisto," Gabe said, ignoring his comment, "*negotiates* with the Guardians. Don't ask me what that's all about because I don't have a clue. But if they're fucking around then Mephisto needs to know about it."

"Negotiates?" That caught his attention. "How the fuck does he *negotiate* with those little shits?"

"Beats me." There was a grim note in Gabe's voice. "But he managed to stop them persecuting Aurora because of her trans-dimensional heritage. And averted Armageddon," he added, as though that was a minor afterthought.

He wasn't in the mood to discuss Mephisto. "Are you going to take this stuff or what?"

"Sure." But Gabe made no move towards him. "You look like shit, Az. What have you been up to?"

"Hunting day and night has that affect." Fuck it. He hadn't even showered before taking Rowan in his arms. She had looked and smelled like a water goddess and he, in the not-so-immortal words of Gabe, *looked like shit.*

"The operative?" Gabe said in a suspiciously neutral tone.

"That's right." He sounded belligerent and didn't care. Let Gabe make what he liked of it.

"What's so special about this operative?"

Why the fuck were they talking about Rowan? He had no intention of discussing her with anyone. "Did I say there was anything special about her?"

Gabe shrugged one shoulder. "Didn't have to. The look on your face was more than enough."

The look on his *face*? He glowered at Gabe. "Shut the fuck up. You gone soft now you've devolved?"

There was a time when Gabe would have responded to any kind of personal insult by ramming the perpetrator up against the nearest wall and smashing his fist into their face. *This* Gabe didn't even blink. Just kept on staring, like he was seeing far more than he had any right to.

He heard movement upstairs and light spilled down the stairs. Gabe's face softened momentarily, and whoever had been moving around stopped and killed the light. His eyes narrowed. Gabe had lost his telepathic ability to communicate with fellow archangels when he'd lost his immortality. But apparently he still retained a telepathic link with Aurora.

A crazy thought surfaced. Was it possible *he* could initiate such a link with Rowan?

"Screws with your head, doesn't it?"

Azrael ditched his instinctive response to tell Gabe he had no idea what he was talking about. There was no point. Gabe had been there, done that and by the gods look at the price he'd paid.

"Falling," Gabe added as if he thought he needed further clarification.

His chest tightened and it became hard to breathe evenly. He'd watched archangels fall in the past and seen their devastation when their beloved died.

Just months ago he'd ripped into Gabe, all but accused him of being a masochist for falling in love with Aurora. *She's mortal. She's destined to die.*

And every time she does, your heart will die too.

There were no words to express the tangled mess of emotions that clogged his head and tore his heart like an insidious virus. And even if there were, he'd rip out his tongue before he said them to Gabe.

"Is she a vampire?"

"No, she isn't." He could barely push the denial out. Because she was a dhampir. And nine hundred years ago, he had slain her people with scarcely a second thought.

Gabe frowned. "She's *human*?" He sounded like he'd never come across an archangelic/human pairing before, when eleven thousand years ago virtually all the archangels who'd fallen had fallen for a *human*.

Aurora herself was. And now, so was Gabe.

He should get out of here. But some newly discovered masochistic tendency compelled him to remain. "She's half human." He glared at Gabe, wanting to provoke a fight so he could lose some of this black terror that engulfed his reason. And despite not wanting to talk about any of it, his deepest fear spilled into the space between them. "She's destined to *die*."

"She'll be reborn." Gabe's gaze shifted and he stared over Azrael's left shoulder. "You'll find her again."

Find her again? "The way you found Eleni?" His voice was harsh. "Sure, that's a plan. It only took you eleven thousand years, didn't it?"

Gabe glanced back, compassion glittering in his eyes. He didn't need Gabe's fucking compassion. He was an archangel. Gabe was only a human and Rowan—

When she died, how the hell could he wait *eleven thousand years* for her to be reborn?

"It won't be that long for you." Gabe sounded so sure. But Rowan was half-vampire and vampires didn't possess souls.

Even with her human heritage she might not have a soul to return to him, even after eleven thousand years.

"When you were immortal how could you stand it?" The words tore from his throat. "The *knowing*?"

Gabe shifted and looked as if he wished he'd never brought the subject up. But the question was out there, and he damn well needed an answer. No matter how he protected her or kept her safe on his planet she was destined to die.

How long did dhampirs live? From memory all those he'd killed in Romania had been young. Nico had told him dhampirs under Sakarbaal's rule didn't live to a great age. Was that because of how Sakarbaal used them? Or a genetic inevitability of their mixed blood?

"You can't think about it." Gabe's voice was rough. "You just have to take each day and live it to the full."

What psycho-babble crap was that?

"Worked for you, did it?" Derision dripped from every word but what had he expected? Some magic formula that would wipe away the feeling of dread and helplessness that was eating him from the inside out?

"No." The admission was stark. "But it's all you can do if you want to hang onto your sanity."

CHAPTER 35

AZRAEL

*A*zrael stood on the veranda outside his villa, waiting for Rowan to finish in the bathroom, but for once he didn't see the majestic range of mountains or the lush valleys below. Gabe's words haunted him. They would haunt him always.

For the first time since discovering Gabe had lost his immortality, and that his and Aurora's life-forces were entwined, Azrael saw the advantage.

Because when Aurora died, so too would Gabe.

It was insane to think that an advantage. He had no desire to be mortal, no wish to lose his archangelic abilities. Involuntarily he spread his wings and savored the light breeze that caressed his feathers. Even the threat of losing his wings was enough to curdle his gut.

Rowan walked over to him.

"I could never tire of this view." She wound her arm around his waist and rested her head against his shoulder. He tugged her close and wrapped his wing around her, enveloping her in the protective mantle of his… immortality.

"Good." Just as well, since once they'd seen Nico and discovered the secrets of Rowan's amber acid, he had no intention that she'd leave this planet again. "Are you ready?" Nate was picking them up to take them to the vamp at any moment and what a pain in the ass that was. What did Nico think he was going to do if he knew the whereabouts of his home?

"Yes." She turned to him and held out her free hand. The phial lay across her palm. "The sooner we know what this stuff is, the better."

He picked the phial up and smothered the shudder that threatened to attack. Earlier he'd virtually had to force Gabe to call Aurora downstairs so she could siphon some of its contents, and the remainder he intended to give to Mephisto. Even without that plan he had no intention of handing it over to the vamp. He owed him enough as it was.

"No need." He shoved the phial into his pants pocket and steeled himself against the unnatural vibrations that radiated from the shimmering black. "I've got it covered."

She threaded her fingers through his and he resisted the urge to press her hand against his heart. It was bad enough Gabe had guessed his feelings for Rowan. He wasn't up to having Nate catch him doing something so... revealing.

"If Nico's scientists discover how to recreate amber acid, I think he intends to manufacture it for wider distribution." Hope glowed in her beautiful eyes. "I was taught the Strigoi despised dhampirs to the point they'd kill us on sight. But that's not true. Sakarbaal might be an evil bastard but maybe his discoveries can be used for some good after all?"

He could only imagine how much she longed to help her fellow dhampirs who scrabbled in the gutter without the magical elixir that subdued their primitive nature. It went against the grain to think Sakarbaal's existence had been good for anything but the fact remained.

If not for the Enclave's scientists, Rowan would probably be dead.

Before he could respond, Nate arrived. His surly expression didn't alter when he glanced at Rowan.

"Ready," he said. It wasn't a question. And then he teleported them to Nico's.

Rowan

ROWAN GLANCED around Nico's laboratory, located on the top floor of his home—the Strigoi HQ? It looked every bit as sophisticated as the ones of the Enclave.

Nico led her, Azrael and Meg farther into the lab. The other archangel, Nate—the one who looked at her as if he'd like to drive a stake through her heart—had remained downstairs flirting with a Strigoi hunter.

"Octavia is our chief scientist," Nico said. "Her findings are... interesting, if not wholly unexpected."

Rowan looked at Octavia, who perched on the end of a stainless-steel bench and regarded them as though they were next up on her to-do list. Her deep auburn hair was pulled back from her beautiful, flawless face in a sleek French plait and her white lab coat was open, showing off a figure-hugging jersey dress. The woman wasn't a vampire and yet there was something about her. Something Rowan couldn't put her finger on, and inexplicably a spooky sense of familiarity trickled through her.

"We've identified all the elements," Octavia said, as her assessing glance rested on Rowan. "In a nutshell, this substance was created for two specific purposes besides being a synthetic blood substitute. Not only is it designed to make the user irrevocably addicted, but it also renders the body physically incapable of ingesting fresh blood." Octavia paused for effect. "A strange drug to hook dhampirs on."

"That can't be right." She battened down the panic that threatened to swamp her. "It's a substitute for blood because we can't process it raw." She glanced at Meg for backup, but the vampire was glaring at Octavia as if she'd like to rip out her throat. "*Meg?*"

Meg turned to her, and Rowan realized she was absolutely furious. And her fury wasn't directed at Octavia.

Disjointed memories tumbled through her mind. How many times in the past had Meg urged her to try some fresh blood? As if, deep down, she'd never believed Rowan was unable to take it?

"I was never convinced dhampirs were physically unable to drink blood," Meg said. "I thought it was another of the High Council's ridiculous discriminatory edicts. But I never thought it was the medication itself that was the cause of your… *allergy*."

"It's more than an allergy," Nico said, coming to stand beside Octavia. "The samples we took from Rowan yesterday showed this substance is entwined with her DNA. It's as much a part of her as the fact her blood type is the rarest on Earth."

"It's corrupted my DNA?" She kept her gaze fixed on Nico, when all she really wanted to do was fall into Azrael's arms and hide from the horrible truth. She'd finally accepted the fact she was a dhampir. Did she now have to face she was a mutant as well?

"In utero," Octavia said. "I'd say your mother was medicated with this from the moment of conception. Your genetic material was manipulated to Sakarbaal's specific modifications."

Her stomach churned and she clenched her fist in a futile effort to stem the pain from flooding through her body. She wasn't just the daughter of Sakarbaal. She was his genetically modified freak.

"And you knew about this?" Azrael turned to Nico and barely leashed fury sizzled beneath every word.

Nico bared his fangs in a mockery of a smile. What the hell was the matter with them? Couldn't they leave their bloody macho egos buried for even a *moment*?

"I knew he was selectively breeding dhampirs."

She tried not to let his bald comment affect her, but it was hard. After all, Nico only spoke the truth. Sakarbaal *had* bred dhampirs for his own use.

It was just science. Don't react.

But they're talking about me.

"Go on." Azrael's voice could have split diamonds.

Nico spared her a fleeting glance. She wondered if she imagined that glint of compassion in his golden eyes.

"This time, unlike nine hundred years ago in Romania, he wanted only those who carried his own DNA." Nico sounded reluctant to admit it. "We long ago discovered his dhampirs all possessed the same rare blood type and the maternal lines were chosen with care. His victims were never random."

"That's all you meant when you said they were genetically engineered?"

When had Nico said that about her? Didn't they care they were ripping apart every shred of her identity?

She'd always been an outsider. But now, when she'd finally come to terms with her hybrid blood, Fate had one more twisted hand to play. Because she wasn't even the person she'd spent her whole life trying *not* to be.

"It wasn't I who used those words." Nico shrugged, as if he didn't care that Azrael had quite obviously read more into that bizarre conversation. "I will admit I thought Sakarbaal had developed a way of enhancing specific pheromones, but Octavia assures me that's not the case."

Azrael took her hand and gripped her fingers tight, as though he half expected her to flee. "So as far as you can determine, the drugs have no bearing on preventing dhampirs from devolving into their natural state?"

Her heart pounded, echoing against her skull, as unformed fear swarmed through her mind. It was only when she finally dragged her reluctant gaze from Azrael's face that the silence hit her.

But it was more than a natural pause in conversation. The

silence throbbed with words unsaid, and raw malignance tainted the air.

"Tell me, archangel," Octavia said, and there was an undercurrent of hostility in her voice. "What *natural state* would that be?"

She shoved her self-pity aside and stepped forward. "You know what he's talking about. As soon as I stopped taking that stuff I—" The words locked in her throat, but she forced them out. Everyone in this room knew the truth. "Turned into a mindless creature consumed with bloodlust."

Azrael squeezed her fingers in silent support and once again stood by her side. It was crazy to draw comfort from such a small gesture. Yet it wasn't a small gesture at all.

"Yes, you did," Nico said, but he didn't sound happy about it. "Because your body can't function without the drugs. You're not simply addicted to it, Rowan. Your body will collapse without it. But understand this. That mindless creature is not your natural state."

A bitter laugh scraped along her throat. "That's easy for you to say." He'd shared his memories of that night in Romania with her. He knew, as well as she, that dhampirs hadn't evolved at all in the last nine hundred years. "But you know it isn't true."

Octavia pushed herself from the bench and came to stand in front of her. She scrutinized her as if she was a sample under one of her microscopes and Rowan fought the urge to squirm.

"I've accessed your file," she said. "On paper your intelligence is unquestioned. In the flesh I'm having a hard time believing it."

"Watch your mouth," Azrael snarled. Octavia merely smiled at him, before returning her attention to Rowan.

"I've been working on the Sakarbaal project for more than forty years," she said. *Forty years?* She only just stopped herself from gaping. Octavia barely looked thirty. *But she wasn't a vampire.* What other species of immortal could she be? "We've known for a long time that brainwashing was part of the educational package his dhampirs received. So look beyond that,

Rowan. Look at the facts logically and objectively. You suffered from acute withdrawal symptoms. Your body turned on itself and yes—you nearly died."

If we could just get past the withdrawal Brad had said. God, he'd been right. So right. But even he hadn't guessed the full truth. That they never could get beyond the withdrawal symptoms—because their bodies couldn't survive without the drugs.

"I craved blood." Her voice was hoarse. "In the end that's all I could think about. It was like I was trapped in a tiny corner of my mind, watching the rest of me… disintegrate."

"Sakarbaal's methods to keep you under his jurisdiction were simple," Nico said. "And very effective. If any of you did escape, you'd be dead within a week. And you're a dhampir. Of course you crave blood. Once the suppressants in the substance wore off your natural instincts came to the fore. You'd never experienced them before, so how could you expect to handle it? But that has nothing to do with your withdrawal symptoms."

He paused, and she sensed the internal battle that raged as to whether he should continue or not. "The dhampirs Sakarbaal gathered in Romania nine hundred years ago were treated like cattle. They lived like animals and that's… the reason they responded like animals."

"But I don't—dhampirs don't have fangs." She shot Azrael a glance, but his face was impassive. Although it was hard knowing she'd been sucked into a vortex of lies her entire life, some things just didn't add up. Surely there had been some glimmer of truth, no matter how tiny, in everything she'd been brought up to believe? "The amber acid was a substitute for the real thing so we wouldn't prowl the streets and rip open an innocent's throat in a bloodlust frenzy."

"A specific manipulation." Octavia's voice was clipped, but a flash of something that looked like anger glinted in her eyes. "His geneticists took away the means to feed and then they spun a web of lies around the offspring so they could pump you full of a synthetic blood substitute." She took another step closer and her lips parted. Rowan caught sight of the tips of her fangs and reeled back. Octavia was a *dhampir*?

No wonder she'd experienced that sense of familiarity when they had met. She couldn't sense the presence of a dhampir the way she could a vamp, but the primal awareness of one of her kind had alerted her senses all the same.

She just hadn't recognized it.

She looked at Nico, but like Azrael his face was an unreadable mask. She spread her fingers over her thigh and hoped no one could see her legs shaking.

All her life she'd been so sure the Strigoi loathed dhampirs to the point where they'd not hesitate to kill them on sight. But they didn't hate half-bloods. She doubted dhampirs of the Strigoi were experimented on while still in the womb, and they certainly didn't die as a matter of course in their twenties. They weren't reliant on drugs to allegedly curb their primitive urges and lack of self-control.

They were educated. Respected. Held positions of power within the vampire hierarchy.

And they had fangs.

She'd been wrong when she thought Nico wanted the secrets of amber acid so he could help dhampirs surviving in the shadows. There was no need.

It was only the dhampirs of the Enclave of the Phoenix who needed help.

CHAPTER 36

ROWAN

"The other night you asked me about the phoenix connection."

Nico's words jerked Rowan back to the present and she shot Azrael a probing look. He'd told her that nine hundred years ago Sakarbaal had captured a phoenix and had somehow manipulated its essence to distort the astral planes. Before Nico had discovered the death of his child, he'd been as close to Sakarbaal as a son. It made sense he'd know of the captive phoenix. But why bring that up now?

"Yes." Azrael's voice gave nothing away. "You refused to answer."

"I had no intention of telling you anything except for that one piece of information I conveyed," Nico said, and realization dawned. He was the one who had told Azrael the truth about her. He glanced at Octavia and a silent message appeared to pass between them. "Circumstances have now changed."

"There was something else in the substance," Octavia said. "Something Nico and I had hoped to discover, but even so its purity was still a shock."

She stared at her in disbelief. Was Octavia suggesting—

"Phoenix essence." Azrael's voice was grim. "He's hooked his dhampirs on phoenix essence."

Her muscles tensed at the disgust in his voice, at the way he'd said *his dhampirs*, but pain still lanced through her heart. Not that she blamed him. It *was* disgusting. And it seemed there was nothing she could do about it.

He pulled his hand from hers and slung his arm around her shoulders, pinning her to his side. Until that moment she hadn't even realized she'd physically flinched at his words.

But he had noticed. And his actions, the way he held her as if he was prepared to take on the entire Echelon to defend her if necessary, spoke far louder than any words he might have said.

"Whether the dhampirs of the Enclave are hooked on phoenix essence or not is irrelevant." Octavia's glance lingered longer than necessary on the possessive way Azrael held her. "It's an integral element of your DNA."

"But why?" The words choked her, but she had to know. Wasn't it enough that she was a hybrid human/vampire? Was she now also part mythical *bird*?

"There's no scientific reasoning for its inclusion." Octavia folded her arms and for the first time looked faintly embarrassed, as if realizing Rowan wasn't just an interesting anomaly but a real person. *But am I a real person when the essence of phoenix corrupts my DNA?* "I've studied phoenix essence for decades, but only possessed ancient trace elements until now. It doesn't bind the other components of amber acid together and as far as we can tell it hasn't altered your genetic code. But here's the thing. It only fully integrates if the blood type is AB Negative. What I'm saying is—it's simply a part of you."

Azrael's grip on her tightened. "It's binding with the soul."

She pulled back, incredulous, and stared at him. "*What*? Why would you think that? How could that even be possible?"

"That was Sakarbaal's obsession a thousand years ago," Nico said. "He confided in me, back then. Things he shared with no one else. He told me that when he'd been turned, in those moments as his body regenerated into an immortal, he soared through the celestial heavens."

"The astral planes," Azrael said.

"He spoke of a hidden power. Said he'd witnessed the soul of a phoenix resurrect. He was consumed by the desire to enter that highest realm again and harness the unimaginable forces there. But despite trying for almost a thousand years, he'd never managed to ascend higher than any trained mortal spiritualist."

"What?" Azrael's voice was harsh. "How could he ascend into the astral planes without a soul?"

Nico offered him a mirthless smile. "Vampires aren't the soulless creatures of your nightmares, archangel."

Azrael sucked in a sharp breath. "He captured a phoenix in the belief it would help him reach that highest realm. What function do the dhampirs serve?"

"The dhampirs are central to his plans. He spent decades harvesting the purity of the phoenix essence and force feeding it to his pitiful slaves. He was convinced that in due course, with enough dhampir souls entwined with the phoenix essence, they'd serve as a gateway."

"And be able to drag him into the highest realm."

"Yes. In Romania he could never understand why less than one percent of the dhampirs who died gave him only an elusive glimpse of the realm he craved to conquer." He glanced at Rowan. "As technology advanced so did his knowledge. Using phoenix essence, he can manipulate only those who possess the rarest blood type on Earth."

Nico paused, allowing her a moment to digest everything he'd just thrown at her. A *moment*? She'd need the rest of her life. "He's also revised his strategy of invasion. My guess is he plans to release all the souls he's harvested over the years at once. That way he'll flood the astral planes, not just with the essential phoenix essence, but also his bloodline. There'll be no stopping him from gaining his objective then."

How could Sakarbaal have captured the souls of all the dhampirs who had died over the years? What did he possess, some kind of homing device for dhampir souls?

It was a horrible thought.

"You appear to know a great deal about Sakarbaal's plans." Meg sounded completely pissed off. It was obvious Nico's prior research and insider information rattled her.

Nico gave her a mirthless smile. "Sakarbaal isn't the only one with spies."

The silence after his words was suffocating. She'd always known of the Enclave's international spy network, even if she didn't know all the individuals involved. Logically she'd also known that spying went both ways. But it was still a shock to hear Nico confirm it so casually.

Was anyone she knew, someone she'd considered a friend, a spy for the Strigoi?

Considering what she'd discovered over the last few days she couldn't condemn them for their treachery. Because just who exactly was the enemy here?

Nico indicated with a sweep of his arm towards the door that their time in his lab was over. As Azrael turned, she pulled back. "I just want a minute."

He gave her a probing look. "I'll be right outside."

She waited until Meg flounced after him before turning to Octavia. There was no way of telling how old she might be. But she was the first dhampir she'd ever knowingly met who wasn't hooked on amber acid.

"I've never known another dhampir who lived beyond twenty-seven." It was a confession but sounded like an accusation, yet Octavia didn't bristle with offense. Rowan resisted the urge to cross her arms. She didn't want the other woman to know how defensive she felt, even if it was brutally obvious by her words. "Is that the life expectancy imposed on us by the amber acid?"

Octavia regarded her for a moment in silence. "Nothing I or my team discovered would indicate there's an expiry date written into the drugs. And as I explained before, the phoenix essence simply *is*. If, as both Nico and your archangel believe, its sole purpose is to become one with your soul then, theoretically, it shouldn't impact on your life expectancy at all."

"But what if the phoenix essence was removed? Would we still be able to fully function?" Because when she found and destroyed Sakarbaal, there was no way in hell she'd let a phoenix continue to suffer such unspeakable torture.

For the first time Octavia looked uncertain. "I don't know." It clearly hurt her pride to admit that. "We can't detect any addictive qualities but that aside there's no way of telling how it might impact your physiology."

It wasn't reassuring but she'd guessed as much. She glanced to the door and saw Azrael lounging against the architrave, watching her. He looked relaxed but she wasn't fooled for a second. If Octavia made the slightest wrong move, her archangel would be by her side before she could blink.

Some of her tension seeped away. She might be a biological nightmare, but he hadn't turned his back on her. And she knew she stood a better chance of ending Sakarbaal's reign with Azrael's help than she would on her own.

She offered him a small smile. He didn't smile back but an odd feeling of warmth encased her heart, obscurely reminding her of the time he'd wrapped his coat around her shoulders to keep out the chill of the night.

Once again she turned back to Octavia. There was something else she wanted to ask. Something she'd never imagined asking before because the suspicion had never arisen.

"Have you ever heard of an Enclave dhampir called Belinda

Carson?" Her friend Belinda, who had allegedly been murdered by the enemy while deep undercover in the Strigoi Echelon.

A guarded expression crossed Octavia's face. "What about her?"

So it was true. Belinda's cover had been blown. Otherwise how would Octavia have known of her? And if the Enclave had told the truth about Belinda's last mission it stood to reason they'd told the truth about her death, too.

She struggled to conceal the ridiculous feeling of betrayal that knotted her breast. The Echelon might not be the enemy she'd always believed, but they'd still killed Belinda when her cover became compromised.

There was nothing more to say. She would just turn her back and return to Azrael. But before she could stop herself the accusation that thundered through her mind tore from her throat.

"She was only following Sakarbaal's orders. She didn't deserve to die for it."

Understanding flashed in Octavia's eyes. "Belinda fell in love with one of our warriors. She wanted to defect. But before Nico had the chance to consider her request, we can only assume that the Enclave's Elders found out." She hesitated and dread coiled through Rowan's heart. "I'm sorry, Rowan. Belinda killed herself."

Azrael

Rowan walked towards him, looking perfectly composed, but something was wrong. What the hell had that fucking dhampir said to her?

He slung his arm around her shoulders as she paused by his side.

"Okay?" His voice sounded harsh when all he wanted to do was offer her some comfort. But what comfort could he give? How could she be feeling when she'd just discovered how fundamentally that bastard Sakarbaal had manipulated her genetic identity?

"I'll be fine once I've decapitated Sakarbaal." She gave him a brittle smile, her green eyes glittering with what looked suspiciously like tears. His grip on her tightened, and he refrained from reminding her there was no way she was ever going near Sakarbaal again.

"Join the queue," Nico said, tossing her a look Azrael didn't care for at all. What right had the vampire to look at her as if they shared a private connection?

They entered the same room where he'd waited for Nico to save Rowan's life—was it really only yesterday? Rowan and Nico did share a special connection. The vampire had shared his blood with her.

"Is he still in London?" After his first meeting with Nico, he'd researched the Enclave of the Phoenix. He'd traced its history to Bulgaria six hundred years ago, but he was damn sure its origins went further back in time than that.

For more than four hundred years the Enclave had thrived in London, Paris—hell, in every major city in Europe, and a couple of centuries ago it had appeared in New York and New Orleans.

During the last nine hundred years Azrael had searched the ruined castle in Romania maybe a dozen times. He'd never discovered anything new. Had never heard a whisper of a rumor as to Sakarbaal's current whereabouts.

He'd been so fucking blinded by the past, he had never imagined Sakarbaal would embrace technology or sink his claws so deeply into the civilized veneer of human capitalism. While Azrael had kicked over the ancient stones of a long-deserted castle, Sakarbaal had been building his empire in plain view.

"No." The blonde vampire—Marguerite—spared him a disdainful glance before standing in front of Rowan and frowning into her face. "He returned to Romania after Rowan disappeared."

"Romania? Why? There's nothing there." At least, *he'd* not discovered anything through his research that led back to Romania.

"That's the heart of the Enclave," Rowan said, turning to him. "That's where the Electors issue their archaic edicts."

It didn't mean Sakarbaal had set up his Council in his former lair. The castle was inhabitable. He'd seen it himself less than a month ago.

"He rebuilt," Nico said. "And he doesn't rely on an inadequate dhampir army to protect his castle."

Azrael recalled the strange, wraith-like mist that had obscured the ruins and his gut tightened. The bastard had cloaked his castle with a glamour. *And I fell for it.*

He tugged Rowan closer, and the vital warmth of her body had a strangely calming effect. "This time I won't underestimate him."

Not ever again. This time he would succeed. Because now it was personal. She might not have been born if not for Sakarbaal, but she would never be free until he was destroyed. He still intended to free the phoenix. But first he'd ensure to stockpile enough of the medication for Rowan's personal use. How much would she need?

"This time," Nico said, echoing his words with barely concealed contempt, "you won't have the chance to. I'll be there."

"Sounds like a plan," Nate strolled into the room, with the satisfied air of an archangel who'd just been thoroughly laid. "Count me in."

He didn't object to Nate's company. But the vampire was something else. "Two archangels are more than enough to finish this for good."

Nico didn't respond. At least not verbally. But the curl of his lip conveyed how little he thought of Azrael's strategy.

Rowan gave a silent sigh before she pulled away from him and went to pick up a katana on the coffee table. Marguerite had presented it to her when they'd arrived earlier, and Rowan had been clearly thrilled by the return of her sword.

No wonder she'd taken his katana the other day. It was her weapon of choice.

"How's Lily, Meg?" she asked, as she fixed the scabbard at her waist and sheathed the sword. Dressed in black jeans and a jade cable knit sweater and with her hair tumbling over her shoulders she looked an unlikely combination of innocence and aggressor. Deja vu crawled along his spine at the way she stood in the middle of the room. It reminded him of the night they'd met. When he'd thought her so cute and vulnerable—and yet even then she had reminded him of a warrior. It was an inherent element of who she was.

Marguerite gave a theatrical sigh. "I do not know. When Sakarbaal and his entourage left they took Brad and Lily with them."

The names meant nothing to him, but Rowan's stance altered, so subtly he doubted anyone else was aware of it. But he saw. Not only that but he felt it, an imperceptible shifting in the atmosphere that surrounded her.

In that moment there wasn't the slightest doubt in his mind that, at her core, she was a warrior. And while he would never allow her to put herself in danger again, pride burned through him at the knowledge.

"Lily's in no state to travel." Her voice was even but he detected the thread of alarm beneath her words. "Why would Sakarbaal take her to *Romania?*"

"Don't worry," he said. "We'll find her."

"I won't let her die." Her fingers curled around the hilt of her katana, but he had the strongest sensation she was unaware of her action. "I didn't save her once to let her down now."

"You won't let her down. I'll bring her back safely."

Her gaze sharpened on him. "I'm going with you, Azrael. I can bring her back myself."

He didn't want this conversation now, not in front of a couple of vamps and Nate. "We'll talk about this later." He needed to return to his villa to arm himself.

And ensure Rowan was somewhere safe.

"No." She didn't raise her voice. Didn't sound belligerent or outraged. She sounded as though she was having a perfectly reasonable discussion. Didn't she understand there was *nothing to discuss?*

"We're leaving." He took a stride towards her and then stopped dead as she raised her hand in a classic gesture to halt.

"Azrael." Her voice was gentle. She appeared supremely unaware that they were the center of attention. "Please believe me. I understand your concerns. But I must go to Romania. I have to help save my friend and my—brother." She hitched in a breath, as if until now she hadn't thought of Brad as her brother.

Damn it, he understood her reasoning, too. But that didn't mean he had any intention of allowing her to go.

"I need your word that you won't try and stop me," she said, shattering his pounding thoughts. "Otherwise I'll have to get to Romania some other way—with Nico."

Adrenaline flooded through him, without reason, as though he was about to launch into battle. He sucked in a sharp breath, but the shot of oxygen didn't help, didn't ease the violent hammer of his heart or the primal danger spiking through his brain.

It wasn't rage that she refused to obey his word. If only that was all it was.

This was worse. So much worse.

The room contracted, faded, blinding him to everything but Rowan. And within a second she also vanished as his cursed vision sucked him into its relentless vortex.

Rowan, brandishing her bloodied katana, in a deadly battle with Sakarbaal. Red and gold flames licked around the great stone walls. It was the dungeons of the castle in Romania.

Sakarbaal plunged his sword through Rowan's heart and she staggered backwards, crimson staining her jade sweater. For a second she looked directly at him, her green eyes filled with shock and something else. Something he wanted so fucking desperately but something he knew now could never be his.

He tried to reach her, to save her, but she stumbled back, and the fire claimed her. All he could hear was the roar of the flames, the laugh of the vampire, and the petrified screams of the woman he had failed when she needed him most.

CHAPTER 37

ROWAN

*R*owan expected Azrael to disagree with her decision. But he didn't say anything. Wild terror flashed across his face and raw agony glowed in his eyes, as primal fear pulsed from him in wretched waves. She had the frightening certainly that while his body remained rooted in the present, his soul had vanished to another time and place.

His unearthly silence rocked her more than any words he could have said. She darted towards him and cupped his jaw between her palms. His skin was oddly clammy, and his harsh breaths scorched her face.

She was dimly aware of Nate's voice, demanding to know what the fuck was going on. But Azrael ignored the other archangel and gripped her hips in a punishing embrace.

She knew he was going to teleport, knew there was nothing she could do to prevent it. But now, unlike a few seconds ago, she was his willing partner.

They materialized in the living room of his villa, but his grip didn't loosen. The savage gleam in his eyes didn't lessen and then he ground out one tortured word.

"No."

His erratic breathing eased, and terror no longer pounded in the air between them. She traced her thumbs in a gentle arc over his autocratic cheekbones and the tension seeped from his rigid muscles.

He held her as if their lives depended on it.

"Azrael." Her voice was soft. She didn't know what had happened back at Nico's, but something had. And until she knew what it was, neither she nor Azrael could move on from this moment. "Tell me."

He bit out a harsh laugh. "There's nothing to tell. Nothing to discuss. You're staying here."

"You know I have to go."

His arms wound around her waist. If she'd been pure human, her bones would've shattered. But he didn't appear to realize, and his burning gaze bore into her, searching for secrets she didn't know existed.

"It won't happen." His voice was brutal, but she had the strangest conviction that he wasn't responding to her gentle rebuttal. "It's not written in stone. Fate can be altered."

Unease whispered through her. He sounded as though he was speaking literally. As if he confronted a power she knew nothing about. "Fate?"

His gaze roved over her face before once again pinning her with a laser sharp look. "You're safe as long as you stay here. I won't allow you to die."

"I know you won't." Her hands slid to his shoulders and she gripped him, trying to force him back to the present. Because although he no longer radiated that bone-grinding fear, he still hadn't wholly returned to her. "I have no intention of giving Sakarbaal the satisfaction of watching me die."

She'd meant to lighten his mood but instead rage whipped across his expression, darkening his eyes. "This isn't a joke, Rowan."

He all but spat the words at her and for the first time fear uncoiled deep in her gut. Not fear of what he might do to her. But an inexplicable fear of this strange intensity that consumed him.

"Then what is it?" She pressed her palm against his heart. "You can't know for sure that I'll die if I come with you to Romania. I could just as easily have an accident here and die. You know it's true."

He bared his teeth and actually growled, and the savage look was back in his eyes. "I saw, Rowan. It's never happened like this before, but fuck it, this time there's something I can do about it. This time I *will* change the future." He grabbed her arms as if he feared she might vanish if he loosened his grip. "If you stay here then your destiny is irrevocably rewritten. *The vision is not infallible.*"

A chill of foreboding inched along her spine. "You had a vision—of my death?"

"It's my curse." He glared at her and she replayed his last tortured words through her mind.

This time there's something I can do about it. This time I will change the future.

The truth came to her in a blinding wave. He'd lost someone he cared about in the past. Someone whose death he'd foreseen and been unable to prevent. And he didn't want the same thing happening to her.

It was a bittersweet revelation, and although she shouldn't care that he'd loved other women in his past the knowledge still stung.

"Did you tell her of your vision?"

A frown flicked over his brow, momentarily narrowing his eyes, as though he didn't have the first idea what she was asking.

She took a calming breath that didn't calm her at all. There was a reason for her question, and soon he would see that. "The woman you loved. Did you tell her of your vision, so she was forewarned?"

"What woman?" The words punched into her mind, but it was the undertow of bafflement in his voice that really stunned her. "I've never fallen. There's never been a… woman I loved."

She didn't miss his hesitation. Or the way his gaze momentarily dropped from hers. And couldn't help replaying his words like an addictive refrain.

I've never fallen.

But there wasn't time to savor those words. Even if they wound around her heart and flooded through her bloodstream. Azrael had never fallen in the past. He might still be unable to voice how he felt about her to her face, but his actions were everything.

"Then who are you talking about? Whose death did you foresee?" She didn't know why it was so important for him to tell her, she only knew that it was.

"It doesn't matter." The words were savage. "It was long ago."

She crossed her arms and threaded her fingers through his, where he still gripped her biceps. Whatever had happened might have occurred long ago, but the gleam of madness in his eyes proved the memory was still vivid in his mind.

But it was more than that. He didn't have to say anything for her to know he was eaten up by guilt by whatever had happened. And the guilt was misplaced. It wasn't his fault that he had visions of death. And it wasn't his fault if people died in the manner he'd foreseen.

He wasn't responsible. She had to make him see that.

"It does matter. You can't take the blame for something that's beyond your control. Just because you see something doesn't mean it's within your power to forewarn."

"It was within my power to forewarn." He ripped his hands from her and swung around but didn't storm off as she'd half feared. "I should have known—should have done something. But I was blinded by my devotion for *her.*"

Pain seared her heart and she molded her body against his

back, nestling her cheek against his shoulder. He didn't push her away, but the coiled tension in his body vibrated like caged lightning.

She didn't say anything. Just wrapped her arms around him in a loose embrace. To let him know she was there. That she would always be there, for as long as he needed her.

A tortured breath raked through him. "Our goddess created all her archangels with the express wish for us to worship at her feet. In my eyes, she could do no wrong, even though she hated the fact some archangels fell in love with mortals. That some even had children with their mortal beloved."

Fragments of myths and legends stirred in her mind.

"The Nephilim?" Weren't they cursed? But Azrael spoke of them as if they had been dearly loved.

"Yes." His voice was bitter. "Back in those times there was an advanced civilization where we made our home, and archangels lived openly on Earth." His hand covered hers where they clasped at his waist. A simple gesture yet somehow profound. "The visions began as half-forgotten dreams, but after a decade or so they became more frequent. Until I could no longer dismiss them as nightmares but accept them for what they really were. A prophecy of an apocalyptic future."

"But how did you know they were prophetic? Did you often have visions of the future?"

"I've been cursed with only two recurring visions in my life. Until now."

Shivers chased over her arms. She'd assumed he often saw glimpses of the future. To know it was so rare made the fact he'd foreseen her own death somehow more significant.

"What did you see?" Her voice was hushed.

"Devastation swept across the face of the planet, wiping out most of humanity. For years I believed I was merely seeing the inevitable destruction caused by Earth resetting her celestial clock. The fall of that ancient civilization had been foretold for millennia that this would occur. Long before archangels were created."

She'd grown up among those whom humans would consider immortal. But Azrael spoke of mysteries hidden deep in prehistory. Events that had become little more than myths and legends. Yet he had lived through them. The lifespan of the vampires she knew were insignificant compared to how long Azrael had walked the Earth.

"Even you couldn't stop something so elemental." Her voice was gentle, hoping she could make him see he couldn't possibly be held accountable for such a catastrophic event.

He turned in her arms, and the despair in his eyes squeezed her heart.

"No, I couldn't have stopped it." His voice was hollow. "We knew it was coming which is why it took me so long to realize I was seeing more in those visions than the decimation of humankind."

"What more did you see?" But in her heart, she'd already guessed. The Nephilim had died, too.

"It was an accepted fact among archangels that when the time came, we'd save our beloveds and our Nephilim. There was another planet in this solar system then, Nibiru, the place of our creation. They'd be safe there. *They would survive.*"

But they hadn't survived. His gaze was fierce, compelling her to ask the question locked in her throat. She didn't want to make him relive the agony of that time. But it seemed he had never left. She swallowed and pushed out the words. "What happened?"

"Our goddess appeared in my later visions." His lips flattened and eyes went scarily glassy. "The glory of her love for her archangels glowed throughout the scenes of fire and flood. She embraced us, as she always did, and the devastation on Earth was left behind."

He closed his eyes, and she could only imagine what he saw in his mind's eye. Silence echoed between them until he finally looked at her once again. "I took her presence to mean she'd accepted the Nephilim. All I felt from her in those visions was benevolence. I misinterpreted them because I didn't go deep enough. If I had, I would have seen what my visions were really trying to tell me. That she planned to use the apocalypse to wipe out the Nephilim."

"You couldn't have known that." Desperate, she searched for elusive words that would make him see the truth. "Hindsight doesn't mean you missed something."

His smile was beautiful, and so sad she wanted to weep.

"The signs were always there. They weren't hidden. I chose not to see because it would have meant everything I cherished about our goddess… was false."

"But…" For a second she floundered. How could she make him see it wasn't his fault? His goddess was the only one responsible for her own actions. Just the way Sakarbaal was. "You weren't the one who killed them, Azrael."

"I spent years searching the archaic ruins of long dead cultures, trying to piece together forgotten knowledge. I hoped to find the answer as to why I was haunted by those images of death. Although we'd planned for their safety, there had to be a reason why I was being shown an alternate future. I could have warned the others. I *should've* warned them that I'd had visions of the Nephilim dying. If I had, we wouldn't have responded when *she* called us home to Nibiru. But I didn't, and none of us imagined it was a trap. She immobilized us, in the one place where she could wield such power over all of us at once—the place of our creation. And we could do nothing while the Nephilim were destroyed."

Azrael

HE'D NEVER SPOKEN of those visions before. Because who could he tell? A fellow archangel? How would that make anything right?

But when she'd asked, it had all come pounding through his brain, as if he'd experienced the vision and horrific aftermath just days ago, instead of eleven thousand years. When he'd opened that wound, Rowan was a salve, listening to his confession, and not condemning him for his sin.

But now she would see how futile it was to tempt fate. If she went to Romania, she would die. If she stayed here, she would live.

There were no maybes.

"I should have done something, Rowan. Instead I believed in the word of our goddess and because of me the Nephilim died." So many times those words had haunted him. But he'd never spoken them aloud.

"Azrael." Her voice was soft, persuasive, and sank into his mind and soul like a soothing balm. Now she understood. Now she would no longer fight him on this, because there was nothing to fight. He would give no quarter. "My precious archangel."

His heart jerked at her endearment. He'd been called many things over millennia, by countless women, but nothing had ever pierced him as deeply as those whispered words from Rowan.

He cradled her face between his hands. She gave the impression of being so fragile, so easily broken. And although he would never allow her to face danger again, he also knew the truth.

She wasn't as vulnerable as she looked. Her delicate human veneer hid a core of vampiric steel. And he would have her no other way.

"I won't pretend to understand how you feel about what happened," she said, still in that soft, mesmeric voice. Gods, if only he could stay here forever with her in his arms. Why was that too much to ask? "But how could anything have changed, if you'd told the other archangels of your vision?"

Jagged splinters of reality cracked his hypnotic trance. How could she even ask that?

"It would have changed everything. We could have transported the Nephilim before our goddess called us home. We could have *saved* them." Hadn't she understood anything he'd told her?

"Do you believe your goddess would have allowed that?"

His instant response that his goddess could have fucked herself choked in his throat. Because for the first time he considered that. Doubt crawled through his mind.

No, she never would have allowed it.

For centuries their goddess had existed in blissful ignorance of the existence of the Nephilim. Had been oblivious to the fact that some of her archangels had not only fallen irrevocably in love with humans but waited for their beloved to be reborn life after life.

But when she'd discovered the truth, her wrath had been mighty. She had bided her time for the inevitable destruction on Earth to align with her plans, but if that hadn't worked would she have discarded her single-minded determination to eradicate the Nephilim from the annals of history?

His hands fisted, and Rowan's hair tangled around his fingers. "At the very least," he ground out between his teeth, "it would have given us all a fighting chance."

She didn't answer. But she didn't have to. He stared into her oh-so-deceptively-innocent eyes. How had he ever imagined she was anything but a warrior born and bred?

A warrior who used words to cut to the heart of the issue, as easily as she used her katana.

Maybe, if he had understood the full impact of that vision eleven thousand years ago and shared it with his fellow archangels, they could have saved the Nephilim. Or maybe the harsh reality was that the Nephilim had never been destined to survive.

Where had all these *maybes* come from?

The stark truth was he would never know. But for the first time he accepted that his misinterpretation wasn't—had never been—the only factor that had decided the fate of the Nephilim. He might just as well blame himself for the loss of the ancient civilization that had taught archangels so much in their youth. Or shoulder responsibility for the near extinction of humankind that had occurred as a result of the Earth's upheaval.

Something deep in his heart unfurled. As if by sharing the great error he had made, had somehow allowed him to gain perspective.

Rowan didn't say a word. He tightened his grip on her hair, but she didn't gasp in pain. But then, she wouldn't.

"This time there was no mistake." His voice was little more than a growl.

She didn't pretend to misunderstand him. She knew damn well he was referring to the vision he'd had at Nico's.

"What you saw might not be literal." Her words were still gentle, still soothing and if he didn't know better, he'd imagine she was about to capitulate to his every demand. "Maybe it was a vision of how things could be—not how they will be. You said yourself it's not written in stone."

Sakarbaal had plunged his sword through Rowan's heart. How much more literal did she want to get?

"And you told me Fate couldn't be cheated." Fine, so she hadn't said that in so many words. But that had been her intent. And damn her, he'd seen her point. To the degree where he could now face those events of the past without acidic guilt searing his soul.

Yes, he would always regret. The guilt would never entirely die. But finally, by spilling his guts, he'd been able to look at what had happened and see it through unprejudiced eyes.

Rowan's eyes.

But did she seriously believe, for even a second, he would take her to the place where he'd foreseen her murder?

"Maybe not," she conceded, and for one misguided moment he thought he'd won. "But you've given me foreknowledge. Knowing of your vision I can make an informed choice of staying here or going to Romania. Maybe Fate can't be cheated. But maybe sometimes it can be… manipulated. Why not? Look at me. I'm living proof sometimes things can be changed in ways you can't imagine."

He didn't need to ask her whether, with foreknowledge, she'd changed her mind. She was as determined to go to Romania now as she had been back at Nico's.

She couldn't leave this planet without his help. He could leave her here and there was nothing she could do about it. And when he returned, would she ever again look at him the way she was now?

Would she ever again confide in him, take him in her arms, tell him he was *her precious archangel?*

Dread seeped through his veins, but it was mixed with a wild sense of pride. Pride that Rowan, despite everything, was still determined to face her vampire lord—*her father*—to exact justice.

It wouldn't come to that. He'd protect her from Sakarbaal in Romania whether she knew it or not. Still gripping her hair, he looked into her eyes and saw his own… mortality.

He wasn't a mortal, and in all his long life he'd never come close to falling. But she was his vulnerability and he was inextricably bound to her, his warrior dhampir.

His nemesis.

CHAPTER 38

AZRAEL

The castle loomed in front of Azrael as he and Rowan, and Nate with Nico, teleported into Romania. But as they breached the forest, the eerie fog that had clouded his mind the last time he'd come here evaporated, and the castle sure as hell wasn't an abandoned ruin.

The half dozen or so luxurious sports cars parked on the castle forecourt scraped along his nerves. They were a discordant visual reminder that the vampire he had long ago hunted was far from the primitive bloodsucker he recalled.

The grounds were well tended. The castle façade well maintained. No pitiful dhampirs lurched from the shadows to prevent their progress and the midday sun penetrated weak rays through the cloud-laden sky.

"Let me guess." Rowan trailed her fingers over the bonnet of a Porsche. "Romanian dhampirs aren't kept in chains or used as blood slaves for the Elector High Council."

He wasn't sure whether she was asking a question or stating a fact.

"More mind games," Nico said. Tolerating daylight was apparently one of the advantages of being an Ancient One.

Rowan thinned her lips. And Azrael knew the fact she'd been taken in by yet another lie merely fueled her determination to exact retribution.

The great arched timber doors, with their huge iron hinges, swung open. Azrael slid his fingers over the hilt of his katana as two figures, dressed for the frigid weather, strolled towards them.

Their approach wasn't inherently aggressive and that alone was enough to raise his hackles. Where was the preternatural security? All he'd seen was cameras and traps. Sure, they were top of the range and no mortal could hope to get anywhere near the gates without triggering a dozen alarms. But even if they'd been enhanced by vampiric technology, he'd still been expecting some kind of army to greet their arrival.

Not two... he double checked their auras. They were *human*.

"Someone's not expecting us." Nate's caustic remark hung in the frosty air. "I'll take the one on the right."

Before he could tell Nate he wanted info from them, the one on the right dropped to the snow crusted ground in response to Nate's mental blast. With a muttered curse, he felled the second human before she could draw a breath. Rowan stepped over the prone body without a second glance and strode towards the open doors.

He was by her side before she crossed the threshold. He might have conceded to her wish to accompany them, but he'd be damned if he'd let her enter the enemy's lair before he'd checked it out.

The dank decay of the Dark Ages was gone. Intricate Persian rugs covered the flagstone floor and elegant antique furniture and artwork graced the interior. All hiding the bloody past. This display of wealth and opulence grated.

Almost as much as the arrogance that led Sakarbaal to imagine that here, in the heart of his web, he was safe from immortal interference.

Then again, aside from Azrael, why would any immortal want to confront him? He shot Nico a calculating glance. In all the centuries that had passed, why hadn't the vampire confronted Sakarbaal before now? He'd obviously been keeping track of Sakarbaal's movements.

But before they'd left London, Nico hadn't even argued when Azrael had informed him that Sakarbaal was *his*.

From nowhere, a dozen young warriors appeared. All brandished gleaming weapons and protective gear. All possessed black hair and a striking beauty. Dhampirs. And if everything the Strigoi had said was true—they were also Rowan's half-siblings.

Her katana was drawn but then her eyes widened, and grip slackened, as if she'd just realized she had to fight her own blood to the death. There was silence and then one of the advancing dhampirs stalked forward, blade extended, then spun around and decapitated the warrior next to him.

A rogue?

A roar rang up and the clang of drawn weapons filled the air, but the rogue dhampir ignored it, marching forward and dragging Rowan aside. She gripped his free hand.

He strained to hear their conversation above the clash of swords.

"Christ, Rowan. I thought you were dead," the male said. *Brad?* "I don't know what they've done to Lily. I'd just gone to check on her when I saw you out of the window. I thought I was hallucinating."

As they spoke, two warriors hurled towards them. Azrael whipped out a dagger, slung it in Rowan's direction. It embedded deep through the brain of a dhampir and she decapitated the other warrior without a second's hesitation.

"Is she okay?" Rowan asked. "Can you keep her safe until—?"

"No," Brad said. He chanced another glance at them. Brad looked sick and he knew it had nothing to do with the carnage unfolding around him. "She's not. You need to help her."

Azrael caught the desperate glance she threw his way and jerked his head. *Go.* In his peripheral vision he watched her and Brad race up the curved staircase and relief spiked at the knowledge she was no longer in the midst of the battle.

Nico materialized by his side from a swirling black fog. "The Electors have joined the fun." There was grim satisfaction in his voice. "Nate and I will keep them busy. You go and finish this with Sakarbaal."

He knew how Nico loathed Sakarbaal. Why would he willingly relinquish the chance of destroying the vampire lord himself? Nico bared his fangs, as if he could read the question in Azrael's mind.

"I can't destroy him." The words were bitter. "He Made me, and the bond is unbreakable. Why else do you think I haven't hunted him down and slaughtered him for the bastard he is?"

Empathy for the vampire stirred. It must have wrenched his heart to have admitted that. "I'll get him."

Rowan

ROWAN FOLLOWED Brad into a chamber that, despite the worn stone floors, possessed cutting edge medical equipment. A couple of humans were unconscious on the floor and a makeshift timber stake, in the center of a pile of ash, told its own story.

"As soon as I saw you, I got rid of them." Brad indicated the fallen with a jerk of his head. "She's through here."

She stepped into the adjoining chamber and terror gripped her heart. Lily was propped up on a bed, sweaty, pale and barely conscious. Blood stained the sheets and Rowan gripped Brad's arm.

"Is she—the baby—"

"I don't fucking know." He tossed her a wild look. "I only

glanced in here after I knocked the others out. Then I came for you."

She sheathed her katana and forced her feet to move. She'd rather face an Ancient One in combat than what she feared awaited her in Lily's bed.

"Keep a look out, Brad." Her voice was hoarse. She reached the end of the bed and her heart slammed against her ribs in a panicky tattoo.

Lily's baby, silent and unmoving, lay on the bloodied sheets, still attached to its umbilical cord.

She had no idea what she was supposed to do, but instinct took over. "It's me, Lily," she said, forcing a light tone in her voice. "Rowan." She grabbed a roll of sterilized thread and with shaky fingers tied off the cord before cutting it with her dagger. "You have a beautiful daughter."

Lily made no reply, and still the blood drained from her body.

She glanced over her shoulder at Brad. He'd positioned himself at the door and was alternating between looking out into the corridor and looking back at Lily. He caught her glance and she saw the same horror reflected in his eyes.

She broke her stupefied trance and dragged open drawers, rifling through the contents. She found a pile of soft blankets, and hurriedly wrapped the chilled baby. Was she doing this right?

"Lily." She couldn't help the tinge of hysteria in her voice as she bent over Lily's deathly face. "Look. Here's your daughter." She wedged the bundle between Lily's chest and arm. "I'm going to heal you, Lily. Just hold on. Please hold on." As she spoke, she pulled her amethyst bracelet from her wrist and tugged the necklace over the top of her coat. They were all she had to assist with her weak powers of healing, and deep in her heart she knew they weren't enough.

But she had to try.

"Rowan." The whisper was hoarse as Lily's eyelashes flickered open. Rowan froze and anguished hope surged. "You have to stop this. Stop it for… ever."

"I will." She leaned over the younger woman and held her hand. "You're going to be all right. I promise."

Lily's breath wheezed, a terrifying sound of life escaping. "No. You have to stop *him*. Never let this… happen again."

"I will stop him. But first I have to—"

Lily gripped her hand. It was the grip of a desperate woman, a woman on the brink of death. "Promise me one other thing."

Tears clogged her throat. "Anything."

"Promise me… look after my baby, Rowan. She's human, too. Just like you."

I won't cry. That wouldn't help Lily. "I promise." *And I promise that somehow, some way, I won't let her life be consumed by the need for amber acid.*

Lily's hand slipped from hers. Her head tipped to the side and she looked at her tiny daughter for the first time. The ghost of a smile touched her white lips. "My baby," she whispered. "My beautiful Willow."

Silence quivered in the room after Lily's words. Rowan battled the rising panic that threatened to suffocate her as she desperately recalled every healing ritual she'd studied. But they were futile. Lily was beyond her help now and finally she took the baby—Willow—into her arms.

The emblem of the Enclave was a phoenix sitting in a willow tree. Did Lily know? But the phoenix was not a myth, and she'd do everything in her power to ensure Willow was the last child born during Sakarbaal's existence. She turned around and Brad was staring at her, looking as shell-shocked as she felt. A thousand questions and accusations pounded against her skull but in the end she asked the only one that mattered.

"Why did he bring her here?"

He glanced in the corridor before turning back to her. "Something about wanting backup, even if it was inferior quality." He glared at her. "He was more than happy to bring me to Romania. Turns out he's sent out a call to every Enclave HQ, ordering all dhampirs to be sent here."

Shudders ripped along her spine. What had Nico said? That Sakarbaal wanted to release all the souls he'd harvested at the same time into the astral planes?

Did he intend to include the souls of dhampirs who had not yet *died*?

She'd wondered how Sakarbaal had captured all the dhampir souls over the years. And now, as she stood with the vampire lord's latest child in her arms—*my half-sister*—a horrifying answer came to her.

Dhampirs did not die in their beds. They died while out on assignment. Their bodies were transported back to their nearest HQ and were then disposed of. Sure, they held private memorial services but for all she knew the coffins that entered the crematorium could contain anything.

Or nothing.

"He had them all brought here." She stared at Brad's uncomprehending frown and her suspicion solidified. "Over the last fifty years, Brad. He had every dhampir who died brought here so he could control their souls." Another horrible thought hit her. "But when you die, your soul leaves the body, right?" She'd never much thought about it before, and from the way Brad glowered at her neither had he. "Shit. I think Sakarbaal had all the dhampirs transported here *before they died*. And he's been somehow keeping them alive until the right moment."

"Nothing he's done would surprise me." Brad's glance flickered to the baby before once again focusing on Rowan. "The dhampirs here know a lot more about what's going on than we ever did. It's common knowledge *here* that any dhampir who becomes romantically involved with a human has signed their death warrant. The order comes from Sakarbaal. The Elders in all the HQs are in on it. It's never had anything to do with the

Strigoi, Rowan. That was all part of the web of lies to keep us in line."

She'd guessed as much. "I'm going after him. I need you to stay here and look after Willow."

He recoiled. "I'm not a babysitter."

"No, you're a warrior. You need to make sure Willow's safe. She can't be taken by any of the Enclave's Elders."

He didn't look happy about it, but he didn't try and argue the point. She put Willow in a sterile looking crib and her heart ached. Such a tiny little thing. Such a tragic heritage.

She'd spend the rest of her life making up to Willow for everything she had lost.

Rowan kissed the baby on her forehead, drew her katana and left the chamber.

CHAPTER 39

AZRAEL

*S*akarbaal was in the dungeons. But it wasn't the dungeon of Azrael's vision. It was a high-tech laboratory and seven transparent columns soared from flagstone floor to scrubbed stone ceiling, each one filled with twisting orange-gold flames.

The vampire's piercing emerald eyes glinted. They looked nothing like Rowan's gorgeous green eyes. But even as he denied the truth to himself, he could see the likeness between them.

The luxuriant black hair. The aristocratic bone structure and striking beauty. The air of otherworldly power that he'd so long failed to identify in Rowan.

Sakarbaal curled his lip. "The *uniilă* returns at last."

"Did you ever doubt it?" He flexed his fingers around the hilt of his katana. Unlike nine hundred years ago when he'd burst in on Sakarbaal, he wasn't filled with fury and disgust and revulsion. An icy calm filled his mind. He was here for Rowan. For the dhampirs Sakarbaal had sired.

The dhampirs he had slain in the past.

He was even here for Nico. And this time he would not fail.

Sakarbaal stroked his thumb over the bejeweled hilt of his

sword. It was a deliberately idle gesture as though he considered Azrael's presence little more than a minor irritation.

"Tell me. Did you enjoy fucking my daughter? I taught her well in the arts of seduction. A pity she failed her final assignment, but she served my needs to the best of her ability."

His words, intended to provoke, had the opposite effect. Because it was clear Sakarbaal had no idea she was still alive.

He forced a derisive laugh. "Was that the best you could do, bloodsucker? Send a girl to try and subdue me with shit you obtained from the Guardians?"

Sakarbaal responded with a mirthless smile that showed his gleaming fangs. "The Guardians have a vested interest in my plans, archangel." He made the word sound as offensive as *uniilă*. "They also covet entry into the celestial heavens as they believe it's a gateway to parallel universes. Foolishly they assumed I would share my knowledge with them in exchange for road testing their experimental serum… on you."

For a second Sakarbaal's comment threw him off balance. Had the vampire approached the Guardians or was it the other way around?

He kept his expression blank. "As you see, it didn't work."

Sakarbaal shrugged. "You're here now. And you will not be leaving."

He unfurled his wings from the glamour and launched himself at the vampire. Sakarbaal didn't waste time meeting his thrust. He dissolved into black vapor, his mocking laugh echoing in Azrael's ears.

"Coward." Azrael ground the word between his teeth, as he flung a mental blast around the chamber. It ricocheted off the stone walls and slammed back into his chest with enough force to rattle his ribs.

Two could play that game. He flung up a glamour to conceal his presence but as the vampire continued to shift from solid form into vapor, frustration stirred deep in his gut.

Even when his katana sliced through flesh, it was no longer flesh and no blood was spilled. They could circle each other like this for eternity, and neither would be the victor.

To liquefy a brain, he needed to get a secure lock. But every time his mental probe brushed Sakarbaal, the vampire dissolved.

There had to be way around it. If he could paralyze Sakarbaal with a mental thrust and simultaneously cripple him with a physical blow, theoretically it would give him a precious second while Sakarbaal was immobilized to finish this once and for all.

He waited for the moment. Sakarbaal was clever but he was arrogant, and his maneuvers weren't as unpredictable as he imagined.

Almost there.

The door to the dungeon lab crashed open and ice speared through his heart as Rowan burst through, her bloodied katana raised. What the hell was she doing? She'd gone off with Brad to help her friend. He hadn't for a second thought Rowan would leave her. He'd thought she was safe. But instead she'd charged into the one place he feared he might be unable to protect her.

Sakarbaal materialized just feet in front of her and Azrael catapulted a blast of energy directly into the vampire's brain. It bounced off his skull, as if he'd just tried to neutralize a fellow archangel.

He hadn't fucking expected that reaction. Sakarbaal might be an arrogant son of a bitch but he also had formidable power.

With an infuriated curse he rematerialized next to Rowan.

"You survived the archangel's wrath." Bizarrely, Sakarbaal sounded pleased. "Your warrior soul glows brightly, Rowan. The braver the dhampir, the more intrinsically the phoenix essence bonds." He flashed a mocking smile. "Twenty-seven years on the mortal plane is the optimal age. Any longer and we discovered the phoenix connection degrades."

"You bastard." Rowan's voice vibrated with rage and grief. "You won't get away with any of this." Before he fully realized her intention she leaped at Sakarbaal, but at the last second she twisted sideways, as if she'd hit an invisible wall.

As a look of shock spread across her face and Sakarbaal's scornful laugh echoed around the chamber, Azrael knew the truth. He'd once joked with her that the bond of blood wasn't everything, and she'd laughingly disagreed. But she'd been right. Because she couldn't kill the vampire lord any more than Nico could.

"Get out of here, Rowan." His voice was harsh as he shoved her back towards the door. "Leave this to me."

Sakarbaal raised his sword, his focus only partially on Rowan but his intent clear. Instinctively Azrael spread his wings, a protective gesture, and then the world turned a crimson maelstrom of unimaginable agony as the vampire's blade severed his feathers.

He doubled over, clinging onto his katana only by sheer instinct. Every feather throbbed, every nerve in his body screamed, and pain such as he had never imagined stabbed through his brain, distorting his vision.

Through the wild cacophony that thundered in his ears, he heard her horrified scream. But even as he tried to straighten, tried to face the vampire, disbelief hammered through his crippled senses.

How had the vampire's blade sliced so easily through his wing? Only the blade crafted by an immortal of the highest echelons could achieve such a thing. How in hell could the vampire have stolen such a weapon?

"Fuck you, bloodsucker." Fury and terror warred for dominance in Rowan's voice and as he staggered backwards, as he tried to calm his mind enough to heal his injuries, he saw her slash her katana through the nearest transparent column.

"No, Rowan!" His yell was too late, as fire burst from its constraints and sucked greedily at the oxygen filling the chamber. Rowan, her lips pulled back in a snarl, backed away from

Sakarbaal who no longer appeared amused by events, and struck out at a second column.

Red and gold flames spilled into the chamber, snaking along the floor and up the walls in an unnatural wave. He glared through the vibrant flames, where the shadow of Sakarbaal stalked Rowan.

He'd get the vamp now. While he was focused on Rowan. He pushed forward through the fire, his damaged wing dragging a bloodied trail along the floor. She danced like a possessed fire goddess between the columns, destroying them one by one, taunting Sakarbaal and causing his guts to knot. Why wouldn't she just get the hell out of it?

"That's enough, dhampir." Sakarbaal's low hiss caused the flames to leap higher and as she once again tried to reach him with her katana, the vampire plunged his immortal-forged sword through her heart.

CHAPTER 40

AZRAEL

*T*ime ceased to exist. The world shrank. All Azrael could see was Rowan as she looked through the flames at him, her beautiful green eyes filled with shock, with disbelief... *with love.*

Crimson stained her sweater as Sakarbaal brutally wrenched his sword from her body. Still clutching her katana in one hand Rowan pressed her other to her breast, and her blood gushed over her fingers.

This wasn't happening. *This couldn't be happening.* He had told her of the vision and therefore he had changed her destiny.

This isn't her fucking destiny.

But he remained rooted to the burning floor, unable to move, unable to breathe, unable to believe the evidence of his eyes as Rowan, *his Rowan*, the woman who possessed his heart and soul staggered back into the depths of the raging furnace.

Denial clawed through his mind, but his throat was locked and all he could hear was the roar of the flames, the laugh of the vampire, and the petrified screams of...

His beloved.

The knowledge erupted from deep within his soul. Erupted

and flooded through him and he teleported into the flames to save her—except he remained welded to the spot, his injuries too severe.

"*No.*" He didn't know whether the roar was only in his mind or whether it rocked the walls of the chamber, but he leaped for Sakarbaal and the vampire's blood coated his blade before the bastard turned to vapor.

Blindly, he blundered through the flames, his wings smoldering as they dragged on the floor. Where the hell was she? She had fallen right here. What had Sakarbaal done with her?

"A pity about Rowan," the vampire taunted, rematerializing for a fleeting moment before once again vanishing. His disembodied voice clawed along Azrael's senses. "Her soul was strong. She would have continued to serve me well forever."

Rage pounded and he embraced it. Because rage he could deal with. Rage he could channel into hunting the vampire. Rage would sustain him and keep at bay the screaming vortex of insanity that offered sweet oblivion within its bottomless black depths.

Eternity passed. He'd been battling the vampire forever. There was no past and he had no future, but nothing else mattered. He'd drawn blood several times, as had the vampire, but nothing fatal and he had the detached certainty they could battle for all time and still no killing blow would fall.

"Give it up, Archangel." Sakarbaal materialized a few feet from him, sweat dripping, clothes ripped and bloodstained. Azrael lunged, hacked through flesh and bone and the vampire once again turned to vapor.

"Go." The vampire panted from behind and he swung around, chest heaving. The vampire's damaged arm hung at his side. "You can't destroy me any more than I can destroy you. There's no need for this endless foolishness."

He didn't waste his breath responding. Sakarbaal had murdered Rowan. The thought hammered in time with his heart, and again madness beckoned on a not-so-distant horizon.

How tempting. But first he would exact justice. No matter how long it took.

Behind Sakarbaal the fire grew brighter. Unbearably so. He reared back, unable to look away, and inexplicably the knot in his chest tightened.

Shadows moved within the flames. Sakarbaal belatedly realized his attention had slipped and he frowned before glancing over his shoulder.

He froze.

From the flames Rowan emerged, black hair tumbling down her naked back, her skin unscathed, and in her hands she held her katana—now a weapon forged of fire.

He stared, mesmerized. *Rowan didn't die?* Vaguely he was aware she wasn't alone. That the dazzling dhampir soul he'd encountered on the astral planes was by her side and above Rowan's head appeared a fiery phoenix.

Rowan looked directly at Sakarbaal. The vampire lord appeared to have lost his power of speech as he stared at her as if she was something from his worst nightmare.

"Hello, Father," she said softly. "My mother named me well." And then she plunged her katana of fire through his heart.

Sakarbaal staggered back, a look of indescribable shock etching his features. Azrael leaped forward, swung his katana and decapitated the vampire, but still the look of utter disbelief remained fixed on his face as his head fell to the floor.

He stepped over the rapidly decomposing body, his gaze never leaving Rowan's.

"I thought I'd lost you." His voice was rough, and his glance dropped to her breasts. No gaping wound marred her flesh. Yet he'd seen the vampire thrust his sword through her heart. It was impossible she could have healed such a devastating injury so swiftly.

She couldn't have healed it at all. He couldn't have healed her. The wound had been fatal. Even for a dhampir.

"You did." Her voice was still soft, and he pulled off his coat and gently draped it across her shoulders. She gave a faint smile as she slid her arms into the sleeves. "I died, Azrael."

His heart jackknifed, although he couldn't think why. She couldn't have died otherwise she wouldn't be here now, in front of him, wearing his coat for gods' sakes.

"No." His voice was thick. Was she telling him she was a spirit? And now that Sakarbaal had been dispatched to his own brand of hell she was leaving?

He gripped her arms. She felt warm, alive. He wouldn't believe she'd died. Wouldn't believe he was going to lose her again. *I won't allow you to leave me again.*

She pressed her palms against his chest and his heart beat for her, and only her.

"My body perished in the flames. I felt it, Azrael. But after the first few seconds of agony it changed. The fire was still there but I was outside my body. And then I wasn't here at all. I was somewhere else, with the phoenix—somewhere beautiful and tranquil."

The astral planes where, after the death of its body, the soul retreated to heal itself from mortal trauma. It still didn't mean she had *died*.

"That's where Belinda found me." She turned to the dhampir soul who no longer emanated such hopeless desperation. "She discovered what Sakarbaal was doing, what he intended for her. She took the only way out she could."

Had the soul of Belinda sought him out because she knew of his connection to Rowan?

He loosened his grip on her and glanced at the phoenix. It was circling the lab and left a fiery trail in its wake.

"The phoenix is free," Rowan said, following his gaze. "Its essence was trapped in the columns."

Nate, followed by Nico, entered the chamber and it was only when they stopped dead and stared at her that he realized the flames had drawn back from her, encircling them all in a fire-free sphere.

"It's done," Nate said with a fleeting glance at the ash strewn floor. His glance took in Azrael's ripped and bloodied wing and he visibly blanched before fixing his gaze onto the floor. He appeared unable, or unwilling, to look directly at Rowan. Nico, on the other hand, couldn't take his eyes from her.

"What happened to you?" Nico said. The faintest hint of awe threaded through his words and Azrael took an instinctive step closer to her. "I can no longer... *feel* you."

The spirit of Belinda enveloped her in an ethereal hug, and he caught a sense of peace drifting from her as she slowly faded. The phoenix swooped low, brushed its wings along Rowan's face and then soared through the open door and vanished.

She looked shell-shocked, as if mystical secrets had been shared during those few brief seconds. She didn't reply to Nico but turned to look at him.

"When I died in the fire," she hesitated, as if she couldn't find the words to explain. He gripped her arms, and even through the leather of his coat could feel the heat of her skin and although it couldn't be possible, the heat sank into his blood like a healing elixir. She blinked, as though emerging from a trance. "The phoenix essence in my blood, in my soul, swept through my body like an internal blaze. It was like I was being purified. So I could be reborn."

Like the phoenix, she had been consumed by flame and risen again from the ashes. He simply stared at her, drinking in the sight of her face and eyes and hair. But none of the external mattered. It wasn't her physical beauty that had ensnared his heart and captured his soul. Rowan had returned and he'd been given a second chance to deserve her love.

"I sense nothing from you." Nico sounded unnerved. "You're

no longer a dhampir, Rowan. My blood doesn't flow in your veins. Neither does Sakarbaal's."

She didn't move from his embrace. "My mother named me Rowan." Her voice was little more than a whisper. *"To prevent the dead from rising.* That's what she wrote in her journal. But isn't that what I've just done? Risen from the dead? *What am I, Azrael?"*

Before he could reassure her that he didn't care if she was now a full blood vampire, she glanced at Nico. "Sakarbaal's dhampirs he sired over the last fifty years are in stasis chambers. They're not dead, but I don't know if they can be revived."

Nico inhaled a long breath. "We'll bring Octavia and her team here. If anyone can save them, she can."

"Let's get out of here." Azrael wrapped his arm around her shoulders. They'd collect Brad and her friend Lily and then he had no intention of returning to Romania again.

CHAPTER 41

ROWAN

*M*eg turned her gaze from Brad to Azrael and finally to Willow who lay peacefully in Rowan's arms. She hadn't known where else for Azrael to take them but Meg's private apartment in Sloane Square, since there was no telling what reception they'd get back at the London HQ. Meg, uncharacteristically, had listened without interruption as she'd given her a brief summary of what had occurred in Romania.

She'd downplayed the whole resurrection bit.

"Lily's parents should know what happened to her." She glanced at the sheet wrapped form of Lily, who lay on Meg's chic sofa. Of course, her parents couldn't be told the whole truth, but would it be kinder to let them know of their daughter's death, rather than have them wonder, forever, if she was still alive somewhere? Could they ever be told they had a grandchild, a child who was only half-human, a child who—at least for now—was addicted to a preternatural cocktail containing the essence of phoenix?

She had no doubt that Octavia and her team—and maybe even some of the Enclave's scientists—would create a viable substitute for when the stockpiles ran out. And if, as Sakarbaal had implied, a dhampir's physiology began to reject the phoenix essence after twenty-seven years, there was hope that at least she and her half-siblings would not be forever hooked on that element of amber acid.

Meg blinked. "There are a great many things the Enclave will have to do now Sakarbaal has been destroyed."

"Starting with hunting down any of the Electors who escaped Romania," Brad said, the savage note in his voice a sure indicator that he'd willingly spend the rest of his life hunting those members of the High Council who'd fled the castle.

Meg stepped closer and frowned down at the sleeping baby. Instinctively her hold on Willow tightened, even though Meg had made no move to take the baby from her. Or even touch her.

"You were barely an hour old when I first saw you," Meg said. There was an odd note in her voice, as if looking at Willow brought back nostalgic memories. "I wasn't close to your mother, Rowan. But when I looked at you—she must have seen some-thing in my eyes. Because it was then she made me promise."

Her heart ached for the mother she had never known. Azrael slid his arm around her waist, offering his silent support. Had her mother requested the same deathbed promise from Meg as Lily had from her?

"She made you promise to look after me?"

Meg made an expressive gesture with her hand. "Of course. But I had already decided you would be mine. That promise was unnecessary." Then she sighed. "She was lucid in those moments, with no medical personnel around. She asked me to find her journal that had been taken from her, and to ensure that you had it when you were older."

The journal she'd given Lily to read. The journal that had roused Lily's suspicions.

For all the good it had done her.

"The edict from the Elector High Council, that dhampirs were not permitted to keep anything from their mothers, was presented as an act of mercy. The Enclave was their only family for surely there was no place for them in human society." Meg gave a derisive sniff. "When I held your mother's journal, and knew I would go against the Elders wishes, it struck me. The real reason why they never allowed the children any personal mementoes. It was to keep you isolated."

In their gilded prison.

"Your mother said she hoped you would one day understand. I did not know what she could mean. I read the journal, Rowan." There was no hint of apology in Meg's voice. "There was nothing in it I could see that was so important. And yet," she hesitated. "Her last entries haunted me. Over the years they fed the seeds of doubt I had about the Ancient Ones. Yet it gives me little pleasure to know my suspicions were not unfounded."

She stared into the sleeping baby's face. She possessed black hair and Rowan knew she would also have green eyes and a striking beauty. She had no journal of her mother's, but she would know the truth of her heritage through Rowan.

The whole truth.

Rowan's mother hadn't known the truth, but she'd tried to explain something inexplicable to her as yet unborn child. It was her mother's words that had jolted Lily into refusing her medication. And those same words had pushed Rowan into breaking into the Enclave's medical records and discovering the link between the dhampirs and their rare blood type.

Maybe, after all, her mother's journal had helped to save her life. And allowed her to finally lay to rest the innocent souls who had been killed by Sakarbaal.

Goodbye, Steven.

"You won't be returning to the Enclave?" Meg asked.

She wanted to stay with Azrael. But if that wasn't her destiny then she still wouldn't return to the place she'd called home for the last twenty-four years. "No."

Meg held out her arms. "Then give me the child. I will ensure she comes to no harm."

She stiffened, even though she knew Meg would never snatch Willow from her. "Can I have a moment alone with Azrael, Meg?"

Was it her imagination or did he tense by her side? Meg shrugged and she and Brad left the room. Azrael turned to face her, his hands molding her hips.

Her heart ached as she looked once again at his broken, bloodied wing. He'd assured her it would mend in time. Had even told her it didn't matter if his wing was permanently deformed. But all she could think whenever she caught sight of it was—it was all her fault. He'd lost half his wing because he'd protected her from Sakarbaal's blade.

She knew, in her heart, that he loved her. Even though he had never said the words. But did he love her enough to accept Lily's child in their life?

Azrael

UNEASE STIRRED deep in his heart. Why was Rowan looking at him as if this was the last time they'd be together?

He battened down the overwhelming urge to contact Nate and get him to teleport them to his planet. At least there he knew she couldn't escape him. At least there he'd have all the time in the universe to make her see that she belonged by his side.

"Azrael." Her voice was husky. "I made a promise to Lily."

His gaze slipped to the baby in her arms. He could guess what she had promised.

"To care for her child." The baby's perfect little mouth twitched, as if disturbed by bad dreams, and something deep in his chest constricted.

He'd ensure with everything he was that this little one would have nothing but sweet dreams in her future.

"Yes. I know Meg would care for her. I know Willow has a home at the Enclave. But that isn't what Lily wanted." She hesitated, but before he could respond she rushed on. "It isn't what *I* want. Willow deserves more than that, Azrael. I want her to have something I never did. A chance for a normal life."

He wasn't sure how much of a normal life a dhampir could have with an archangel as her father and Rowan, who had died and then resurrected, as her mother but he was more than willing to try.

"We can do that." As the words left his mouth light filled his chest. Hope. As if the remnants of guilt, that had remained buried deep inside his heart since confessing his sins to Rowan, had finally faded.

He'd once believed dhampirs should never have been conceived. But he had fallen for one, and another had stolen his heart in less than a moment, in a way he'd never imagined possible.

In all his long existence the thought of having a child had never crossed his mind. And instantly fear choked him. Fear that something might happen to the baby. That he'd be a lousy dad. But most of all the fear that crippled him was that both Rowan and the baby *would some day die.*

She stiffened and took a step back. His hands dropped to his sides and he stared at her, uncomprehending. A wary look was in her eyes, as though his pledge meant nothing.

"It's all right." Her voice was soft but couldn't hide the thread of pain beneath. "You don't have to pretend. I'd never try and force you to accept Willow. But it doesn't mean we can't still see each other, does it? We could—work something out."

Work something out? What the hell was there to work out? He'd seen unquestioning love in her eyes in that terrifying moment before she'd fallen into the flames. It had simultaneously been the most wonderful and horrific moment in his life.

"You're not going anywhere." The thought of her not being by his side when he woke in the morning or went to bed at night didn't bear thinking about. "You belong with me."

A faint smile curved her lips, as if she found his macho display endearing rather than commanding. "I know. And I want to be with you. But I won't leave Willow. We can make it work. If you want it to."

He rolled his shoulders and attempted to ignore the white-hot agony that shot through his damaged wing. There was a time, not long ago, when the state of his wing would have consumed him with horror. But it was only his wing. Eventually, it would heal. And even if it didn't, right now he had more important things to worry about.

"Why would you leave Willow?" He didn't want to ask but had to know the truth. "Don't you trust me with her?"

The smile slid from her face. "It's got nothing to do with trust. She's a dhampir. I know how you feel about dhampirs. But her parentage isn't her fault."

He glared at her and tried to convince himself the ache consuming his chest was connected to his damaged wing.

Except it wasn't. The pain was deeper than mere physical. It seared the elemental essence of his being and shamed the depths of his soul. Because Rowan still believed he despised the race of her birth.

"I was wrong." It hurt to admit, but not as much as the knowledge she'd thought he was still entrenched in his former prejudices. "Gods, Rowan. I was so wrong. I should have known from the start. The Nephilim were condemned as anomalies of nature, but only by the ignorant and only because of their parentage. How are dhampirs any different?"

"Sakarbaal is her father."

He reached out and gently traced his finger along the baby's soft cheek. "I'm her father."

Rowan's bottom lip wobbled. "But the look on your face just

now—of horror—as if you couldn't imagine anything worse than—"

"No." He cradled her face between his hands. "It had nothing to do with the baby's heritage. It was—" The words lodged in his throat. How could he begin to tell her of the fear that engulfed him every time he thought of her mortality? Yet if he didn't, she would forever wonder. "I can't bear the thought that you and Willow—" It was no good. He couldn't say the words. What had Gabe told him? *You can't think about it.* You just have to take each day and live it to the full.

He'd do that. He could do that, for Rowan and for Willow.

An odd expression crossed her face. "You can't bear the thought of us dying?"

"Don't even say it." The horror of Sakarbaal plunging his sword through her heart would haunt him always.

She hitched the baby closer to her breast, and with her free hand she slid her fingers between his. "Azrael. Willow could potentially live for centuries. And as for me—I've already died. I shouldn't be here with you now, but the phoenix essence inside me changed me in the fire. I'm no longer a dhampir. I'm not human. For all we know I could be as immortal as you. But whatever I am, I'm still *me*. And I love you. I'll always love you."

Her words flowed through him, healing the pain, vanquishing the fear. He didn't care if she was some unique new species because she was right. She was Rowan. And Rowan was his everything.

He, who had lived for millennia, who had visited countless worlds in a dozen galaxies, couldn't find the words to tell her what she meant to him.

There were no words. But he could tell her this. "I love you."

A single tear escaped and trickled down her cheek and soaked into his thumb. "Forever?" Her voice was husky.

He leaned towards her, mindful of Willow, and his lips brushed hers. "Forever."

~

SALVATION

A REALM OF FLAME AND SHADOW NOVEL
BOOK 3

I just spent the best night of my life with the hottest guy I've ever met. Too bad he turns out to be my deadliest enemy – the Archangel Nathanael...

Half-demon Isabella has dreamed of bringing archangels to justice and there's no way she'll forgive Nate for his deception. Except it turns out he has no idea who she is... can this be the chance for retribution she's been searching for?

There's only one rule I live by. Never trust a demon.

Close to finding a rogue demon he's been hunting for millennia, Nate's not looking for any distractions. Until Isabella turns his world inside out and leaves him wanting so much more. But when he uncovers her true heritage, her betrayal rocks him, and he faces the choice of leaving her to her fate or breaking the only rule in his book.

With dark secrets threatening their survival, there's no way an archangel and a half-demon can work together. But with the clock ticking, and danger stalking every move they make, the only way to save themselves might just be to save each other.

ACKNOWLEDGMENTS

Although I wrote the first draft of this book several years ago, it was never published. But after I received the rights back for **Redemption**, book one in the *Realm of Flame and Shadow* series, and prepared it for publication, I couldn't wait to dive in and revise Azrael and Rowan's romance. As always, I owe massive thanks to my incredible editor, Amanda Ashby, whose ability to peel back the layers and find the heart of the story never ceases to amaze me!

I'm eternally grateful to Sally Rigby and Cathleen Ross for your eagle eyes and for asking the hard questions. Thank you!

A big thanks also to Caleb, who answered my many questions regarding weapons and their applications. All mistakes are my own, although I hope I can get away with them seeing as the weapons are wielded by an archangel and a dhampir!

And to Mark and our beautiful family, I couldn't do this gig without you all.

ABOUT THE AUTHOR

Christina Phillips is an ex-pat Brit who now lives in sunny Western Australia with her high school sweetheart and their family. She enjoys writing paranormal, historical fantasy and contemporary romance where the stories sizzle and the heroine brings her hero to his knees.

She is addicted to good coffee, expensive chocolate and bad boy heroes. She is also owned by three gorgeous cats who are convinced the universe revolves around their needs. They are not wrong.

Printed in Great Britain
by Amazon